THE PERFECT BLEND

Teresa Purkis

Best Wishes
Teresa (Terry) Purkis

For Gill.

My friend, My soulmate. My wife.

Thank you for putting up with me for over thirty years and allowing me to pursue my hobby.

Love you loads

Acknowledgements

I would like to thank the following for entering the fun time pun time competition. Becki, Sue, Sam, Gaynor, Chaela, Linda, Luce, Dot, Julz, Kate, Claire, Niki, Laney, Lilian, Angela, Natalie, Jo, Wilma, Heather, Sarah, Justine, Eileen, Steve, Gill, Kathleen, Sharon, Jane, Rosy, Sazz, Teresa, Gillian, Ann, Rachael, Emily, Vera, Astrid, Tammy, Abby, Julie, Rainie, Deb, Ana, Barbara.

Thank you Paula Burns who was the winner and, as promised, has a character named after her. Some others might also recognise their names within the said chapter.

I would also like to thank KC Luck and all the other writers who took part in the "60 to 60" writers challenge. Without their support, kindness and encouragement, this novel would still be on the back burner. Hopefully, this mutual support will continue well after the allotted sixty days. Best wishes everyone with your projects.

Finally, I'd like to thank everyone else who made this happen. From those of you who read through my drafts, to those who helped choose the cover. I am truly blessed.

Synopsis

This workplace lesbian romance explores the relationship between two older women. A heart warming, slow burn, late in life, friends to lovers story.

Georgina owns an independent coffeehouse. Her co-owner, ex lover and sometime friend with benefits, has recently died in a car accident. Grieving, and trying to keep the business going, she finds out the half share has been willed to a complete stranger.

Catherine has flitted from job to job, always searching for an important missing piece in her life. Dumped by her boyfriend, jobless, single, penniless and soon to be homeless, Catherine receives a letter which could solve all her problems.

Georgina has said she would never again date a straight woman. So why is Catherine continually invading her thoughts? Catherine knows she isn't gay. So why is she feeling something more than friendship towards Georgina? Will Georgina let her past control her future? Will Catherine acknowledge a future different to her past?

Set in a coffeehouse on a busy, bustling main thoroughfare into Bristol. The Perfect Blend introduces us to the owners and characters who frequent the establishment.

CHAPTER ONE

Catherine

Catherine opened the front door to her flat and, sighing loudly, picked up the post that was lying on the doormat. She flung the post on the small side table, quickly followed by her keys into the bowl. Her handbag was unceremoniously dumped on the settee, accompanied by another sigh. She quickly removed her coat and hung it on the peg, her old, knitted scarf draped over the top.

After kicking off her classic court shoes under the side table, she moved into the kitchen area in her stockinged feet. She pulled out the chilled bottle of wine from the fridge and collected a glass from a cupboard, narrowing her eyes, gritting her teeth, she slammed the doors closed as she did so.

She made her way back into her living space and plonked herself down next to her handbag.

Catherine unscrewed the bottle top and poured a full glass. She raised the glass to her lips and poured the contents down her throat in one large gulp.

"Shit," she spoke out loud. "Shit. Shit. Shit." She poured herself another glass and the contents was gone in two gulps this time.

"Shit. Shit. Shit. Shit. Shit. Shit. Shit," she repeated, as she slammed the glass onto the coffee table.

She leant back and her head rested on the cushioned support of the settee. She fell sideways, pulled up her feet, and lay prone on the seat, her legs entangled with the strap of her handbag. Annoyed she kicked out and the bag and its contents tumbled to the floor.

She gently touched her eyebrow and felt the bump. It felt as though it was the size of a tennis ball and she wondered why every ailment felt bigger than what it was. She carefully explored the surrounding area, flinching at a particularly tender area. She took a deep breath and exhaled long and hard. Screwing up her eyes, she tried to blink away the tears that threatened to fall.

Failing miserably, she brushed them aside with the knuckle of her forefinger as her thoughts played over the events of the day.

The buzzing noise seeped into her consciousness. She wiped the sleep from her eyes as she tried to focus on the display of her clock. She squinted to bring the digits into focus, closing first one eye then the other, as neither would obey her commands.

"Shit," she shouted as the digits came into focus and realisation dawned.

She had overslept, not by minutes but by a good hour. Cursing to herself she jumped out of bed quickly, ignoring the advice she had read about giving her body time to adjust to being awake. She suddenly felt light-headed and took a moment, holding onto the chest of drawers, to regain her equilibrium.

Still cursing she stumbled to the bathroom, and sacrificing her usual shower, she stripped washed as quickly as possible.

Swiftly dressing in the normal pencil skirt and blouse. She grabbed a pair of tights and fought with them as normal, pulling them up, making sure they weren't twisted or wrinkled. One of her nails must have been jagged as it caught on the sheer material and a hole appeared.

Swearing and cursing to herself, she pulled them off quickly and threw them in the general direction of the laundry basket. She nibbled at the offending nail, retrieved a new pair of tights and succeeded in pulling them on with no other mishaps.

She grabbed a cereal bar from a kitchen cabinet, praying that she would reach the bus stop in time to catch the bus. Knowing if she did, there would be time for a reviving cup of coffee at work before the day began.

She pulled on her coat, and wrapping her scarf around her neck, as she slipped her feet into a comfortable pair of small, heeled court shoes. She closed the door behind her with a click and dashed down the two flights of stairs as quickly as her knees would allow.

Exiting the building into the cold and damp late spring day. Her shoes click, clacked on the pavement as she strode along the two streets needed to get to the main road. She pulled her scarf tightly around her throat and her hands pushed deep into the pockets of her coat. Head down, she hurried on her way.

As she neared the end of the road, she heard the familiar sounds of a bus.

Please don't let it be mine, she pleaded silently.

Catherine broke out into a run as she saw a bus pass by. The type of run that showed that she was trying to hurry but was no faster than the quick walk she had been doing. Her pencil skirt limited her speed of movement and length of stride.

She turned the corner and gazed at the retreating back of the bus. Her eyes tried to focus on the number displayed. She squinted as she ran, yet still, the numbers appeared blurry. Was it the number sixty or eighty-nine? She tried to hitch her skirt higher, to take longer strides, but the attempt was futile.

"Wait for me," she cried out, waving her arms frantically to be noticed.

But either she wasn't heard or was being ignored, for as she reached the back of the bus, the doors closed and it pulled out into the traffic. Cursing to herself she stopped the run-walk she had been doing and started to amble the few paces to the actual stop.

She felt herself stumbling as her footstep hit an uneven paving slab, and the ground seemed to give way under her. Whilst she frantically tried to stop herself from falling, she slammed into the bus shelter and her head connected with the metal.

Cursing, she wobbled into the shelter and sat down on the plastic bench between two women.

"You okay?" one of the women asked.

"Yeah," Catherine replied, as she gingerly felt the small bump that had grown on her eyebrow. "I must have tripped on something."

"You might need a cold compress for that. You're going to get a black eye. I can see one forming already."

The semi-enclosed plastic structure gave protection from the cool breeze that was blowing.

Catherine looked at her watch.

Another woman, who was frequently waiting at the same stop, suddenly sensing her presence, turned to look at Catherine. She took out her headphones and said, "That was your bus. Sorry, I didn't see you coming or I would have tried to slow it down."

"Thanks, anyway," said Catherine.

The woman looked at Catherine's face as she continued to touch the sore spot.

"That looks sore. Are you alright?" the woman asked.

"I think so. I stumbled and head-butted the shelter."

"I felt the vibration, I thought it was a lorry thundering by. You must have given it a real good whack."

"Could my day get any worse? First, I oversleep, then I miss my bus and finally, I miss my footing and head butt the shelter. What else could go wrong?" Catherine's words sounded resigned.

"You'll be okay now. They say bad luck comes in threes."

"Let's hope so. I've been trying to play catch up since waking and I desperately need a coffee."

The younger woman laughed, "Yeah, I'm useless without my morning fix."

She was about to put her headphones back in but instead asked, "Are you going to the high street?" Catherine nodded assent.

"Don't wait for your next bus. Get on mine. There's a great coffee shop right where the bus stops. Get yourself a takeaway and walk the fifteen minutes to the high street. You should get there at the same time as the next bus and you will have had your coffee fix."

Catherine smiled, "I might do that. I'm going to be late anyway so why not. At least I'll get a decent coffee. Thanks."

The woman smiled back. "I hope your eye doesn't swell up any more," she said as she put her headphones back in.

Catherine glanced at her watch as the door automatically opened. Five minutes late. Not too bad. And I managed to grab that coffee.

She entered the building and smiled at the woman sitting behind her desk.

"Good morning, Lily. A bit chilly out there."

"Morning Catherine. Phil's looking for you," Lily said with a grimace. "He stormed out of the office with a face like thunder. He told me to tell you to see him as soon as you get in. Sorry."

"Do you know why? Did he give any hints?" She paused, shrugged her shoulders, grimaced, then continued, "So it's no use pretending I arrived on time."

"Not this time," Lily replied with a shake of her head, as she scrunched up her face. As Catherine walked closer, Lily stared at her.

Catherine was of average height. She had short, thick, blond wavy hair that moulded her perfectly sculptured skull.

Her blond almost non-existent eyelashes outlined her deep blue piercing eyes, which appeared slightly too wide apart. Laughter lines etched at the corner of her eyes, as though a joke was close to the surface, ready to bubble forth. The eyes shone beneath the blond eyebrows that grew almost together, forming a level line that moved expressively as she spoke, making her forehead furrow.

Her nose, slightly crooked as though a minor accident had caused the damage, hung between pronounced cheekbones and above thin lips, that matched the playfulness of her eyes.

A strong square jaw was set firm, courting no awkward questions. Her neck was beginning to show sign of age as her jowls had lost their tightness.

She asked accusingly, "What have you done to yourself?"

Catherine again touched the tender spot on her eyebrow, and shrugged, "I had a run-in with the bus shelter. As you can see the bus shelter won."

"Come closer. Let me look."

Lily's tone of voice brooked no refusal so Catherine walked over to the petite woman.

"Sit down so I can get a proper look."

Catherine sat as Lily gently moved the blond fringe out of the way and lay her fingers around the inflamed area. Still looking at the contusion she asked, "What happened?"

"You should see the other guy," Catherine replied trying to make a joke of her clumsiness.

Lily looked at her and again asked, "No. No more of your flippant answers. What happened?"

"Okay. I was running for the bus and then I tripped on something and as I said, I barrelled straight into the bus shelter."

"Thank goodness you didn't fall into the road." Lily shivered at the thought of what could have happened. She continued to study the damage. "I think you'll have a shiner tomorrow. Colour is already beginning to show. Have you a headache?"

"No. Not really. Only my normal headache of having to work and try to be nice all day."

Lily patted Catherine on the shoulder and said, "You'll live."

"I'd best go and see what he wants," Catherine answered, as she pulled off her coat and scarf.

She made her way through to the back office, putting her outside wear onto the coat stand as she passed by the staff room that resembled a small cupboard.

Catherine stood outside the office door, took a deep breath and knocked.

"Come," Phil's dulcet tone rang out.

On hearing the reply she took another deep breath and opened the door, walked in with her head held high.

"Please Catherine, do take a seat." Phil said, "I think you know what I'm going to ..." His words caught in his throat as he saw the state of her face. Instead he asked, "Whatever have you done?"

Catherine fingered the contusion.

"I tripped as I neared the back of the bus and stumbled into the bus shelter."

"Is that why you're late?"

Grabbing hold of the lifeline she had been given, she replied, "Yes. The bus driver didn't notice. By the time I came out of the shock of hurting myself, the driver had already pulled out into the traffic. So sorry for being late."

Phil's features softened. "Okay," he said, sympathetically. "I'll make an exception this time." He looked at her again and continued, his voice becoming harsher, "But remember you are on your final warning. Keep your nose clean. I can't back you anymore. What with the threat of cuts hanging over us? And I need that report on my desk by four o'clock. There is no margin for error."

She bit her tongue, holding back her frustration but sighed and said, "I know Phil. Thank you. I'll repay your faith in me somehow."

"Just do your job and get here on time. Now go before I change my mind."

Catherine got up from the chair and made her way from the office. A smile played on her face. Her job was safe for a while longer. The threat of not being able to play the rent this month receded into the background but had not gone away. She hoped she would get a response from the advert for a flatmate today.

Catherine sighed and looked down as Lily finished with an enquiry. She glanced at the clock on the screen. She had an hour to finish the report and get it to Phil. Then she would be able to relax and catch up with the normal mundane tasks. One final push was all that was needed.

She sighed again. She had the last table of results to include, the conclusion to finish off and a final read-through. She knew she was cutting it fine but she was pleased with the results so far. Then she could pass it on to Phil. Her finger hovered over the save button as the phone began to ring.

"Good afternoon. Harper and Davis, Catherine speaking, how may I help?"

She listened to the voice at the other end.

"Hold the line and I will transfer you."

Catherine turned back to the screen, forgetting to press save and opened the window that contained all the table of results. She found the one she was looking for. She inserted the table into her document and was repositioning and resizing it when all the lights flickered and went off, along with all the electrical appliances.

"Shit. No. No. No. No." exclaimed Catherine. "No this can't be happening."

"It's only a power cut. I'll look out and see if it's just us or the whole street." Lily replied as she walked towards the front door.

Just as she was about to poke her head outside all the electrics came back to life.

Lily turned and saw a look of panic on Catherine's face, who was frantically clicking on various buttons.

"No," she screamed out. "It's gone."

Lily stood behind Catherine and said, "Reload your last saved copy."

"I can't."

"What do you mean, you can't?" She sighed, shaking her head and felt foolish. "I'm telling you I can't."

"Why ever not? You'd only have lost about ten minutes worth of work." Lily looked at Catherine's stricken face. "You turned the autosave off, didn't you?"

Catherine nodded. She could feel tears of frustration gathering in the corners of her eyes.

"Why the bloody hell did you do that for?" Lily asked brusquely.

"It was annoying me. I kept on having to wait for it to save." Catherine's voice broke as she admitted her mistake.

"And you kept forgetting to save it manually?"

All Catherine could do was nod. She closed her eyes and blinked away the tears that threatened to fall.

"Please tell me you've got a fair chunk of it saved."

Catherine shrugged her shoulders.

"When did you last save it."

Catherine's face took on a look of pain, as she shook her head in resignation. "I don't know."

Lily tried a reassuring smile as she continued, "Oh Catherine." Lily placed a reassuring hand on Catherine's shoulder. "Let me see if I can find a temporary file of it somewhere. Up you get."

Lily took Catherine's seat and started to delve into the system. "What file name did you give it?"

"MAHolding711"

"He's going to fire me for this. I know he is." Catherine groaned as the enormity of her mistake began to sink in. "How could I be so stupid. I knew I was on borrowed time. I won't have time to be able to rewrite it again. What am I going to do?" The last sentence came out as a whine.

Both women sensed the other person at the same time.

Phil spoke sharply, "Catherine. My office. Now."

CHAPTER TWO

Georgina

Rachel put the lid on the cup and placed it on the counter in front of the customer.

"Enjoy." Rachel smiled,

The customer raised the cup as if in a salute and smiled in return then walked out into the damp morning air. She returned her attention to the next customer. After dispensing the required drink subconsciously wiped her hands down the front of her apron, pleased that the early morning rush had abated for a second.

Rachel took a deep breath and let it out slowly as she composed herself. It felt as though she had already done a full day of work. She knew she would be busy, but this morning was insane. She looked around the room. Every table was stacked with dirty cups, mugs and plates.

Sighing, she picked up a cloth, spray and a tray and she extricated herself from behind the counter. She quickly set about clearing the debris left behind by those who had resided inside whilst tasting the delights of the early morning tonic of their choice.

Soon she only had a couple more tables to clear. She passed comments with a couple of regulars as she transformed the room back to its pristine default setting.

The bell above the door chimed and not looking up she called out, "I'll be with you in a sec."

"Take your time," the voice called back.

Suppressing a scream Rachel, still armed with a cloth and spray picked her way through the table and chairs and flung her arms around the older woman who had walked through the door.

"Get off me," the woman pleaded, as she tried to bat away the arms that held her in a warm embrace.

A smile played on the woman's lips as Rachel continued to embrace her.

"What are you doing here," Rachel asked. "I didn't expect you back this week."

When Georgina spoke, a lump started to form in her throat and her voice changed as she swallowed hard. "I couldn't let you do it all by yourself. It's hard enough sometimes when it was the three of us."

The last couple of words seemed to lodge in her throat as a small sob escaped. Rachel pulled the woman tighter and gently replied, "I'll be fine. Simon will be here soon, and Molly is coming straight from school. We've got it covered. You don't need to be here. Why don't you go back home? I've got it under control."

Georgina Turnball gave a weak smile, "I'll feel better being here."

Rachel stepped back so she was an arm's length away and scrutinised her boss, who was older than her by a good twenty years, and for once the extra years showed.

The lines around Georgina's eyes, her slightly sagging jawline and the lack of definition of her muscles seemed more pronounced.

Dark shadows had formed under her slightly puffy eyes and she seemed to have lost a few pounds. She looked tired and sad, yet Rachel felt her intelligence, her strength and her effectiveness oozing out of her pores. She had an air of confidence that surrounded her, a confidence that had nearly all been sapped from her.

Georgina had a slightly rounded chin enclosing thin, delicate lips, the lower lip slightly fuller than the top. One of the corners turned up slightly. The lop-sidedness gave the impression of a mischief-loving smile, not quite a grin, that in better times, would allow laughter to escape.

Her nose implied a Roman style, and the deep brown eyes probed hers, looking for clues. The cropped hair contained different shades of reds and browns, interspersed with many flecks of grey. The grey colour was denser at her temples and fringe. The close cut emphasised the noble look of her skull.

Wrinkles framed the high chiselled cheekbones, and accentuated the eyes, drawing Rachel in, mesmerising her. Georgina, uncomfortable with the scrutiny, looked away and broke the spell.

Rachel gently lifted Georgina's chin with her forefinger and raised her eyebrows in another silent question. Concern and worry radiated from her eyes.

"I'm okay," Georgina reiterated.

"Sure?"

"Sure," Georgina nodded. She looked at the pile of dirty dishes and asked, "It looks like you were busy?"

"It did get a bit hectic. Everyone seemed to come in together."

Georgina, still in her coat, started stacking the dishwasher. Between them, the coffeehouse soon returned to normalcy.

"Thanks," Rachel said as she again took the time to study her boss. "You look exhausted. Why don't you take yourself home? The rush is over. I've got this."

Georgina placed her hand on the younger woman's arm. The hand showed the beginning signs of ageing. The skin looked thin and small brown spots were beginning to show. A couple of her knuckles were starting to protrude with a hint of arthritis.

"I know. But as I said I'd rather be here. I have to do something. I'm going stir crazy staying at home. But as it's quiet I might do some paperwork out the back."

Rachel nodded her understanding. She had never seen Georgina look so lost and defeated. She had expected sadness but this was something more, as though her whole world had been rocked to the core. Her heart went out to her boss and friend. She showed her support by saying nothing but communicating everything.

Georgina walked towards the door marked private. She keyed in the code and as she pushed open the door, she turned and said, "Let me know when your cousin arrives so I can thank him for stepping in."

"Will do," Rachel looked deeply into Georgina's eyes and the unspoken question was asked again.

Georgina smiled a little, visibly touched by her question, and said, "I'm fine. Stop worrying."

Rachel gave another understanding nod and busied herself behind the counter. Georgina watched her employee begin to rearrange the cakes and other assorted goodies. She closed the door and sat down behind the desk.

She sighed as her eyes fell on an old, framed photograph. A smile played on her face as she remembered when it had been taken.

The two women in the photo both looked so young, dressed in black trousers and white blouses. Beaming smiles and sparkling eyes shone out. They were standing in the doorway to a shop, this shop. Each of them had an arm raised and pointing to the sign above. They had finally, after years of saving and procuring funds, managed to persuade the bank manager to give them a mortgage when no other company would.

And almost thirty years later the shop was still thriving. And for the first time, last month, the coffeehouse was mortgage-free.

But would she be able to carry on by herself? She knew the business plan that was in place was sound. Yes, it needed updating, and discussions had taken place on the best way to move forward. But now the circumstances had changed, would they still be possible?

She let out a sigh. A noise she had heard all the more often recently, but usually interspersed with an occasional sob. But today was different. She felt stronger. Still sad but stronger.

She looked around the office. It was big enough to hold the two desks and a two-seater settee. Glimpses of the two of them working at their desks and snatches of conversations flashed through her thoughts. Almost as though she had been transported back in time. Back to a time when excitement coursed through their veins. Before life had got in the way.

"Oh, Laura. I'm sorry. But why did you do it." The words came out in a suppressed groan.

She sighed again and this time a strangled sobbed accompanied it. She moved around her desk and sat down.

She looked at the pile of bills mounting up knowing that everything had changed. She would see what the solicitor had to say tomorrow. But she also knew that no matter what obstacles were thrown her way, she would have to work around them. She couldn't afford anything else.

She opened up the laptop, pulled the box of receipts towards her, and got down to sorting out the accounts. Georgina looked down at the pile. How she hated doing the book-keeping. She had always managed the shop whilst Laura looked after the accounts and stock. It had always worked well. They both knew their strengths.

Georgina brushed away a tear that threatened to escape

with a knuckle. She knew that for the time being, she had no other choice but to step up and take over all the reins. She had wanted to begin to distance herself from the hurly-burly of coffeehouse life. To gradually wind down during her later working years. To perhaps go part-time. Now she had no idea what next week would bring, let alone next month or next year.

With a sigh, she picked up the top receipt and tried to work out where she had to enter the data. How she hated using the computer. She was much more comfortable using a ledger. Over the next half hour, she worked her way through the pile.

A gentle knock sounded on the door and Rachel's cousin Simon pushed the door open and peaked his head around.

"Come in." Georgina beckoned, as she rolled her shoulders.

"I'm so sorry, Mrs T." Simon grimaced as he spoke quietly.

Georgina lifted her hand in acknowledgement and nodded her head. Pain and sorrow flitted across her eyes as she said, "Thank you for stepping in to help, Simon. I don't think I'll be a genial host at the moment."

"Happy to help. You know I'll do anything I can. I've got a two-week break until I start my new job, so I'm ready to step in anytime." He gave a small smile saying, "The extra money will always come in handy."

Georgina again gave a slight nod of her head and continued, "And how many times have I told you to call me Georgie or Georgina."

"And how many times have I replied that I can't change the habit of a lifetime. You're Mrs T to me and that's how you'll stay. Ever since our Muh would bring me and our Rachel in for hot chocolate every Saturday morning." A smile shone in his eyes as he continued, "That seems like an eternity away now."

"And look at you now. All grown up, with a family of your own." Georgina smiled at the memory.

Simon had fair hair and a handsome face which was marred by the evidence of an old crooked broken nose. His blue eyes held the hint of a smile.

"How is Jean and the twins?" she asked.

"They're good. Jean's glad I'm helping out here as she says it gets me out from under her feet. She says I mess up her routine." Simon laughed, and for the first time since a police officer had broken the news, Georgina's smile reached her eyes.

Simon took a breath as if to say something, paused and studied Georgina, then asked, "Do you need a hand with anything upstairs. I can take anything to the charity shop or tip after my shift. All I need to do is give Jean a ring, let her know I'll be late."

Georgina shook her head.

"Thank you but not at the moment. I have no idea what will happen to it, whether I'll be expected to sort it out or whatever. It is going to be a waiting game until everything gets worked out," Georgina replied. Then with a smile, she asked, "Are you still okay to cover tomorrow's early morning and lunchtime shift?"

"Of course, Mrs T. I'm sorry I couldn't help out earlier but I couldn't get out of my meeting."

"I know," Georgina replied. "Both Rachel and I, are grateful that you could step in and cover the shifts you are doing."

"My pleasure, Mrs T." Simon again studied the older woman and asked gently, "Do you know what is going to happen with the flat? The business?"

Georgina shook her head as she said, "I'm seeing the solicitor tomorrow. The message from them seemed a little cryptic. The PA wouldn't, or couldn't, answer my question. She just requested my company tomorrow at three. Hopefully, I'll have a better idea of what I'm dealing with."

"Good luck with that."

"Thanks."

Simon stood up and said, "Time for me to get to work. And if you need me to do anything, and I mean anything, give me a shout."

"I will. Thanks, Simon." Georgina gave him a big smile.

Simon gave a salute and walked back out to the bustle of the coffeehouse.

Rachel hesitated before she opened the door to the office. She listened and could hear soft sniffling as though the person on the other side of the door was trying their best to keep their emotions in check.

Rachel keyed in the code, turned the handle and gently pushed the door open. She sidled inside and made her way to the woman whose head lay on her arms on the table.

Rachel tenderly touched her shoulder.

The woman started and said, "You scared the living daylights out of me. I didn't hear you come in."

"I'm only checking to see if there is anything you want. Coffee? Tea? Cake?"

"I'm fine thanks," Georgina said as her breathing returned to normal.

Georgina looked at the younger woman standing in front of her and tried to smile. Rachel's blond hair was cropped short at the side and flopped forward on top. Her very expressive face showed the empathy she felt for the older woman. Long thick lashes enclosed blue striking eyes, and yet without mascara, they would be ignored. Her lithe body showed the hours spent at the gym.

Rachel studied Georgina. Her usual pristine appearance looked dishevelled, as though she had run her fingers through her hair one too many times.

"You know you can tell me anything. I hope you think of me more than your employee because to me you're my friend, surrogate mum and mentor. And I do know what you felt about her. I wasn't blind."

Georgina tried desperately not to let another tear slide down her cheek. Her face scrunched up in emotional sadness. She blurted out, "I loved her."

"Oh Georgie, I know you did." Rachel gave her shoulder another squeeze. "But now you can start to live your life as you want. Not clinging to that crumb of hope she would occasionally give. Expecting the result would be different, that it would turn into something more. She loved you as a friend. And it was wrong of her to lead you on for all those years."

Georgina's voice, sounding strangled in sadness, responded, "Why wasn't I strong enough to send her away all those times when she came to mine after a few drinks. Why did I forgive her and let her in? Why did we play out the same circle of life every single time? Why did she keep on asking me to give more of myself, when she would give nothing back? Why didn't she just leave me alone? Why?"

"Because she was selfish. She was unhappy and depressed. She didn't love herself so she wanted everyone to go through what she was going through."

Georgina nodded, "Why didn't I realise she was so unhappy? I could have made her happy. I could have helped her with her sadness. I would have put her on the pedestal and worshipped her for the goddess she was to me."

Rachel's face showed the empathy she was feeling. "I know you wanted more. You wanted her to love you as you loved her, but she couldn't give you what you wanted. It was a pipe dream. All it did was make you unhappy."

Rachel gave Georgina's shoulder another squeeze.

"I wasn't unhappy."

Rachel rolled her eyes.

Georgina conceded, "Well perhaps a little."

"So now it's your turn to start being truly happy." Rachel smiled at her. "Start to love yourself. You've still got years ahead of you to find that true love. Don't go wasting time on unrequited love. You've done that for too long."

"What chance have I got to make a relationship work? I've hankered after this one for the best years of my life. She meant everything to me. Even though she treated me as a plaything to toss into the corner when the mood suited. Why couldn't she be true to herself? Why pretend all these years that I meant nothing to her? That we couldn't be a couple."

"Perhaps her fears were too deeply rooted."

"But her family were dead to her."

"And yet their prejudices continued to influence her actions."

Georgina closed her eyes and breathed deeply. "I've been such a fool to waste my life on her."

"You are no fool." Rachel bent down and kissed her boss on the cheek. "You loved her. That's why. And she was cruel to lead you on."

"So why do I feel so guilty?"

"I know things were bad between you for the last couple of months."

"Yeah. Ever since I stood up to her and told her I wasn't going to put up with her drunken antics. That they were beginning to harm the business." Georgina took a deep breath to control her emotions. "I'm so sorry the atmosphere in the coffeehouse was so bad at times. I thought she would get her act together,"

"That was not your fault." Rachel offered a small smile.

"But she continued drinking, she still kept coming around

being cruel. I should have reacted differently."

"You are not to blame. She kept on pushing and pushing you. Needling you for a reaction. She didn't hate you, even though I heard her say it enough times, she only hated herself."

"So I should have been there for her. Is that what you're saying?"

"No." Rachel shook her head "How many years did you stand by her side? How often did you put her to bed when she didn't have a clue where she was or what she was doing? You didn't force her to drink."

"But I could have tried to stop her."

"No, you couldn't. She was on a path of self-destruction. There was nothing you or anyone else could have done. She gave no thought to the outcome of her actions." Rachel became angry. "Thank goodness no one else was involved. I know it's horrible to say bad of the dead but thank goodness she hit the tree and not the bus shelter further down the road. Imagine what injuries she could have caused."

"But I was to blame." Georgina whined, "She called around and I told her to only come back when she was sober. I could have stopped her. I could have sobered her up. She wouldn't have died."

"This time. But she wouldn't have stopped drinking. She didn't think she had a problem. So don't you dare blame yourself? You didn't make her drive that fateful night." Rachel paused for a moment. "I will say it again. You... did... nothing... wrong... You couldn't make her love herself."

"I know."

Rachel looked at her boss and said, "Stop hankering over what is now definitely in the past. You are not her puppet anymore and she cannot keep you dangling, dancing to her tune. Those string are well and truly been broken. Go and grab life by the horns and enjoy the ride of your life."

Nodding, Georgina replied, "Someone said to me once that I would understand why it never worked out between Laura and me when someone else walks into my life. And at that moment my life will change. My mind might not know it straight away, but my body will. That I will ask for nothing, expect nothing, but suddenly everything I want is standing in front of me. That it may not be easy but it will be worth it. I think they were talking bullshit. I'm fifty-six. I think the time for that to happen, has well and truly passed me by."

"That's not old."

"Rachel please. Look at me. I look and feel like a washed-up hag."

"But..."

Georgina held up her hand to stop Rachel from continuing. "I know you are going to say some platitudes, but I have eyes and I have a mirror. My body is sagging and getting fat, my hair is turning grey and I'm getting wrinkles on my wrinkles. A real catch." She laughed sardonically.

Rachel shook her head and smiled at her boss. "You're tired, that's all it is. Some sort of fitness routine will get you back on track."

"And where will I find the time to do that?"

Rachel dismissed the words with another shake of her head. "You can always put a colour in your hair but I think the way it is now, makes you look distinguished. And as for your wrinkles... I call them laughter lines. They are what makes you, you."

"Anyone would think you fancy me."

"And why wouldn't I?"

"One, you are twenty years younger than me. Two, you are like a surrogate daughter to me. Three, you have a gorgeous husband and two charming boys, or should I say, young men. Four, it would be just weird. And five, you are not my type."

"So you've given me five reasons. All fairly valid. But I admire the inner beauty that I see in you. Everyone's good looks fade over time, but the beauty which is in here," she put her hands over her heart, "will always keep you attractive. You could be gay or straight. Man or woman. And everything in between. It doesn't matter to me. All I see is a wonderful person with a heart of gold. Who would not want to be a part of that? And I am proud to call you my friend, I look up to you as I would my Mum, and as such I love you."

Georgina gave a slight nod. "Thank you for those lovely words."

The friendship that developed, and over the years had held them together, was there for all to see. The two women looked at each other as mutual respect passed between them, and they smiled in recognition of the fact.

Rachel looked at her watch. "It's past closing time. We're all clean and tidy out there. I've put the closed sign up. The tables are cleared and the chairs are stacked on them. I've told Molly to go. So there is only the pair of us left. So are you sure you don't want a coffee or a cake?"

"No thanks." Georgina gave Rachel a genuine smile.

Rachel walked over to the coat rack and picked up both hers and Georgina's coat.

"Come on," she said. "Let me take you over the road and let us have a glass of wine to celebrate her life, rather than her death."

"Okay." Georgina gave a small cough, trying to disguise the lump that had formed in her throat.

Rachel helped Georgina into the coat and stated, "You're seeing the solicitor tomorrow."

Georgina nodded.

"So cross whatever obstacles are put in front of you then. This evening let's go and remember the good times and not the troubled soul she had become."

CHAPTER THREE

Catherine

Catherine looked at the screen. A small smile played on her lips but disappeared as quickly. She thought about not answering but knew the caller would keep on trying until she reached her. She swiped to answer and listened, as her childhood friend, Sue, her usual partner in crime dove right in.

"Hi, babes, the twins and I thoughts we should kick our blokes into touch. Let the CATS meet up and have some girly time. How about a night of drunkenness and debauchery on Wednesday? Are you up for it?"

The twins were Anne and Tracy, but they weren't twins, not even related. They were born three days apart and their parents lived next door to each other. And whilst they were growing up, they hardly spent a day away from each other. The exception was family holidays, and even then, they managed to persuade their parents to allow them to accompany each other.

They both had the same features. Long blond hair, chiselled cheekbones and striking blue eyes. Anyone looking at them would think they had either the same mother or father. Yet neither was the case.

They were the popular girls at school but were never mean or disrespectful. Everyone seemed to gravitate towards them and had many friendship groups which had changed in intensity over the years. But the closeness between them, Sue and

Catherine had stood the test of time. And through all the relationships, marriages, divorces and being unattached, their friendship tethered them all together.

"So?" Sue prompted. "Are all the CATS coming out to play?"

"Sorry," Catherine realised that Sue had asked her a question.

Sue sighed. "Are you sorry you can't make it or sorry for something else?"

Catherine sighed as well, then asked, "What are you going on about?"

"Wednesday?"

"What about Wednesday?"

"Us. The twins. Meeting up. Wednesday."

Silence greeted her.

"Catherine?"

Silence. She looked at the screen to make sure the connection hadn't been broken.

"Catherine? Are you there?"

"Yes. I'm still here." A huge sigh escaped, her eyes filled with tears as Catherine sobbed, "Oh Sue. I don't know what to do."

"Give me half an hour and I'll be there. Okay."

"Okay," the strangled voice answered.

"I'm at the top of the road armed with a bottle of wine. Get the door open and get ready for a hug."

The line went dead as Catherine gave a weak smile through her tears.

Catherine pushed herself up from the settee, swept all the tissues into the bin and walked down the stairs to the front door. On seeing the shadow closing towards the frosted glass, she opened the door.

Sue pulled Catherine into a hug as Catherine burst into more tears.

"Aw, sweetie," Sue spoke softly as she kicked the door behind her closed.

They stood together, with Catherine pulled into a tight embrace. Gradually the sobs subsided. Sue moved away to arm's length and gave Catherine an encouraging smile.

"Unless we are going to stand here all night, I suggest we make our way up to your flat."

Sue followed Catherine's slow climb up the two flights of stairs and entered the flat.

Sue looked around. "You go and sit yourself down. I'll get myself a glass."

On autopilot, Catherine walked to the settee and sat down. She downed the last of the wine in her glass, leant her head back, and closed her eyes. Her lips trembled as though she was on the verge of tears again.

Sue shrugged off her coat and hung it on the hook. Retrieving a glass from the cupboard, she opened the new bottle and poured herself some wine. Taking a slurp she sat at the other end of the two-seater settee, pulled Catherine's legs onto her lap and proceeded to give her feet and calves a massage.

"Catherine Mary Munden. Are you going to tell me why you have drunk a full bottle of wine and got through, what looks like, a whole box of tissues, and it's not 7 o'clock?"

"Oh Sue, my life is such shit." Catherine's voice came out as a plaintive cry, as more tears threatened to overcome her again.

Sue waited patiently.

"I screwed up at work." Catherine continued. Her sorrowful tone accentuated the depth of her emotions.

"You can sort it out though. Go in extra early and work on it. If anyone can sort out work problems it's you." Sue worked on a knot in her left calve then slid her hand down to work on the arch.

"Not this time." Catherine felt her bottom lip begin another cycle of trembling as tears again threatened to escape.

"Why ever not?"

"I've been sacked." The words came out emotionless.

"What? How? Why? What did you do that was so bad?" Sue asked with concern for her friend pouring out of every pore.

"I screwed up big time, and it wasn't the first."

Sue studied her friend and noticed worry lines etched on her face where there wasn't any before. Dark circles surrounded her eyes and, even though the crying had made them red, swollen and blotchy, her eyes appeared sunken. Her cheeks appeared as though she had lost some weight.

Catherine squirmed under her friend's scrutiny. "What?" she asked.

"Tell me what happened, " Sue questioned softly.

Catherine had a battle raging within herself. She hadn't spoken to Sue for a month and so much had happened. She didn't know where to start.

Did she start with her breaking up with boyfriend Ben, and all the hurtful barbs he had flung her way?

Or did she admit that she had been duped by a con artist after binge shopping on an internet site and that she was now behind on her rent?

Could she divulge how going through the menopause was playing havoc with her sleep patterns and that she hated feeling moody, snappy and grumpy? Should she reveal that everything she did seemed too much trouble?

Should she let slip that she was on antidepressant tablets, but the side effects were worse than the good they were doing?

Or did she admit that she needed a good bonk because she

hadn't felt satisfied in years? But again Ben's caustic comments rang in her ears.

Or did she just talk about work?

"Please speak to me. You look more worried than I've ever seen you." Sue reached across and took both of Catherine's hands in hers, and said with a smile, "A woman with your talents will find a job fairly easily."

Catherine gave a small shrug, that could be taken any way.

"Okay," said Sue. "So there is more going on. Do you care to tell me? Let me help. What does Ben think about it all?"

"Hah." The noise came out like a strangle.

Sue frowned at her friend. "What do you mean by hah?"

Catherine pursed her lips together and let out a deep sigh. "We split up about six weeks ago..."

Sue butted in, saying, "Six weeks ago... and I'm only hearing about this now because..."

"Don't start." Catherine held up a hand to silence her friend.

Sue kept quiet for a moment then asked in a gentle tone "What else haven't you told me, your best friend, your forever friend. Your friend with whom we have shared all our deepest secrets. Your friend who loves you. Quirks and all."

Almost as a whisper, she said, "I thought he'd come back."

"Is that why you didn't want to speak last month?"

Catherine nodded. Her face crumpled some more.

"Do you want to tell me about it?" Sue prodded.

"Not really. I'm embarrassed."

"Why? You never get embarrassed. The things you've told me things over the years have made my toes curl. And not in a good way." She smiled as she looked at her friend. Not seeing the usual rolling of eyes or laugh in return, asked, "Do you need a cuddle?"

A small smile reached her eyes as she replied, "I need more than a cuddle, but as you are a woman, and my best friend, a cuddle will have to do."

Sue nudged Catherine's shoulder as she scooted over. "So you need a good bonk, is that it?"

"If only."

Sue frowned, as she asked, "I've told John to put the kids to bed so I've got all night. Well, perhaps not all night. But at least until midnight."

Sue wrapped an arm around her friend who was soon nestled into her shoulder. They cuddled together for some moments. Sue could tell that her friend was building up to saying something by the way she kept taking deep breaths and then opening her mouth. Then taking more deep breaths. Sue waited patiently, knowing that if she pushed, her friend would clam up like last time they spoke.

Finally, Catherine said, "My life has become one huge piece of shit. I'm forty-eight. Live in a grotty flat. Have no significant other. I'm menopausal. I'm grumpy, grouchy, depressed, skint. I've just lost my job. Even though I hated it, I enjoyed going to work. And to top it all I need some mind-blowing sex."

Sue squeezed her friend's shoulder.

Catherine, again, blew out her cheeks, and continued, "Actually I think I need more than a good bonk. I need a whole new life."

"I'm listening."

"I'm so tired all the time," Catherine sighed.

"Have you been to the doctors?"

"Yeah. He's given me some tablets to take."

"What like sleeping tablets?" asked Sue.

"No. He knows I won't take those. He's given me some antidepressants."

"Okay. Why? How long have you been taking them?"

"About two weeks. But that isn't the real problem."

"So what is the real problem?" Sue asked, gently rubbing her friend's arm.

"One of the reasons I'm feeling like shit is..." she paused and took a deep breath before she continued, "I'm embarrassed that I've been so gullible."

Catherine closed her eyes and shook her head. Sue waited patiently.

"You'll think I'm a complete and utter prat. But I've done something stupid which is likely to have consequences for a while to come."

"You're pregnant." Sue joked.

Catherine sloshed her arm, "Yeah, yeah. It's been a few years since I last had my period, thank goodness. And anyway, can you imagine this train wreck of a woman bringing up children. I'd be a pensioner and well into my dotage before they could take me to the pub." A look of panic played across Catherine's features. "Good grief I hope I'm not. I don't need any more worries. I can hardly cope with looking after myself."

"You would've made a great mum. My kids adore you."

"And I adore them, that's why I'm content with being a godparent to yours."

Catherine stopped talking and different images passed before Catherine's eyes. She sighed deeply and she felt anger at herself start to build.

Sue noticing the change asked, "What have you done?"

Catherine gave an embarrassed smile, "A few weeks ago when I realised Ben wasn't coming back, I bought some stuff off the internet."

"Okay..."

She huffed out a breath, "I was so stupid. I normally check

and pick up anything dodgy, but I just needed some retail therapy and they looked like a bargain." She shook her head, "The stuff hasn't arrived and the site is no more."

"Oh no. How much did you pay out?"

"About thirty quid."

"That's not too bad."

Catherine burst into new tears.

"Oh sweetie, it's only thirty quid. Everyone buys stupid stuff every once in a while."

"They wiped me out."

"They've wiped you out?" Sue asked in shock.

Catherine brushed away a rogue tear with her knuckle. "The money that would cover my rent for the next couple of months is gone."

"Gone?"

"Yeah, every penny in my current account."

"What is your bank doing?"

"There's nothing they can do. I permitted them to take the money out. I've put a stop on any more going out from it." Catherine bottom lip quivered. "And on top of that, I've lost my job."

"So you haven't enough money to cover your rent?"

Catherine shook her head. More tears threatened to come.

"Do you want to sub you your rent? I'd do it willingly."

"I know you would. Thanks for the offer."

"So what are you going to do?"

"Start job hunting first thing tomorrow morning." Catherine looked into her friend's eyes. "And if I can't find a lodger soon, may I take you up on that offer of a sub, if that's alright."

"I wouldn't have offered if I didn't mean it," she laughed. "I wouldn't let my friend become homeless."

No words were spoken for a while, with Catherine taking the comfort of her friend's embrace.

"Why am I so tired all the time. I come home from work knackered and have a snooze. Then as soon as my head touches the pillow. Ping. I'm wide awake. All these different thoughts start to go through my mind. I drop off to sleep and wake up, baking hot and wringing wet. I finally get off to sleep only for my alarm to wake me from my slumbers, feeling as though I have hardly slept."

Sue continued to rub her friend's arm then asked, "Why don't you go back to the doctors? Get him to give you something to tide you over. Explain why you need something."

"Oh no. I can't talk to my doctor about that." Catherine shook her head vigorously.

"Why ever not?"

"Because I can't." Again she shook her head.

"Again I'll ask. Why ever not?"

She sighed, "He comes across as being so judgmental. I can't talk to him about my sex life."

"How did we get from you being tired, to your sex life. I thought you broke up with Ben six weeks ago.

"We did. But it was problems with our sex life that caused the split. I don't know whether I miss him or not. I miss having someone around." Catherine shrugged. "Even though we weren't living together, he stayed over most nights. I don't miss the loo seat being up, or stubble in the basin, or wet towels being left on the floor, or his other annoying habits."

They again sat in silence.

Finally, Sue asked, "Do you want to tell me what happened between you and Ben? He seemed like a nice bloke. You two looked good together."

Catherine nodded then shrugged, saying, "We had a massive argument."

Sue squeezed Catherine's hand, "You know you can tell me anything."

"I know."

"Did he want to do some kinky stuff?"

"No." Catherine sighed, "But I obviously wasn't satisfying him."

"Was he satisfying you?"

Catherine didn't answer Sue's question. Instead, she said, "He called me frigid. I told him, he was hurting me, that I needed some more foreplay. He told me I was a cock tease and if I wouldn't give him what he wanted then he would find it elsewhere. Again I told him I wanted to, but it was hurting me, that my body needed a little more coaxing. Do you know what he did?"

Sue shook her head, "Tell me."

"He got dressed, told me he was sick of my shit. Said I was the worst lay he had ever had. Chucked my keys at me and walked out."

"That's awful." Sue gave her friend an extra squeeze and said, "Bastard. Do want me to go and give him a piece of my mind?"

Catherine's bottom lip quivered, "No. But, even though we weren't living together," her voice hitched. She composed herself quickly and added quietly, "I miss him. Not particularly him, but I miss having someone around."

"Aw, sweetie. I'm so sorry."

Catherine was quiet for a little while, before saying, "Sue?"

"Yeah."

"You've been through the menopause, haven't you?"

"Yeah." Sue rolled her eyes.

"Did you find you became dry? You know. Down there."

"To a certain extent." She gave Catherine a shy smile as she continued, "We've adapted. John has spent more time adoring my body. Kissing me, kissing my boobs, giving me oral, that sort of thing. It also helped that John started to find it difficult to get it up more than once, so he used his hands, fingers and toys more." Sue laughed.

"So I'm not a freak."

"No sweetie, you are not. And there are creams and stuff you can get to help. John and I include using the cream on each other as foreplay."

Catherine thought her friend's words over, then said, "He would never go down on me."

"Never?" Sue's voice was incredulous, "Who wouldn't?"

"Both. My husband... Ben..."

"Did they ever say why they wouldn't?"

"My husband wouldn't speak about sex. It was either the missionary position or nothing. Ben said it felt dirty."

"Dirty?" Sue looked incredulous, "Dirty? Well, he wouldn't have lasted a second, if he refused to go down on me."

"I thought he wanted it to smell fresher so I made sure I soaked in bubble baths and used my scented soaps before he came over. But still, he wouldn't. And yet he expected me to give him a blow job whenever he wanted it."

"It seems to me that you've dodged a bullet there." She kissed the top of her friend's head.

"Do you really want to be treated like shit? You need someone to love you. Love all of you. But the bubble bath and scented soaps might have been adding to the problem. When I saw my doctor, he recommended that I stop using them as for women our age they can cause dryness."

Catherine raised her eyes. "I didn't know that. Anyway, I

think I'll give up on sex. I know I said I need a good bonk but I've never really enjoyed it."

Sue nudged her friend's shoulder. "You can't give up. You can't beat a mind-blowing orgasm."

In a voice not louder than a whisper, Catherine responded, "I wouldn't know."

"What?" Sue frowned as though she hadn't heard correctly. "Did you say what I thought you said? That you've never had a mind-blowing orgasm. I don't believe you. What about all the years you spent with your old man. Didn't you ever with him?"

"No. Never. As long as he had his five-minute bonk on a Sunday morning, he seemed happy. I pretended I enjoyed it and made all the right noises. But I've faked it for so long, I don't think I'll ever feel it. All I want is to have one. Just one. I'm not asking for much. I'm forty-eight. And if I haven't found someone by now to give me one, I don't think I ever will." Catherine sobbed and wiped the tears from her eyes with her elegant fingers.

Sue pulled Catherine even tighter.

"I'm so sorry. I didn't know. I thought you and that husband of yours were good together. And yes, I know it all went horribly wrong."

"Yeah. We were. That was in all but one aspect. We hardly ever argued. But obviously, I didn't satisfy him, and he wanted more than the Sunday morning bonk. And yet when I tried to encourage him, he was more interested in the football, snooker or whatever sport was on the TV rather than me." Her bottom lip quivered. "He didn't love me otherwise he wouldn't have packed up his things and disappeared."

Sue kissed her friend on the cheek. "All men are bastards except John, Dave and Stu. Even then the twins moan about their blokes sometimes."

Catherine tried to smile. "Since he left me, I've only been

with Ben. I did try one of these dating sites but no one interested me. I'm sick of looking. It seems all the good ones like your John, or Dave or even Stu, have been snapped up."

"Aww babes, I truly believe there is someone out there for you." Sue pulled her friend into a hug. "Don't go searching too hard for it. You might be pleasantly surprised who turns up and sweeps you off your feet. Keep an open mind. And stop falling for the same type." Sue changed tack and said, "So Wednesday. The CATS. I'll pick you up at seven. Even if you don't want to go, I'm dragging you out."

CHAPTER FOUR

Letters and emails

"I'm downstairs. Double parked. You ready?" Sue asked as she spoke into her phone.

"I'm not sure," came Catherine's reply.

Sue huffed out a breath, "You're not backing out on us now. Okay?"

Catherine smiled as she heard the huff, "I won't I promise but can you come up for a moment. I've got something to show you and I want your opinion."

Annoyed Sue responded, "Can't I look at it in the pub?"

"Please." Catherine pleaded.

"Okay, I'll try to find a parking spot. But I won't allow you to back out."

"I won't. I promise. It would be good to see the twins and get myself away from these four walls. They do know I'm not good for standing a round."

"They know. We've all be in that situation at least once, so don't worry. Be back in a mo. Get that door open."

A little while later and as soon as Sue followed Catherine into her flat, she was handed an official-looking envelope.

"What is this?" she asked.

"Take the letter out and read it. Then tell me what you think."

Sue pulled out the headed letter from the envelope. The quality of the paper caused her to rub it between her thumb and forefinger. She loved the feel of paper, especially expensive paper. She smelt it as she would her favourite books.

"Feels posh, smells pleasant," Sue commented. "Not your average writing paper."

Sue started to read out loud:-

Dear Ms Munden

Re: The Estate of Laura Richards deceased

"Who is Laura Richards?" Sue asked.

Catherine shrugged, "I have no idea. This letter came in the post today, and I have been racking my brain ever since opening it to try to dredge up any memories. But nothing has come to mind." Catherine frowned as though she was still delving into the depths of her memory. She shook her head and said, "Read on."

We are very sad to inform you that Laura Richards passed away on the 17th of March.

Her last Will and Testament has named you as a partial beneficiary of her estate and in accordance please contact us at your earliest convenience.

Yours sincerely

Rupert James Esq

Sue looked studied the letter heading and asked, "The solicitor's address is in Bristol. Who do you know in Bristol?"

Catherine shook her head, and replied, "I don't know anyone in Bristol. Well, I don't think I do."

"Have you ever been there? What about your parents?" Sue

prodded.

"No, and no I don't think so. Mum might have. Dad only knew the local pub. And the pub near their place in Benidorm." She gave a small laugh. "Do you think it's a con?"

"The stationary seems a bit posh for a con. Have you googled this Laura or this solicitor?"

"Not yet. I haven't had the time."

"So it arrived today?"

"It was here when I got home tonight after my interview. I'm going to give them a ring tomorrow."

"I don't think we have time to investigate now." Sue looked at her watch. "Come on we're going to be late if we don't get a wriggle on. Bring the letter with you and we can think about some more. I think the twins will be as intrigued as we are and have something to say. "

The bell above the door didn't jingle, it clanged, as the door was flung open. Rachel watched as the whirlwind flounced through, stormed across the shop floor, a couple of chairs tumbled in the wake. The numbers were bashed onto the keypad to the office.

Rachel stared in disbelief at the face of her boss. She had never seen her look like thunder before. She appeared as though she was at the end of her tether. Like she was getting ready to fly away from what was anchoring in place. Not yet ready to embrace the gathering storm that circled her.

Rachel looked at the customers to see if they had seen anything that could have a detrimental impact on their future custom.

A few of the regulars glanced up and gave Rachel a curious look. She shrugged her shoulders and made a face that implied that they knew as much as her. Luckily, the only other two women in the room sat in one of the booths and were so engrossed in each other. They were holding hands and staring intently at each other. They seemed oblivious to the angry woman that had stormed through, knocking over chairs.

Rachel heard an animalistic noise come from the office as the door closed. It sounded somewhere between a growl and a howl. It was closely followed by the sound of something being thrown and smashed.

Rachel turned to Simon and asked, "Can you stay awhile longer?"

"Yes go. I'll text Jean and let her know. Leave the chairs I'll tidy them."

"Thanks." Rachel gave her cousin a grateful smile.

Rachel stood by the door with her ear pressed against it. Stomping and swearing could be heard. She rolled her eyes at her cousin, grimaced and said, "It doesn't sound good. But I don't think anything else has been thrown. Wish me luck."

When there was a break in the noise, she quickly entered the code and slipped through the door. She saw the photo frame, which usually had pride of place on the shelf, was now on the floor just inside the door. The smashed glass by her feet, and the photo upside down close by. She gingerly stepped over the glass and retrieved the photo and frame from the floor.

She peered into the room and decided not to switch on the overhead light. The small window allowed the diminishing daylight to flood a corner of the room, good enough for her purposes.

Georgina sat in a crumpled heap on the floor by her desk. Her head rested on her bent knees and her arms were wrapped around them.

Laura's knickknacks that normally were carefully arranged on her desk had been swept on the floor. The broken bits lay haphazardly on the opposite side of the room from where Georgina lay huddled in pain.

Rachel put the frame down. She rooted around in a pocket and brought out a small pack of tissues. Rachel surveyed the floor and carefully sat down next to Georgina, handing her the tissues. Rachel pulled Georgina into a hug and started stroking her hair. Huge sobs escaped and Rachel let her cry until there were no more tears to shed. Pulling her in tight and secure.

Rachel planted a tender kiss on the top of her head. "Do you want to tell me about it?"

Georgina blew her nose and dabbed at her eyes. Her shoulders rose and fell in sobs but no more tears fell.

Finally, Georgina spoke, the sound came out in gulps. "And she's still haunting me from the grave. Did she think that little of me?"

"What has happened? What did she do?" Rachel asked gently as she again kissed the top of the older woman's head.

"I could lose everything."

Rachel frowned. "What? Why?"

Georgina let out a huge sigh. Her shoulders sagged in defeat. Tears threatened to overwhelm her again. She closed her eyes and in a monotonous tone replied, "A couple of weeks before the accident she changed her will."

Rachel took hold of Georgina's hand and squeezed it.

"I don't understand," Rachel said finally when nothing else was forthcoming. "Why would she do that?"

Georgina's face crumpled again as another bout of tears fell. Her hands clenched into fists. Suddenly, she slapped her thigh hard in anger, and it made Rachel jump.

"How could she leave her half of the business to some relative she didn't know, and I've never heard of. I can understand leaving the flat, but the business."

Rachel gasped as she took in the news, "Do you know their name? Is it a man, woman? How old they are? Are they thinking of selling?"

Georgina shrugged her shoulders and gave out a sigh. "All I know is that her name is Catherine and that the executors are awaiting her instructions before proceeding. This woman has to agree to these certain terms, or Laura's estate reverts to me." She took in a breath. "Well, the business does. Not the flat."

"I don't understand. What terms?"

Georgina felt Rachel's hand on her arm, gentler than before. She tried to avoid her eyes as she said, "Neither do I fully. The solicitor only gave me the gist of the Will as per Laura's instructions as it affects me directly. The complete reading will take place next week.

"Then it could work out okay." Rachel gave an encouraging squeeze and smile.

"And then again it might not." Georgina closed her eyes and took a deep breath. Rachel could feel Georgina was getting angry again. "It's all my fault. I shouldn't have pushed her away. We had words. We said some nasty things to each other. And yet for once, we were both true to ourselves. I could still feel the love between us. And still, after all this time it boils down to her not trusting her heart. And her not loving me enough to push aside her demons."

Rachel again pulled Georgina into a comforting embrace.

"She was such a tortured soul," Georgina admitted. "I wanted to help her, but she only let me see glimpses of the real person. I could have helped her more."

Rachel looked directly into Georgina's eyes meaningfully. She spoke as she squeezed her hands, "And as I said yesterday. None of this is your fault. People will only give easy access to what is comfortable."

Georgina's bottom lip began to quiver and tears again sprang into her eyes.

Rachel kissed the top of her head and suggested, "If this

woman accepts the conditions of whatever is on offer, can't you offer to buy her out?"

Georgina shook her head in desolation, "Not an option. Knowing our mortgage was almost paid I used any spare money I had when we bought all that new equipment last year. And I can't see myself getting a new mortgage. Not at my age. Especially with the multinationals that have moved within walking distance. I don't know what to do. I suppose I could get a second mortgage on my house. But even then, I doubt whether it would be enough."

"Oh, Georgie. I'm so sorry. But don't do anything daft. Be patient. But you'll think of something. You always do. You were the brains behind this encounter."

"But Laura had her hands on the money side of things. I don't know if I can cope with doing the accounting alongside everything else. What if this woman wants to sell her share? I'm going to lose everything we spent over thirty years of our lives working towards."

"I'm sure it won't come to that."

"But what if it does?"

"Then you'll have to cross that bridge when you come to it. In the meantime hold onto the thought that this woman might not want anything to do with a small independent coffeehouse in Bristol. And that the terms are unacceptable."

Georgina wiped at her eyes and mumbled, "Okay."

Catherine noticed that the email had arrived from the solicitor as promised. Her conversation over the phone seemed strange. She had been told that she was being left some property and a half share in a small business. But there were conditions she had to agree to before the half share converted into her name.

She was intrigued. Nothing had piqued her curiosity like

this for a long time. She had been going through the motions, bumbling from one position to another. Not fully involved in any project. Always searching for something different.

Being sacked and unable to pay the rent had been a wake-up call. Perhaps now was the time to get a bit of stability into her life. To settle down like her close friends. The meet up with them on Wednesday had her questioning her decisions.

Did she want to go into her dotage still searching for that elusive something? Especially since she had no idea what she was searching for, or even what was missing. And yet this restlessness had followed her around all her life.

The last couple of job interviews had shown that her age was beginning to catch up with her. Both times they had opted for the twenty-year-old, whom they could mould into the workings of their corporation, not the set in her ways, old hag.

She looked at the email in her inbox. Could this be the change she needed? She spoke out loud, "Okay. Let's see what is on offer."

And with that, she clicked it open. Two attachments came with the official blurb. She opened the first document.

Catherine,

I have followed your path through life firstly through the eyes of your Mother and latterly through my own eyes. I know life has been difficult for you. I was sorry to hear about your problems and your divorce.

'How does she know that I have problems.' Catherine thought as she looked at the date the letter was written. 'One month previous. I still had my job then. I wonder what she is alluding to.'

You might not know but your mother provided me with the start-up capital for my half share of a coffeehouse. And

I would like to repay her faith in me all those years ago by giving you the same courtesy. I would like you to have my half share of the business. However, you will have to meet certain criteria for it to be finalised. My solicitor will explain to you the finer details but a rough outline is described in the 'criteria to be met' document.

Catherine looked at the other document and it was indeed labelled 'Criteria To Be Met'. She laughed. If she had noticed the filename, she was sure she would have opened it first. She carried on reading.

Your skillset and the variety of posts you have filled make you an ideal candidate to take over my reins in our small but thriving business. I hope you will love working there as much as I did and will continue to make it a success.

If you take a full and active part in the running of the business and thriving community hub, I can only see it going from strength to strength. I know you will do your best but if it is not for you, please ensure you do nothing to harm my business partner or the business. I will give you one year from the date you sign the agreement. If you fulfil the criteria listed your name will replace mine. If not, my share will be given to Ms Georgina Turnball. Your future rests entirely in your own hands.

Please do not dismiss this chance of a lifetime. It could be the making of you.

No matter what, on my death, the flat above The Perfect Blend coffeehouse, Gloucester Road, Bristol will become yours with no strings attached, to do with as you will.

Kindest regards

Your Great Aunt

Laura Richards xx

Catherine paused for a moment taking in all the implications of being given a property and half share in a business. She decided to concentrate on the property as this was a given. She ticked off different ideas in her head about what she could do with it.

The three main ones came down to move in, rent or sell.

If she moved, she would always have a roof over her head. Okay, it was Bristol, but there were worse places to be. By renting it out, the money would give her a buffer, allowing her time to get another job. The problem was immediate though. She needed money for this month's rent. Perhaps she would have to ask Sue for a loan to tide her over.

She could sell it and use the money to cover her rent. But with the cost of living in London, that would soon be frittered away and, more than likely, she would be in the same position she is now.

Perhaps she should sell and try to find a small place in the suburbs, where it was cheaper. But that would be no different than upping sticks and moving across the country.

She tapped her pursed lips as she continued to think and for the first time in ages, she felt positive about where her life was going.

Aloud she said, "Another get together with CATS is needed." She grinned then berated herself, "Okay, you have wasted enough time. Don't be a chicken and open up that other document."

Criteria to be met:-

1. To work the required hours each week.

She nodded. "To be expected."

2. To work mutually beneficial shift patterns with the co-owner Georgina Turnball.

"Sounds reasonable."

3. To bring the business into the twenty-first century by introducing an up to date electronic stock control and accounting system

"Easy. What I was doing for one of my previous jobs"

4. To keep the accounts and produce the tax returns on time.

"And this"

5. To hold monthly meetings with our accountant for the first year.

"I hate meeting stuffed shirts. They always wind me up the wrong way" she sighed. "They usually think they are superior to me. But if needs must."

6. To attend a weekly meeting with Georgina, and a monthly meeting with Georgina and Rachel to brainstorm ideas

"As I would expect. I wonder who this Rachel is? I'm sure to find out soon"

7. To design a website to showcase our individuality

"Two jobs ago. Easy"

8. To increase our visibility on social media

"Yeah. Being on social media officially during office hours. Love it."

9. To promote our presence in the local community

"Could be tricky as I don't know the area."

10. To investigate other income streams and see at least two of them come to fruition

"Sounds like hard work, but I should imagine doable. I'll tap up Tracy for some ideas. She's always thinking up new money-making ideas."

11. To liaise with representatives to source more local and sustainable products

"Again, as long as they are not stuffed shirts or real hippy-like, it won't be a problem"

12. To cut our carbon footprint of all goods sold

"Could be difficult but something, deep down, I believe in."

13. To increase the annual profit by five per cent over and above the previous year.

"Impossible to predict. How can I agree to this? I don't know the area, the community, the constraints the local government has."

I predict that if most of the above criteria are met then that should lead to at least an increase in annual profit of five per cent over and above the previous year, and this figure will be the benchmark to whether you take up my share of the business.

"Nope. Impossible. And yet I ticked off most of the criteria as doable."

She reread the criteria, then moaned, "I can't even research the place. Going by these criteria they are in the dark ages. No website. No social media. Nothing. But I can Google the area and see what pops up. That's a good place to start. I can't believe I'm contemplating this. But first I need someone else's perspective on all this."

She picked up her phone and dialled.

"Hi, Sue. Are you busy?"

"What do you want to do. How do you feel about it?" Sue asked after she read the email. "There is nothing there which you couldn't do if you put your mind to it."

"That's what I thought." Catherine pondered for a little while. "But it will be a massive change."

"But do you want your life to stay the same or do you want it to change?" Sue sighed, "Look around you. If you like what you see then appreciate it now because nothing stays the same. If you think it does look at what has happened to you in the past few weeks. What you have here will all be changed next year."

"I know things change. I'm not daft."

"I'm not saying you are. I know you. You need challenges. And if you stay around here, will there be opportunities for you. You told me that you've been looked over for the younger generation in the last couple of job interviews. I say take it."

"Even if it means moving away from you, the twins." Catherine sighed.

"Yes, even if it means moving away from me and the twins, Words, time and opportunities never return once they have gone. Use the inner strength you have. You know things don't get easier, instead, you find the strength to do them better. Allow that strength to grow. Be braver than you think you are. I think it is the ideal opportunity for you." Sue squeezed her knee.

"But what if I'm not brave. That what you see is all show. Bluster."

"It might be a little bit bluster. People won't know you there. You can reinvent yourself as no one has any preconceived ideas of who you are and what you can do. You don't need references. You don't even need to pass a job interview. All you need to do is sign on a dotted line. You will have a blank canvas to paint the picture of your choice. Don't sell yourself short. Make it a masterpiece, not a scribble. Make it a place where everyone wants to see and be seen. Make it the best it can be."

"I'm scared."

"I know sweetie. Make this adventure like a snapshot or selfie. You will be focusing and emphasising what is important at first. For some it is the plate of food in front of them, for many it who they are with, or for others it might be the place they are in. But whatever, whoever and wherever you are, remember to capture the good times within your heart and soul. If something either does not quite ring true, if people let you down, or places don't work out, then evolve from those negatives. Don't be afraid to take another shot and produce a more candid picture of what, who and where you are along your path of life."

"Sage advice. What has happened to my silly, micky taking buddy?"

She burst out laughing and said, "Give her a minute. And she'll be back to her old ways."

CHAPTER FIVE

Letters and Contracts

Georgina had given her name to the receptionist and was soon beckoned into an office and handed a letter.

Rupert James, one of the partners in the firm stated, "There is a reason I called you in early. Laura wanted me to give you this letter, and for you to have time to read and digest it. She hoped it would explain the rationale into why she changed her Will. Knowing the contents of the Will, I also realised you might need time to compose yourself after you have read it, and before meeting the others."

He handed her the letter and left the room closing the door quietly behind him.

Georgina sat down and held the letter in front of her. The familiar writing jumping off the envelope. Trepidation coursed through her veins, as she wondered how all the years had come to this, sitting alone with a letter in an impersonal office.

She became aware of the total silence that surrounded her. A change was coming, but how big would the change be? Would only the hiding cobwebs in the corners be blown away, or was a complete renovation in the making? Would the comfortable security of familiar surroundings be replaced by an unsettling, strange environment?

A deep depression seemed to gather over her head as various emotions invaded her thinking. The air hung heavy as massive storm clouds began to develop in her mind. She could feel it brewing but what type of storm would it be.

Would it be a flash flood, which would be over as quickly as it arrived, but could leave lasting damage in a matter of minutes?

Maybe a large series of storms would be waiting in the wings. Ready to follow each other, but each different enough so their paths were hard to predict. With each storm building on from the chaos previously inflicted.

Perhaps a hurricane would blow in? Ripping up everything in its path to eventually lose its power, after having affected all the surrounding infrastructure.

But then again it may be a continual heavy downpour. Where its persistence enables one to recharge any stagnation and drought. Allowing the sustainability of new growth and improve the resources at its disposal. To breathe new life into the ground packed hard through years of travelling the same path.

Georgina sighed. Did she have the energy left for the change that was coming? Would she be strong enough? Could she cope with major adjustments towards the latter years of her working life? But most importantly did she want to?

This business was hers and Laura's. They had built it up from nothing. Their hearts and souls were ingrained in every brick, in its very being. How could Laura do this to her? How could she pull the rug from under her? Didn't she ever love her? Didn't she ever care for her?

She closed her eyes and took a few breaths to steady the raging emotions that were boiling inside her. She gasped in another deep breath and opened her eyes. She stared at the familiar writing as though it could convey what was inside.

"Oh, Laura. What have you done?" Georgina pleaded to the ghost of her friend who had held a place in her heart. But Laura wasn't there. Hadn't been there for a long time. Her heart was alone, as it nearly always had been.

And yet it continued to beat. The dependable pulsing vibrated through her body. A steadying rhythm, grounding her, guiding her, giving her the strength to face the adjustments that were coming. Spreading its life through her body. Giving hope for the future.

She turned the envelope over and slid her forefinger under the flap. She pulled out the folded pages, opened them out and started to read.

My dearest Georgina

If you are reading this then my place on this planet has come to an end. I found out a little while ago that my time was short and I'm afraid I didn't take the news very well. I just hope my last few days weren't too painful. Some things are going to happen whether we like it or not.

I'm so sorry for the hurt I put you through. I know I was never a good enough person for you. You deserve someone to love you fully and I was never that person. Please realise that I did love you in my way, although the way I showed my love wasn't always kind.

I know you will struggle to keep the business going by yourself so I think I have found someone who is more than capable of taking my place, and I would like her to take over my mantle. To take the business further into the twenty-first century.

She has a wide range of skill sets but will need gentle guidance to get the best out of her. You are that person. She works better when she is challenged. She doesn't suffer fools gladly, but as neither you, nor Rachel, are fools and unlikely to rub her up the wrong way, you should get on well. So keep her on her toes but allow her to fly.

Over the years I have listened to your thoughts on how to take the business forward and have narrowed yours and my ideas into achievable segments. I know she will need to prove herself to you so I have come up with a thirteen-point plan to work towards the final goal of whether she becomes your business partner or not.

If you are still reading then I know that she has agreed to the criteria I set out, which I think bodes well for the future. And if she manages to do this, or even gets close, then I think she will be a worthy partner in the business. If she doesn't then I was wrong but I think it was still worth taking the chance.

Please keep your heart and mind open to new ideas, as we have discussed over the years.

My love for you never changed, but I did. You will always be my dearest friend and sometimes bedfellow. I'm sorry I couldn't be the woman you needed or deserved. But remember I loved you in my way. You were always there for me, even when we were apart.

Yours forever

Laura xx

She read through the letter again. Shocked by Laura's admission that she hadn't had long to live. What was wrong? Why wasn't she told?

Sadness seeped through her, she felt herself become weak,

glad that she was sat down. Laura had always been insular. Putting shields up around her to stop anyone from getting close. But Georgina was the person that was allowed to be intimate occasionally. To break down that barricade for a short while until the barrier was rebuilt, stronger.

Georgina thought back to that night a month or so ago. When Laura had appeared on her doorstep, drunk. Why had she turned her away? Laura must have wanted to open up, to reveal a small beacon of light in the darkness of her mind, allowing a fragment of her soul to find peace. But instead, she was faced with a black hole of anger, where any remaining light got caught and extinguished, and all the dying embers of love and acceptance were sucked into the sphere of nothingness. Where the glowing ash diminished until all hope was gone, and any residual emotions were blown away on the breeze.

"Oh Laura," Georgina wailed in shock, trying to fathom all that she had just learned. "I'm so sorry I wasn't there at the end when you needed me. I thought it was another false dawn. Another time when you divulged your undying love for me, for you to then cruelly snatch it away the next morning. I couldn't go through that again. But I didn't know you were sick. I had no idea."

She shook her head at the memory. "I had to preserve my sanity. You know that don't you. I had to push you away."

Georgina took a deep breath and closed her eyes. "And for the first time, I did push you away... Why didn't you insist on staying? You knew I loved you more than any words could say... But I was only human... There are only so many knock-backs a person can take, and I had reached my threshold. I'm so sorry. Will you forgive me? Did you forgive me? But that is perhaps what you wanted me to do. To stop loving you. Was that your way of setting me free? If it was, it still hurts as much."

Georgina sat for a short while clutching the letter in her

hands, allowing different scenarios and her emotions to play out in her mind. When the feeling of a type of peace won the struggle inside her, she gave a small sigh.

She flattened out the crumpled pages in her hands, turned to the second page and read through the criteria. She could see no surprises. She reread it and shook her head. Most of the criteria seemed fairly achievable, a lot was what they had previously discussed. But an increased annual profit of over five per cent was virtually unheard of. Not in today's climate.

The business was not a start-up. They had a steady stream from local customers. She couldn't envision how this extra revenue could be generated. And although the criteria written down were things they had discussed over the past couple of years, neither of them felt compelled to embrace any ideas they came up with. Each of them was stuck in their ways and their youthful energy had long since dissipated.

Perhaps this is why Laura didn't leave her share to her. Perhaps this was the kick up the backside the business needed, with the multinationals inching ever closer.

She felt herself smile a little through her tears. She blew her nose and dabbed at her eyes. She left the room ready to hear whether there were any other bombshells Laura had dropped.

Georgina sat down next to Rachel. They had left the coffeehouse in the competent hands of Simon and one of the regulars who had helped out previously. She was grateful it was a Tuesday, as it was their quietest day. All she wanted to do was to get the legalities over with so she could get some semblance of order back into her life. So she would know where she stood and could start planning for the future.

Rachel gave her arm a reassuring pat. Georgina gave a weak smile back.

The door creaked open and Catherine walked through followed directly by Rupert James, the solicitor.

Georgina was straight away held like a magnet by the deep blue piercing eyes that locked with hers. Georgina pulled her eyes away and looked the woman over. She was dressed in blue, skinny jeans, a polo shirt and a lightweight hoodie. Her legs seemed to go forever. She pulled off the hoodie as she looked around the office.

A smile played on Georgina's face.

She felt Rachel nudge her leg. Rachel pulled her closer as said, "Stop gawping."

"I'm not."

"You are too." Rachel squeezed Georgina's knee and said, "But it's good to see."

The smile turned into a full-blown grin, as Georgina whispered, "She looks pleasant enough. That's if this is the infamous Catherine."

And so the game began where she needed the answers to unwritten questions, that could only be found in the eyes. And yet by making eye contact she would be at a disadvantage as all her needs and desire would be laid bare. There was something about her. She was drawn to her as if there was a cord attaching her to this beautiful woman. That, from this moment on,their lives would be linked by more than the business.

Georgina's eyes roamed, and avoided looking directly into the piercing eyes, that held a hint of mirth. The woman appeared to be somewhere in her forties. Georgina noticed that the muscle definition was beginning to be lost in her arms and legs. Batwings wobbled as she moved her arms to pull out the chair. Yet it didn't distract from the impression she was having on Georgina.

The instant Georgina thought Catherine had noticed her scrutiny, she quickly averted her gaze. She turned her head, making a show of looking about the office, as though she was casually glancing around, observing everything, Catherine included.

Georgina's eyes resting briefly on the woman's face, appraising her. She was trying to discreetly study her face, perhaps to find the intention behind her attendance.

Catherine became aware of the woman eying her up and down. A small smile played on Catherine's lips. She was used to scrutiny from men but to have a woman taking an unusual amount of interest was different. Not uncomfortable, just unfamiliar.

Their eyes locked, both looking intense yet their desires were different. Catherine allowed herself to focus on this moment, on this woman in front of her. She needed this opportunity. She had no idea what she would do if she didn't take it.

She looked into Georgina's face, as the light from the window, shone in her eyes, and for a fleeting moment, she saw something she hadn't seen directed at her for years. Lust.

She smiled again and before she sat down, she extended a hand in her direction and said, "I'm Catherine."

Georgina grasped the outstretched hand. A slight tingle made its way up Catherine's arm as both hands touched. Catherine frowned at the feeling. She gave Georgina a slight nod and one of the corners of her mouth went up as if she smirked at her.

"Georgina," she smiled back. Their eyes held longer than was usual, both unwilling to break the connection. After what felt like ages but was in fact seconds, Catherine remembered the other woman in the room and broke the hold. She turned to Rachel

"Rachel." Rachel shook the pro-offered hand. "Pleased to meet you."

The solicitor cleared his throat. "Now you're acquainted with each other, let us get down to business."

Everyone settled into their seats and the solicitor shuffled through a few papers. He said, "We are here to finalise the will of Laura Richards. I'll read the Will. See whether there are any questions, and if you, Catherine, are satisfied with the criteria being imposed on you, I will ask you to sign. Georgina, I will ask you to countersign showing your understanding. And finally, both myself and," he looked at the papers, "Rachel will witness."

He looked at the three women.

"Okay, down to business."

He picked up the Will, cleared his throat, and started reading all the legal jargon. Finally, he got to the crux of the matter.

> *I am leaving the residue of my personal account to my business partner Ms Georgina Turnball. I wish you no ill will, and as I explained in my private letter to you, I think you need another person to share the burden of running our thriving business.*
>
> *The gift of my share in the business goes to Catherine Mary Munden. And is in thanks to her mother, sadly deceased, who provided the start-up capital for this venture all those years ago.*
>
> *I know you will do your best to make this work, but if it is not for you, please ensure you do nothing to harm my business partner, Georgina Turnball, or the business. I will give you one year from the date you sign the contract agreement. If you fulfil the criteria and succeed in making a five per cent increase in annual profit, then your name will replace mine. If not, my share will revert to Ms Georgina Turnball.*
>
> *I bequeath the flat above The Perfect Blend, Gloucester*

Road, to the aforementioned Catherine Mary Munden with no strings attached. To do with as she will.

To our employee Rachel Louise Mendoza I bequeath £1000. Please help ensure the smooth transition in the first difficult few months. Thank you for the cheerfulness and insight you brought over the years.

The solicitor continued reading through the rest of the myriad of legalese. At the finish, he placed the document on the table and asked, "Any questions?"

Catherine raised her hand to speak. "So you're saying I have to work my backside off for a year but if I don't reach the magic five per cent increased profit, then it was all for nothing."

"Yes, Ms Munden. That is exactly what I am saying."

"And the flat is definitely mine. I could move in now if I wanted to."

"All that is needed is your signature on a couple of documents."

"And you Ms Turnball? What do you think?" Catherine asked.

"Georgina."

She nodded. "Okay. And you Georgina. What are your thoughts on this whole palaver?"

"Surprised. Hurt." Georgina's voice displayed the multitude of thoughts that had been swirling around in her brain. Thoughts that had magnified since receiving news of firstly, the death of her friend, and secondly, realising she wasn't to receive the half share she was expecting. "And a variety of every other emotion possible."

She continued, "Her share of the business and the flat was to do with as Laura wished. And yes, I know Laura has given me the monies in her account, so I have come away with something. But it is hard to take." Georgina let out a sigh. "I think I understand why my friend and business partner, your aunt, thought I needed someone to work with. I hope, for the good of the business, that we can work together."

"Very diplomatic." Catherine smiled. "I also hope we can work together."

"Rachel?"

"Not my place to say. I am an employee."

"But if you weren't?"

"I would want whatever is good for the business and good for my employment."

"Right." She turned to the solicitor and asked, "Where do I sign?"

CHAPTER SIX

Getting to know you

The bell over the door tinkled as the three women walked through.

"Hi Simon, Bren," Georgina greeted the two standing behind the counter. "Thanks for looking after the place. Any problems?"

"No. A steady trickle. The rain earlier kept us busy." Simon replied, wiping his hands on his apron.

Georgina nodded. She looked around the area, giving all parts an appraising eye, and acknowledged a few of the regulars. She wandered behind the counter and pulled out an envelope and handed it to Bren. "Thanks. It's what we agreed."

"Th... thanks, Muh... Mrs T." Bren responded, shoving the envelope into his jeans pocket. "G... give me a ring if you need help any other time."

"Thanks, Bren. I'll keep you in mind."

Simon asked, "Do you need us any longer or can we go?"

Rachel answered, "Just give me a mo to go to the loo and I'll be right there."

"Before you go, let me introduce you to Catherine, my new business partner. Catherine, this is Simon. Rachel's cousin, who is helping us out whilst he is between jobs. And Bren, who usually sits in that corner seat over there."

Bren grinned, "An... and I can't think of a nicer place to let my creative juices flow."

Catherine quickly studied both Bren and Simon.

Simon's blue eyes held the hint of a smile as he caught her studying him. He towered above Bren.

Bren's brown eyes held a million hues. Her small nose, above thinner top and fuller bottom lips was straight. She was petite, with her straight brown hair tied back in a ponytail.

Catherine raised her eyebrows and asked, "So which of the creative arts are you interested in?"

"I... I write" Bren said as she pulled her bottom lip between her teeth. When nervous or uncertain, she always bit or chewed on her lips.

"Yeah. What sort of thing?"

A blush spread from the neck up. "I... I write Lesfic."

"Lesfic? What's that."

"Um." Bren looked to Georgina for help. Her blush deepened.

Georgina stepped in and hugged her. "Bren writes Lesbian fiction. Women loving women. It's good as well. Can't wait until the next one comes out."

"It... it won't be long now," Bren admitted. "I... I've sent it off to my editor."

"Here's hoping there are no problems."

"I... I hope so t... too."

Catherine looked at the two women, having listened to the exchange, "I've never heard of lesfic before. I've never seen any in bookstores."

"Quite a lot still don't stock them, or if they do, they are hidden in the dark corners. It's as though they've been told to stock them but they don't want to." Georgina admitted.

Georgina nudged Bren's shoulder. "Bren has quite a following around these parts. You wouldn't think someone this shy could write anything so steamy. I love it..." she enthused.

Rachel at that moment came back and asked, "What do you love?"

"Reading Bren's books. They've kept me going through many a lonely night."

Bren started to blush again. "Puh ... please. Ya... you know how I hate people talking about my books. An... and talking about them myself."

"But they are so good. You need to push them more," Georgina retorted.

"Nuh ... no I write because I enjoy it. Nuh... not for any other reason."

Rachel joined in. "I've read all of them." She waved a hand in front of her face as though she was fanning herself. "Wow."

Bren replied, "Y... you have a husband."

"Yes. And before Buwan you also know I liked sex with a woman," she laughed. Rachel pulled Bren into a hug and continued to laugh, "Come here and give me a kiss."

Bren squealed and pushed Rachel's arms away. "G... get off me." She started to laugh, "I...I've told you before that you're not my type. Muh... Mrs T. Hu... help..."

Georgina shook her head, smiling. "I'm not getting involved."

"Suh... Simon?" Bren pleaded.

"Rachel, behave yourself in front of your new boss."

Rachel immediately stopped her teasing. She turned to Catherine and said, "Oh my goodness. I'm so sorry. Whatever must you think of me."

"It looked like two friends teasing each other and having a laugh. Have you known each other long?"

Bren answered "Suh... since secondary school. Wuh... we had to sit next to each other in Fu... French. Wuh... we were both clueless."

"Then we met up again when Bren moved back and started using the coffeehouse to write." Rachel continued.

"It... it's a lot quieter than home." Bren sighed, "I... I love my Dad but I need my own space."

Rachel turned to Catherine and said, "You ought to read one of Bren's books. I think 'Two women on the edge' is the least explicit one."

"What makes you think I don't want explicit." Catherine gasped and covered her mouth with her hand and added, "I said that out loud, didn't I? Why did I say that out loud?"

She started giggling and the other women joined in. Simon rolled his eyes and said, "I think this my cue to leave. Bye. I'll be here for the early shift tomorrow." He turned to Catherine and said, "Don't let them corrupt you."

"Don't worry about me. My girlfriends back home already have. No." She blushed. "Not like that. They are all happily married women. Sorry. I'll shut up now before I put my foot in it some more."

When the laughter died down Georgina, still smirking, said to Catherine, "Come on. Let me show you the shop entrance to your flat, your street one is the black door to the right of the shop."

"Lead on. I'm looking forward to seeing it," Catherine answered.

As they were walking down the corridor to the back stairs Georgina said, "I'm sorry. I haven't done anything to it except I washed the sheets and the rest of the laundry. I've boxed up Laura's clothes, books, photos and the like and labelled the boxes."

"That doesn't seem like nothing. It sounds as though you have virtually done everything. Thanks." Catherine smiled her gratitude.

Georgina continued, "I hope you don't mind but I took a couple of bits and pieces that had some sentimental memories. A photograph and a holiday knickknack. I didn't know what you wanted to do with the boxes so I left them in the guest bedroom. Simon said he would help take anything to charity shops or the tip if you want him to."

"Thank you and that was kind of Simon to offer."

"Yeah. He's a good bloke."

Later, after the coffeehouse had shut for the evening Georgina took Catherine to the pub over the road, for a bite to eat and a drink.

Once they were settled with the food and drinks in front of them Catherine asked, "Was my aunt seeing anyone? Was there a significant other I should know about?"

Georgina's eyes glazed over, as the sadness ran deep. A corner of her mouth turned up slightly, more in a grimace than a smile. "No. No significant other," she admitted, answering without thinking, shrugging her shoulders.

"So she never married?" Catherine continued to prod.

Georgina shook her head and swallowed hard. "I don't think she loved the person enough to do that."

"That's so sad. What was his name?"

Georgina took a deep breath and asked, "Why are you bringing up her personal life? When was the last time you saw her?"

"It was years ago. But I'm interested in why she would leave part of her estate to me. I know she said Mum had given her the start-up money. Did you know my Mum?" she asked Georgina, dumbfounded.

Georgina shook her head and stared intensely at Catherine. "No. Laura didn't tell me how she suddenly came up with half of the funds. One minute she was still a good year away from saving up enough and then the funds were in place. All she told me was that she came into an inheritance."

Catherine delved into her memories. "Laura was always good to me. I only knew her as Aunt Lolly. I had forgotten her surname was Richards. She was only ten years older and she looked after me a lot as I was growing up. She was my favourite babysitter. And then mum and my aunt had this massive argument and I didn't see her again. Mum wouldn't talk about her. I thought she must have died. And now she has. So sad."

"Yeah," Georgina replied as tears started to collect in the corner of her eyes.

"I'm sorry. I'm being insensitive. I didn't mean to upset you."

"That's okay. Can you remember how long ago you saw her?"

"I know I was in working for an accountancy firm and came home for a weekend to find them screaming at each other. So I must have been about twenty... twenty-one. Somewhere around that age. I can remember Lolly left without speaking to me. I asked Mum what was going on and she got angry with me. So I never asked again."

Catherine stayed lost in her memories for a moment, then she asked, "What about you? Are you married? Living with anyone? Seeing anyone?"

Georgina shook her head and getting restless, hoped she wouldn't probe further.

Again Catherine noticed the sadness and she quickly added, "You look as though you are thinking of someone special? What happened?"

"They obviously didn't love me enough," she grimaced and prayed that line of questioning would end.

"I'm so sorry. My best friend Sue says that I ask too many probing questions. She just tells me to shut up and that it's none of my business. She pouts. I sulk. She looks daggers at me. I make a funny face then we're back giggling again."

Catherine got out her phone. Scrolled, and showed a picture of four women. They were all pulling silly faces. "That's me, Anne, Tracy and Sue. We've been good mates forever. We call ourselves the CATS."

Georgina gave her an inquisitive look. Catherine laughed. "It started as a joke. Someone said to us that when we went out, we spent our evening's hunting and playing predator games just like a pack of lionesses. So we started to roar then purr like cats. Tracy noticed that our initials spelt the word cats. And so the name has stayed with us from that day forward."

Georgina shook her head in amusement.

"Roar" Catherine pawed and scratched at the air in front of her.

"So do you still all go out as predators."

"Good grief no. Usually only a sedate evening with something to eat and a couple of wines. All of the others are happily married. I'm sure you'll be seeing them soon. They are too nosey to stay away."

"You are so lucky to have friends like that."

Catherine frowned, "Weren't you and my aunt Lolly like that. I thought you were best buddies."

"We were." Again sadness passed across her face. "We were best friends for over thirty years. We became joint owners in this place. We built this up from nothing to what you see today."

"It seems to be a hub for the community."

"It is."

"So why have I been brought in? What happened between you two? "

Georgina shook her head, "Your aunt was a troubled soul.

She went through very dark times. We were arguing quite a lot at the end."

"About the coffeehouse."

"No. We never argued about the coffeehouse. Whereas I could always pull her out of her melancholy, recently I couldn't. But I don't want to talk about it."

Catherine scrutinised the woman sat opposite her. "Okay," she replied, as she wondered for a moment what she meant. There had been an argument and pondered what had caused the rift. "Not my problem," she thought to herself.

"Hi, babes," Sue spoke down the phone. "How did the meeting go at the solicitor's. Did you sign all the paperwork? Did you meet your new business partner? What's the place and the flat like? How long are you staying over there? Do you think you've done the right thing?"

Catherine burst out laughing. "Slow down and stop bombarding me with questions."

"Sorry babes," Sue snorted. "You know me. I have to get everything out before I forget what I want to say or ask."

Catherine started laughing again. "Okay. The meeting went well and I did sign all of the paperwork, and yes, all of the paperwork. I did as you said to do before the meeting. I drove past, parked up and went in for a coffee. It seemed very popular both with the sit-down crowd and those having a takeaway. I felt as though they were short-staffed but with my Aunts death and the upcoming meeting, it was understandable."

She squinted as though she was remembering the shop. "There was plenty of tables to sit down at, also a small area that had a couple of sofas and a coffee table, and a couple of booths if you wanted a bit more privacy."

"It sounds as though it catered for all tastes throughout the day."

"That's what I thought as well. There was the usual array of coffees, speciality teas, cocoa and chocolate, as well as soft drinks. A few cakes, biscuits and sandwiches were displayed. I also noticed a menu hiding behind the counter but I don't think it is used anymore."

"So were your first impressions good?"

"Very good."

"So no second thoughts? The twins didn't try to change your mind? They both phoned me to get me to try to put you off moving. But as I said to them, it can only be your decision. And whatever you decided we would have to back you all the way. They know you haven't been happy for years."

"They both did phone me, reiterated the cons we talked about when we last met up. But apart from the three of you, there is nothing left for me in London. No job. No flat to live in next week. No prospects. At least here I have a place to live and a job to go to. Whether it is for me or not, I have a year to find out."

"Well, fingers crossed it turns out for the best," Sue replied.

Catherine admitted, "I did have a moment of indecision where my hand hovered over the dotted line. But it seemed too good an opportunity to let slip through my fingers. That means I now own a flat on one of the main roads into the centre of Bristol. And I have a year to work on improving the coffee-house, cafe, whatever you want to call it, to allow me to get a half share in what could be a thriving business."

"So when are you coming back to finish all your packing."

"I'm driving back after the rush hour tomorrow morning. Can you meet up for lunch? I'll send you some pictures so you can tell me what you think."

"Okay. See you for lunch tomorrow. Usual place? Usual time?"

"Yeah, usual place. And hopefully usual time. I'll text you if

I'm going to be late."

CHAPTER SEVEN

First impressions

"So, first impressions?" Rachel asked as they were tidying up and restocking the coffeehouse after the early morning rush.

"My first impression? May I think about it?" Georgina replied as she loaded the tray of dirty cups, saucers and plates into the dishwasher.

"No," Rachel smirked at her. "First impressions are exactly that. Your first impressions. Not a thought-through answer, where you have dissected everything from the colour of her eyes to the type of shoes she wore, or the way she spoke, or whether she had laughter lines and a moustache." Rachel flicked the tea towel towards her, laughing, "But in your head, I expect you have done that already."

"Okay, okay," Georgina smiled back. "First impressions." She tapped her lips with her forefinger and thought for a split second before continuing, "She appears to be a very confident person." She paused. "But how could she make a massive decision like moving to Bristol from London as she did so quickly. Is she moving away from something?"

"Or someone."

"Exactly. And there is also the number of jobs she has had, and that is just the ones either she or Laura mentioned or hinted at. Why didn't she stay longer in those positions? Does she have an issue with staying anywhere long?"

"Or the economic climate didn't allow her to stay." Rachel

countered.

Georgina made a face and shook her head. "Nah, there is something more to it." She thought for a moment then asked, "Did you see the colour of her eyes. They were so striking. I felt as though I was being drawn into her. As though I could look into her soul."

"Her eyes did sparkle." Rachel laughed, "but looking into her soul... I think that was more to do with you fancying her."

"Do not."

Rachel smirked.

"I don't," Georgina argued. Rachel raised her eyebrows. Georgina conceded, "Okay, just a little."

"Tart." Rachel teased.

"But when have you known me to ever act on these feelings."

"Perhaps you should." Rachel reached across and put her hand on Georgina's arm. "You hankered after Laura like a sad puppy dog. Waiting for her to call you up to the flat so you could be her pet for the day."

"I didn't."

Rachel looked at her in disbelief. She squeezed her fingers and said, "I know you loved her. And I know Laura was a good person and your friend, but you and she were not suited. So similar and yet so different. You were always at her beck and call, but was she ever at yours?"

Georgina looked sad and acknowledged her friends' words.

"You are a lovely person with a beautiful heart. I want you to do something about your feelings and attractions. Otherwise, you will end up lonelier and sadder than you already are. There are plenty of women who come in here to take your pick from. I'm sure there are a couple in the Thursday walking club that would jump at the chance."

"Get away with you. There's nobody in the walking club that fancies me." She flicked the tea towel she was holding towards Rachel. "Why do you think that?"

"Boss," Rachel said exasperated, "you might usually be spot on with your gaydar, but you are useless realising when some-one got the hots for you."

"Who has. Who?" Georgina prodded.

"Not going to say. Where would the fun be in that?" Rachel giggled. "I'll enjoy watching you trying to work out who they are." She paused, turning serious, and said, "It's about time you put yourself out there. Yes, grieve over your friend and let your battered heart mend. You have to look forward and stop beating yourself up over the false hopes Laura put you through for years. With you hoping the two of you would somehow turn into this loving couple and have the perfect relationship. I saw the hurt she caused you. And I think you knew, deep down, it was never meant to be."

"My head knew but my heart wouldn't listen," Georgina whispered as she agreed.

Rachel spoke softly, "I know. But you have so much to give to the right person. Why don't you have some fun finding that person."

"I'm too old for all that malarkey."

Rachel put her arms on Georgina's shoulders. "You are not too old. Be the woman I first knew. The outgoing, gregarious woman. The woman who laughed and joked. Not this shell of the loving person I knew."

"I'll think about it." Georgina pouted.

"Good."

"Thank you." Georgina smiled at her friend.

Rachel grinned. "Now back to your first impressions."

"Okay." She tapped her finger against her lips. "She did seem friendly enough. And behind the counter, you have to have an outgoing personality. She knows her way around an accounting system as she shrugged that aside."

Nodding, Rachel said, "As I heard her say she had set up a few web sites. I did look at a couple she mentioned and they looked very professional."

Taking a long breath, Georgina continued, "I know we have to bring the coffeehouse into the twenty-first century kicking and screaming. And Laura and I often discussed it, but neither of us was inclined to do anything. Perhaps, even if she doesn't stay, she will at least do that for us. And I know we need to get on Facebook, Twit thingy, Instamail and whatever." She shook her head. "I hate texting. I haven't one of those posh mobiles, nor even a whatchamacallit."

"Smartphone? iPad?"

"Yeah, iPad. That's it."

"It's Twitter and Instagram."

"Whatever." Georgina waved her hand dismissively.

Rachel smiled at her boss with a shake of her head. "You do need to think about all the good things that the latest technology can help with."

"We have a laptop."

"But it's the work one. And I've only ever seen you work on it. I bet there are no downloaded games on it or any social media sites."

"True. I don't have anything like that on it."

Shaking her head Rachel asked, "How do you cope with no social media to keep you up to date?"

"I talk face to face with people." Georgina sighed, looked at Rachel and asked, "So how am I going to cope if I'm expected to do all this techie stuff?"

"You'd get one of us minions to do it," Rachel laughed. "Or

we will show you what to do every day until you realise it doesn't bite." She paused for a moment then asked, "You're certain she isn't going to stay, aren't you?"

"Yes, I am and that's why I'm worried. Why would a big city girl want to come here? I know Bristol is not the back of beyond and has brilliant things going on. I know I don't go into town often, and I overhear conversations about how good the music scene is, the theatre, the harbourside, et cetera. But it is not the capital."

Rachel replied, "Yeah, but you don't always want to be somewhere big. Where life is busy and can take over. Bristol is large enough to be able to do your own thing, yet small enough to be friendly. Just think about this area. It is on one of the main routes into town, with plenty of buses feeding onto this road. It's thriving with loads of independent shops."

"You're correct. We were so lucky to bag this place all those years ago. The only real difference now is the number of students. The two universities and FE college down the road have certainly helped, although some would say hindered, the dynamics of the area, and the locals do support us."

"I'm worried there won't be enough here to keep her occupied. She seems to have a good friendship group around her where she lives now. I'm afraid she might get lonely moving to a city by herself."

"But you're by yourself."

"Thanks for reminding me," Georgina huffed.

"I didn't mean it like that. I know you enjoy their own company. She might be the same type."

The door dinged and Catherine entered. She acknowledged the two women and moved towards them saying, "Now the rush hour is over, I'll be on my way and have a leisurely drive home. Thanks, both, for everything. You have made me feel welcome."

"Safe journey driving back to London," Rachel replied.

Georgina smiled, nodded then asked, "When will you be back? I need to know so I can get enough cover in until then."

"If that's okay with you I'll be gone about a week to finish sorting out my old life. Shall we say Monday week I'll be ready to get stuck in? We'll chat on the phone to work out some sort of training routine, cos I haven't a clue how any of these machines work."

"Okay. You've got my home number as well?"

Catherine quickly scrolled through her phone to check.

"Yep. Both here and home."

Georgina nodded, "Okay. I'll work out with Rachel your first week's shifts. But we'll take some time training you up with the intricacies of the different machines."

"Dishwasher first please as that looks the easiest to start with." Catherine smiled, "Then I could be chief table tidier and cup washer until I get the hang of the others. Okay, I'm off."

"Bye. See you next week." Rachel smiled.

Georgina also gave a smile as she said, "Have a safe journey and I will wait to hear from you."

"Will do. And thanks for accepting me as graciously as you have."

Georgina gave a slight nod of her head in acknowledgement as Catherine left the coffeehouse.

"Do you still think she'll not stick with it?"

"I do. Let's hope I'm proven wrong."

Before they could continue the door dinged again. Bren walked in. Both women greeted her warmly.

"Thank you for yesterday." Georgina smiled.

"I... I enjoyed myself. I... I couldn't get the hang of the middle machine, but we muddled through."

Rachel replied, smiling, "Yes, it is the most complicated." She pulled down a mug. "The usual?"

"Yuh... yes, please. An... and may I have a danish bun." Bren asked.

"Certainly."

Georgina walked towards the office. "Thanks again," she turned to Catherine and announced, "I can't stand around here all day nattering, I'll be on the phone reordering stock. Give me a shout when it gets busy."

"Will do."

Catherine rushed across the floor. She gave Sue a quick kiss on the cheek and as she sat down, she said, "Hi babes, sorry I'm late. The traffic going past Heathrow was awful. I sat in a queue for ever. You did get my message, didn't you?"

"Yes. I did get your message. A smile played on Sue's face. No matter how early Catherine left, she was always late arriving anywhere. It had got her into trouble in so many places of work. "I swapped lunchtime with one of the juniors, so I don't have to rush. Now sit down and take a slurp of your drink. I got the usual if that's alright. "

"That's good, thanks." She took a sip and said, "Just what the doctor ordered. Mmm."

"What do you want to eat?"

"I'll push the boat out and have something different for a change. No just kidding. I'll have my usual."

"And it is going to be my treat."

"I can't let you do that."

"I can and I will. I know you're getting the deposit back on the flat and you won't have to pay any rent in the future, but your money situation will still be dire for a little while. So let me help you out until you are back on your feet."

Catherine gave a small smile. "Thank you," she said.

When Sue came back from putting in the order she asked, "So tell me how it went? Was your soon to be business partner nice? The photos of the coffeehouse were as I expected. A bit dated, but a good size? And the street it was on seemed like it was bustling with life. What about the flat? Was it a decent size? No mould or anything? Was it properly heated? Did you get the smell from downstairs drifting up?"

Catherine sat back, listening, shaking her head at her friend. Finally, she said, "Are you going to rabbit on all lunchtime or do you want to know how it went."

Sue smiled, "Sorry, but after all these years you know what I'm like. So tell me about it."

"Well." Catherine started to impart her impressions of the day to her friend. "The drive over was good. Motorway virtually all the way, except the last few miles. It's about two hours from Heathrow and however long from there to here. It was busy to Reading then was quite a pleasant drive the rest of the way towards Bristol."

"Two hours isn't too bad for visits." Catherine laughed.

"Who said I was going to invite you."

"Oi. Of course, you are going to invite your best friend forever." Sue started to laugh as she continued, "And even if you don't invite me, you know I'll turn up on your doorstep."

Catherine rolled her eyes and gave her I know you would look. "Do you want me to continue?"

"Of course."

The conversation stopped as the food was put in front of them.

Catherine continued, "The coffeehouse was easy to find as it is on one of the main routes into the city centre. There is street parking on the side streets, but it is loading only outside for certain hours during the daytime. After six you can park right outside."

"Why are you talking about parking?" Sue said in exasperation, "What's the place like?"

"I'm talking about parking because it is important to the footfall. The more people who pass by, the more likely they are to come in."

"Okay go on." Sue conceded.

"I sent you the photos. What do you think?"

"It looks a decent size. I like how there are different types of seating. The decor is a bit dated though."

Catherine nodded. "That's what I thought as well. It won't cost much to do something to it. Nothing major. Just a freshen up."

"I'd love to get my hands on it and work my magic."

"Get your interior design paws off it. You know I can't afford your London rates. Don't forget I won't be getting the London allowance any more. I'm going to be a country bumpkin now. I bet my wage won't be much."

She fought the urge to roll her eyes. "Didn't you ask?"

"It slipped my mind." She gave a small giggle, "You should hear the dialect. When I was at the solicitor's I thought I'd walked into talk like a pirate day."

"I'm looking forward to our chats over the next few months as you pick up the accent. Ooh aarh."

Catherine sloshed her friend's arm.

"Ouch."

"You deserved it."

"Carry on." Sue smirked, "I'll try not to take the piss."

Catherine finished the last bite of her lunch, licked her lips and wiped her hands and face on the napkin. She continued, "The flat is directly above, and can be accessed from both the street and through the back of the coffeehouse. It has a fairly big kitchen and living room areas. Two bedrooms, with a Jack and Jill bathroom between. There is another room at the top of the back stairs but that is part of the coffeehouse. Storage I suspect. The flat is bigger than my soon to be gone one. And quieter. But I did hear quite a few sirens. I think there must be quite a big hospital nearby."

"What about the surrounding streets. What's the housing like?" She placed her empty plate on top of Catherine's.

"I had a quick wander. It seemed that all the streets leading off the main road are old Victorian terraced streets. The people seemed a very mixed bunch. It felt very bohemian, with loads of student-types. But there was quite a few of our generation and older. And very multicultural. So as I said mixed."

"What about the other businesses?"

"Loads of independents. There is a Polish supermarket on one side of us and a hairdresser on the other. There's a pub across the road. It's not a part of one of the chains. I sampled some of the food last night. It was very good. Traditional pub fare. Nothing fancy. The woman who is now my business partner took me over there after the coffeehouse closed."

"So that's where you'll be eating every night?"

"No. I noticed there's a Chinese takeaway and an Indian restaurant/takeaway as well as a Turkish restaurant within easy walking distance. Yummy, all my favourites."

"So..." Sue hesitated for a moment.

Catherine gave her an enquiring look. "Yes?"

"What's she like?"

"Who?"

Sue tutted, her eyes narrowed and were full of impatience. "You know who I'm talking about."

"I think she is a little bit older than me, perhaps, mid-fifties.

She seems to be quite set in her ways, but when she relaxed, her sense of humour came through." She reflected for a moment then admitted, "I thought she was sad. I know she had recently lost her friend and business partner but I felt it was something deeper than that. We'll see.

Catherine suddenly started giggling.

"What are you laughing about?"

"When we got back to the coffeehouse, one of the regular customers was helping out. She's a local author." Catherine started giggling again.

"And? What?"

"Have you heard of Lesfic?"

"Yes."

"You have?" Catherine asked incredulously. "Well, I've never heard of it before."

"And I've read some?"

"Have you?" Catherine again stuttered in disbelief; her mouth hung open.

Sue smiled, "Yes, why not. And close your mouth. It doesn't become you."

Catherine huffed.

Sue continued, "The ones I've read have mainly been good. I even made John read some."

"Did you?" Catherine's voice and eyebrows rose higher in surprise.

"Since then he's become much more adventurous," Sue smirked.

"Shut up," Catherine groaned. "You are making me jealous"

"You ought to read some."

"I was told I could borrow one. But I don't know."

"Go on. Live dangerously." As Sue took the last sip of her

drink, she said, “Tell me. Do you think you will give it a good go to make it work?”

“What? Reading Lesfic?”

Sue slapped Catherine’s knee.

“Oi.”

“You deserved that. Well?”

Chewing the inside of her cheek, Catherine thought for a moment and gave a half-hearted nod, “I think so.”

Sue smiled in encouragement, “You have to go for it. Even if it ends for the good or the bad, it will add to your life’s experience. I can see it getting you out of your rut.”

“I’m not in a rut.”

Sue gave Catherine the look and continued as though she hadn’t been interrupted. “And if it does end badly, then all that you would have wasted is your time. I realise that you have less energy and feel weary from all that life has thrown at you recently. I do know your heart was been broken and you’ve had more disappointments than most. But you haven’t given up.” She paused. “Are you scared?”

Catherine pursed her lips and shook her head. “Not really, no.” She then quickly nodded her head in defeat, “Of course I am.” Catherine said with a huff, knowing Sue would pick up the nuances if she lied.

Sue bumped their shoulders together, and said, “Any change will be scary. But do you know what is worse?”

Catherine frowned and shook her head.

“Regret. That will be worse. Imagine if you allow your fears to stop you from doing this and one year, two years down the line, all you say is what if... you look at your life and rue the missed opportunities. But I don’t see fear, I see a bit of apprehension. But mainly I detect and discern this spark of hope and a smile of optimism, I can see it in your eyes and hear it in your voice."

Sue took hold of Catherine's hands in hers and said, "You have pulled through everything life has thrown at you. And the person you are now has been moulded from your past experiences. Where you are now and where you are in a year will be the most important journey you can take." She looked deeply into her friend's eyes. "What that passage through time looks like is down to you."

A look of worry came into Catherine's eyes, "But what if the challenge is too great?"

"No matter what you choose to do, every day is a challenge. Moving to the other side of the country is a test of your resolve. But it is no different than being an actor walking into an improvised play, where everything from the set, characters and lines change daily. Where you have to create something that you, and the audience, are comfortable with. Embrace and feel comfortable with each scene, each act, each complete play. Surround yourself with an audience who appreciates what you are trying to achieve, who likes you for who you are, and will encourage you to be the best you can be."

Sue squeezed Catherine's hands, "Also make sure they are critical enough to bail you out when the path you've chosen is wrong. Befriend people who will encourage you to keep growing and become an even better version of yourself." Sue smiled into her friend's eyes, "I have tried to be that friend and will always be there for you. It's now time for you to remove the script you know by heart. You cannot stay where you are, and you have no choice but to go somewhere else."

"I know." Catherine's response was quietly spoken. "I have a year to prove I can do it. Going by my previous jobs it's going to be hard."

"Those jobs weren't right for you. You are too talented to be defined by them. You are much more than those jobs said you were." Sue continued squeezing her hand and said, "I love you, now start loving yourself and be happy. Remember, no matter how far you have travelled down a path, you always have the choice to turn around. There will always be a place here for you until you decide to where you want to travel, and for how long."

"Thank you." Catherine nodded and smiled, "I love you, too. And I know you'll always have my back and will tell it like it is."

Sue studied her friend's smile and knew that apprehension still flowed through her. She decided to continue with her words of wisdom, and said, "Each tiny step on the road to progress is a journey in itself. But all you got to do is place one foot in front of the other. Join those steps together and soon the whole trip has been achieved. And when you think you have come to the end of your expedition you can take another step and a different journey opens up. If you see something not working endeavour to change it. Small solutions make for big results. And at the end of the year, you will know whether all the steps you took was worth it. I think it will be."

Catherine gave her friends hand a squeeze back. "Are you sure you are not an inspirational speaker instead of a home designer? And yes, I agree with you."

"That's a first," Sue laughed.

This time Catherine swatted Sue's arm, then held her hands over her heart, gave a mock look of hurt and replied, "I'm wounded to the core," she smiled, "I know I have to do this and it is too good an opportunity to let slip."

Giving her friend a smile of encouragement Sue replied, "Well let's hope everything turns out well. I think it will. Remember how you start is important, so embrace it. Everything you do from the first minute onwards will affect and determine whether you will feel successful. So immerse yourself straight away. Let that inner confidence that has been missing for so long come back to the fore. You'll be in a new place with a new beginning. Leave your baggage here, so grow, evolve and advance on this journey into the unknown, and have the courage to become the woman you were destined to be. Be aware that first impressions are good but lasting impressions are better. Make sure each decision you make will leave a positive, enduring opinion."

"Thank you. I'll try."

"I know you will. I'll miss my best friend living around the corner."

"And I'll miss you, too." Catherine suddenly became emotional as she brushed away a stray tear with a knuckle.

"Aww, sweetie. It's not like you are going to the end of the Earth. You're only a couple of hours away." A pained look came over Sue's face as she looked at her watch. "I don't like leaving you feeling sad but I've got to get back to work. Come and hug me. You will see me before you leave, won't you?"

Catherine's face crumpled but the tears were kept at bay, as she nodded, "It goes without saying. And you will get the first invite. I promise."

"I'll give you two weeks and if the invite has not arrived by then I'm coming down whether you like it or not."

"But you don't know the address."

Sue laughed as she moved away from her friend. "Ways and means," she smiled, "ways and means."

Sue looked back one last time and waved before walking into the sunshine.

Catherine felt a deep loneliness envelope her. She hoped with all her being, that she had chosen to do the correct thing. But it was too late now. The wheels were in motion. Forward was the only way to go.

CHAPTER EIGHT

First shift

Fifteen minutes before the coffeehouse was due to open Catherine stood behind the counter next to Georgina.

"Are you sure for my first shift I can't only clear the tables and use the dishwasher? I'd be good at that."

"Don't be nervous. Let me go over it again." Georgina explained the workings of the till once more.

"Everything we sell can be found on the labels. The brown labels are the coffees, the greens are the teas, the reds are the other hot drinks and blue are our soft drinks. Along the bottom the white labels are the sandwiches, yellow is the cakes, snacks and cookies."

Catherine looked daunted as she stared at the piece of machinery.

"It's easy and will soon be second nature. So you look for each item and press the on-screen buttons for the transaction to apply. Then finally press this button. If you make a mistake and it all goes wrong then this is the cancel button. Find out if they are paying cash or card and press the requisite button. If you realise you have made a mistake after you've totalled the transaction, write down the mistake and I'll show you how to rectify it at the end of the shift, then input the sale again. Okay?"

"I think so."

Georgina smiled at Catherine and said, "You are going to sell me a cappuccino and a latte. Show me what you are going to do."

"Cappuccino and latte."

Georgina nodded.

"They are both coffees so I search for them here. Okay. Latte." She pressed a button. "Cappuccino." She pressed the next button and finished the transaction. "Cash or card?"

"Cash."

"Okay." Catherine finished the transaction and the till opened. A smile played on her face.

"Do you want to try another?" Georgina asked.

Catherine nodded. Soon she had tried a variety of scenarios and successfully corrected any mistakes. Georgina looked up at the clock.

"Don't forget to be pleasant, polite and friendly even when it gets hectic. When someone smiles it's hard not to feel happy back. So make our customers feel happy. People don't just buy goods and services. They buy the whole experience. It could be for friendship, stories and laughter, or even be a voice they hear. Wherever possible try to form some sort of relationship, even if it's just a smile. You might be the only person they speak to all day. Make them feel special. Make the last impression you leave with the customer be the most important one. Make them want to come back."

"Will do." Catherine thought over what Georgina. *'Yeah, I could be the only person they speak to. I've never thought of it like that before.'*

"Okay, are you ready?"

Catherine took a deep breath and said, "As ready as I'll ever be."

"We will work like a conveyor belt Rachel and I will take

the drinks order and make it. The receipt gets passed to you and you ask if they want any extras. The cookies and snacks are good to push for the takeaway customers. The sandwiches and cakes for the eat-in crowd. This first half an hour is quite slow so you should get the hang of it before it needs the three of us behind here. Rachel is due at work at eight. How are you feeling?"

"A little overwhelmed."

"You'll be okay. Try to feel confident, or if you can't, pretend. People will know you are new here, but they won't know anything else about you. Smile and if you make a mistake apologise and rectify it. It won't take long until you get into the swing of things. Okay? Good luck."

"Thank you."

Later that morning Catherine leant against the counter. Rachel asked, "How have you found your first shift so far?"

"It's going quickly. I don't think I've made too many mistakes. The local dialect takes a bit of getting used to. It sounds really strange in my ears."

"Yes. It is a bit unique."

"Apart from different and extra words used, and the r and vowel sounds, what I have noticed most is the way the voice went up towards the end of the sentence, making everyone sound surprised, questioning or looking for reassurance. I also can't get used to being called love, lover or babber." She sighed, "but most of all, my feet are killing me. I think I need to get some comfortable shoes."

"There's a shoe shop about one hundred yards down the road. It's the type that has bargain shoes in buckets in the entranceway. Not the type of place to get your shoes to go with your posh frock, but the cheap and cheerful type. The type you would wear to walk around to a mate's house, or pop to the shops in. I know they do comfy shoes. I got these there." Rachel raised her left foot.

"That's sort of what I was thinking about." She suddenly laughed out loud and tried to cover her mouth with her hand.

"What's so funny." Rachel gave her an enquiring look.

"My friend Sue will think an alien has invaded my body. My shoes always have a heel, and here I am looking at your flats and thinking of buying something similar to yours."

"I bet you have never had to stand on your feet this long either?"

"No, I haven't. I didn't realise it could be so tiring."

"Do you want to sit down?" Rachel pulled out two stools that were hidden under the counter. "When it gets quiet like this Georgina and I would often sit down for a natter."

They sat down and kept an eye on the few customers.

"You should see the heels I wear when my hubby deigns to take me out. They're killer ones. I just can't drink too much when I got them on." Rachel laughed, "Otherwise I spend the night hanging on to my old man's arm to hold me up."

The conversation waned for a moment then Rachel asked, "Will we be seeing a significant other?"

"Nope. I'm single. My divorce came through last year and I split up with my last boyfriend almost two months ago." Catherine shrugged.

"Oh, I am sorry."

"It's fine. This opportunity came at the right time. I was between jobs and apart from my friends I have no ties in London. My parents are dead. So even if it doesn't work out, I have only uprooted me."

Catherine thought for a moment, then asked, "What is Bristol like?

"I think it's a buzzing place. We don't go into town much

these days. We prefer staying nearer home. There are some good pubs and restaurants nearby."

"Georgina took me over to the pub over the road last week. It seemed a nice place."

"It's not bad. The Harbourside area in the city centre is a good place to explore and always seems busy, no matter what time of day. The old town is always worth a wander around. And during the summer season every week, there is some festival or another going on. Take a look at the visit Bristol website if you want something more specific. I love living here. Big enough to have everything you want but small enough to feel part of a community."

"On my next day off I will. What's the parking like?"

"If you are only going into town, it's easier to catch the bus. Then you can stay for as long or as short a time as you want. You'll come to the shopping centre first and then a couple of stops later is the city centre."

"That sounds like a plan." They sat in silence for a while before Catherine asked, "Did you know my Aunt well?"

"Even though I've worked alongside her for years. Your Aunt was a very private person. I did like her. She had a wicked sense of humour but rarely did you see it. If you want to know more about her then Georgina is the person to ask. They used to be as thick as thieves."

"You said used to be. What happened?"

"Not for me to say as I don't know. I have an idea, but..." Rachel shook her head. "Your Aunt changed. She was friendly towards me all the time. And we would chat about everyday things, but the conversation would stop at anything personal, or anything to do with her family. It was as though there was a whole side of her about which she would dodge questions and became dismissive. As I said, if you want to know more about your Aunt you will have to ask Georgina."

"Okay," Catherine nodded.

She was about to ask another question when the office door opened and Georgina, walked out. She went over to the other two women and spoke to Catherine, "As it's quiet may I have a word in the office." Catherine got off the stool and pushed it under the counter. Georgina turned to Rachel. "Give me a buzz if you need me."

"Will do."

Georgina had pulled the chairs from behind the tables and had placed them at an angle close together.

"Please sit and make yourself comfortable," Georgina instructed. As they were getting eased into their seats Georgina asked, "It is nearly the end of your first shift, I hope it wasn't too bad?"

"No. I quite enjoyed it, but my feet will tell you something completely different," Catherine laughed.

"I know. I always find that the first shift back from being away is always the worst. So the morning rush seemed to go smoothly. If you can manage that, you'll be able to manage anything."

"But I was only doing the till and tidying up."

"Baby steps. I don't want you to become overwhelmed." Georgina looked intently at the other woman. "I know you have only done one shift but any thoughts."

Catherine gave a small grimace and didn't respond for a few minutes, then replied, "I don't want to tread on anyone's toes but I think we're missing a trick here."

"We will be joint owners of this establishment so if you have noticed something that can be easily changed then we should discuss it. I think that is why Laura wanted you here." Georgina leant back in her seat and smiled encouragement. "Would you like to explain?"

"Do you visit many other establishments such as ours?"

"No. Well, not recently I haven't. Not for quite a while."

"The coffee shop back home which I used a lot had, instead of a till, what was called a point of sale system. They had brought it in about a year or so ago."

"I've never heard of a point of sale system. What is different between that and a till."

"Customers should be able to use their cash, debit, credit cards, and smartphones to pay for their purchases. I noticed that the morning crowd were mainly young twenty-year-olds. I should imagine they are up to date with all the new technology. If we introduce it here, we might keep them coming in instead of one of the multinationals."

"Explain how it works."

Catherine described briefly how it worked and continued by saying, "I would always pay by using my phone and I would have my receipt sent by email. And for us to have our customer's emails would make our marketing easier."

"What do we have to market? We are the local coffeehouse."

Catherine interjected, "Who might be putting on some specials which the locals might find interesting. Who might start to want to come here during the less busy times?"

"I'm not into all this technical malarkey. Our till works fine."

"You might not be, but I am. And I know the till works fine but as I said earlier, we might be missing a trick." Catherine then asked, "Where is the nearest multinational?"

"About a quarter of a mile down the road."

"So the question is... do we want to embrace new technology or chance losing our trade to the multinationals"

Georgina gave a small laugh, "You don't waste your time trying to change things."

"Well, you did ask for my first impressions."

"That I did."

Catherine gave an apologetic smile, "And as I said, I don't want to tread on any toes."

"You did say that as well. And the only toes you will be treading on is mine." Georgina contemplated the suggestion, as she looked at the other woman. "Why don't you do some research and come up with some figures and we'll discuss it again soon."

"Okay. Will do." Catherine nodded her head then asked, "Is the till ours or do we rent it?"

"We rent it."

"Okay." Catherine continued to nod her head and thought for a moment. "Do you know who with?"

"I'll search for the relevant paperwork and leave it on your desk," Georgina replied.

"Or you can scan it on your phone and email it to me." The look of horror passed across Georgina's face.

"Leave it on my desk." Catherine smiled at her. "Oh, and you need to tell me the alarm code so I don't accidentally set it off. And the code to the office."

"Sorry, I didn't think of that." Georgina wrote the codes on a piece of paper rose and gave them to her. Their hands touched and both women felt a frisson pass between them. They both pulled away quickly and Catherine placed the paper in her pocket then stared down at her hand.

"Can you think of anything else?" Georgina asked as she tried to ignore what she felt.

Catherine looked embarrassed. A strange feeling encompassed her and she shook her head to try to remove the sensation.

Georgina scrutinised her, "Are you okay. You look a little out of sorts."

"I think I'm hungry. I didn't eat much at lunch."

"In that case, why don't you clock off now and rustle something up. Simon will be in shortly to take over from Rachel."

"Okay." Catherine rose and as she was walking Georgina asked, "Tomorrow, will you be okay to work the till for the early shift?"

Catherine nodded in the affirmative. "Yep. I'll be fine when I've had something to eat."

"Good." Georgina continued, "When the early rush is over, we'll show you how to work the different machines. Then when you are confident, we'll sort out our shifts for next week. Okay?"

"Yeah, okay."

"I'll see you tomorrow at just before eight."

"You don't want me in earlier."

"Nah, I can cope by myself for the first half an hour. I have done it often enough."

"Okay see you tomorrow."

Catherine walked out of the office and leant against the closed door and puffed out her cheeks. Rachel looked over to her.

"Are you alright? You look pale."

"No, I'm fine."

"Has Georgina said something?"

"No. Nothing like that. I think I just need a sugar burst. She told me to clock off and to have something to eat. So if that's alright with you I'll go upstairs now."

"No problem. Make sure you eat properly we don't want you passing out anytime soon."

"Will do Mum." Catherine laughed at her younger colleague. "I'll see you tomorrow."

CHAPTER NINE

The swing of things

A week or so later Catherine and Georgina were working together during the afternoon. Catherine was cleaning the tables whilst Georgina was rearranging the counter. She heard Catherine laugh and looked in her direction. The joyous sound made Georgina smile and sigh. She studied the woman across the room. She couldn't tear her eyes from her backside. The trousers fit her perfectly, and accentuated her shapely legs.

Georgina thought to herself *"What am I doing? Stop ogling. I don't want to have a crush on a straight woman. I'm too old to have crushes."*

She turned back to her tidying but glanced over to Catherine who was now talking to another one of the customers as she cleared the adjacent table.

"She does have a way about her. She seems to make everyone feel valued."

Catherine looked up and noticed Georgina watching her. Catherine smiled and was presented with a reciprocal one in return.

Georgina felt her heart skip a beat. She started to have a conversation in her mind. "Don't go down that route. Remember your mantra. Stay away from straight women."

She busied herself behind the counter but she found herself surreptitiously giving the slightly younger woman stray glances. The conversation in her head continued, *"It isn't worth it. All it brings is a mess and confusion. You've had enough hurt and disappointment throughout your life. Don't go there."*

Georgina noticed that the customer had asked Catherine a question. Catherine sat down in the empty chair and became fully engaged in the conversation. She suddenly felt a stab of jealousy as she watched the interaction.

"Start distancing yourself. Don't leave yourself open to more hurt."

Catherine walked back to the counter and was standing before Georgina, smiling her radiant smile. Catherine had noticed Georgina had stolen glances at her all morning, ostensibly to make sure she was all right.

Georgina had decided there was no law against looking, she suddenly felt embarrassed at the thought, and some colour bloomed in her cheeks. And for the first time, Georgina could remember in a long time, her heart felt lighter.

Catherine spoke to Georgina, "I think we need a community notice board in here. That's the second person today who's asked me if I know of a local tradesperson to do a job for her, preferably female. What do you think?"

"Good idea. There's room over there. She pointed to a place on the wall near the corridor to the toilets. It's not in the way and easy to get to. It won't disturb any customers if you want to look at it. After we close let's measure up and see what size board we'll need."

Catherine smiled a happy smile. It was her first suggestion since mentioning the till and it was welcomed with open arms. She thought, *"Perhaps she's not so set in her ways after all."*

The smile Catherine gave her made Georgina's stomach do a flip. *"You've got to convince yourself you see her only as a potential friend, not in any other kind of light. That's what you need to do with Catherine. You can't afford to do anything else."* Out loud she said, "As it has quieted down, do you want to look through the accounts and see if there is a more efficient way of doing them?"

Catherine thought for a moment before saying, "I think I'd rather get our social media sites up and running. I don't have to give that much thought."

Georgina frowned at her, so Catherine continued, "I'd rather look at the accounts when I know there is not a chance of being disturbed. I would like to have an allocated time built into my work schedule to look at them."

"That's what we had for Laura."

"But if you don't mind, why don't I get my laptop set up over there and I make a start on our website." She pointed to a table for one by the counter that was rarely used. "That way if we get busy, I can easily close it down and spring into action, knowing I'm not going to lose anything important."

Georgina nodded.

"I've also looked at a point of sale till. I'd like to run some figures past you, and see what you think?" Catherine continued.

And even though Georgina had known her for only a week, a feeling of intense empathy for Catherine flowed through her. Then without thinking she suddenly asked, "Do you want to go over to the pub for an early evening meal when we finish up here. We can talk about the new till in a bit of comfort. I was going to go there anyway so if you want to join me you will be more than welcome."

The realisation of what she had asked invaded her thoughts and the arguments started again. *"Did you just invite her out for a meal? Just the two of us. Are you crazy? Even though you suggested working it sounded far too much like a date. I thought you wanted to be friends. But that's what friends do, isn't it? Friends go to the pub. Just don't let her know you fancy her."*

"What a good plan. I need to get out." Catherine agreed. "I've been holed up in the flat for too many days. I was going to get myself a takeaway, so a trip to the pub works for me." She smiled her dazzling smile. "You can let me know what I can do on my day off tomorrow. Rachel suggested going to the Harbourside. I'd like to hear your ideas."

"The Harbourside? That's a good shout. There's plenty to do around the area." Georgina paused for a moment then said, "You'll have to tell me what you like to do. I'm sure I can help you with it."

Georgina let out a small gasp, and tried to cover it up with a cough, *"Did you ask her what she liked and that you'd help her? Normally you would only say that sort of thing if you were flirting with her. Stop it. Keep remembering, no arm touching, hand on the knee or anything similar. Does she even know you're a lesbian? You'll have to tell her soon, that's if she hasn't realised already."*

"Are you alright? You seem a little hot and flustered." Catherine's voice interrupted her thoughts.

"Yes, I'm good. I think it's my age."

"Tell me about it. I've been struggling with them myself."

"I thought I'd finished with them. Obviously not."

Georgina saw Catherine looking at her phone with a frown. She asked, "Have I come at the wrong time." *Why did that sound like an innuendo? And why is she smirking at me like she'd heard the same double entendre that I did? She could feel herself blushing. I'm going to be very careful about what I say and how I say it.* "Do you need to take that?"

Catherine smirk continued then it quickly disappeared as she replied, "No. it was a text message from my friend Tracy saying they couldn't visit this weekend. One of her children is poorly so she doesn't want to leave him."

"That's a shame." Georgina sat down and as she placed the two drinks on the table, she asked, "Are you missing your friends?"

"Yes and no." Catherine smiled. "We only meet up about once a month so haven't had time yet to miss them. We will chat on the phone about once a week but since being here I've spoken to at least one of them every night. It's as though they've arranged between themselves who is going to phone." She let out a small laugh. "I've told them I'm okay but I don't think they believe me. I'm quite content to sit at home watching the TV or some films. So the evenings are not much different to normal. Just a different set of walls. But I would have had a different set of walls anyway as I would have had to move out of my flat this week."

"It's good to know they care."

Catherine glanced up to see Georgina biting her lip, eyes heavy-lidded and locked on hers.

"They do. They are like mother hens. They've been worse since I broke with my previous fella and I think they will be like this until one or all three of them come down to see for themselves."

Georgina laughed, "But at least you have someone fighting your corner."

"I would hope everyone has someone in their corner. Everyone needs that person who will help fix a flat tyre or change a fuse. Someone you can call at three in the morning, and they will listen through the tears and will cry with you. The person who can tell from the tone of your voice whether you are okay or not." Catherine paused for a moment then laughed, "That's definitely Sue."

Her eyes had a faraway look as she continued, "Now the twins are both the person who, when they are in your house, will make themselves a coffee, without asking permission. The ones who know my deepest darkest secrets and will often bring them up to embarrass me."

Shaking her head with her memories "They all have, on various occasions, been the one who makes sure my hair is out of the way when I was being sick through drinking too much. The person who loves me even when I have annoyed them." She paused, "They are all my no matter what person."

She studied Georgina. "If you have at least one of those, you indeed are blessed. And although I moan about them, I do feel blessed to have three. What about you? Do you have a no matter what person?"

"I did." Georgina's voice caught.

"Oh my god." Her hand went to her mouth. "I'm so sorry. I've put my foot in it, haven't I."

"It's okay."

"No, it's not," Catherine answered. She then asked sincerely, "Do you want to talk. I've been told I'm a good listener."

Georgina studied the woman next to her, and against her usual reticence, she decided to talk. In a quiet voice, she said, "We met up in our first year at the university. I answered an advert for a room in a shared house. A couple of days later I bumped into her in the shared kitchen. She was making a pig's ear of whatever she was cooking. There were pots and pans everywhere. Somehow, I ended up making the meal, whilst she tidied up the bomb site. Soon we ended up eating together every night with me cooking and her washing up."

"Is this my Aunt we're talking about?"

"Yeah, Laura or Aunt Lolly as you know her. After university, we both got jobs and rented a small flat together. We talked a lot about our hopes and fears. Following one night of drunkenness, I admitted to her that I was a lesbian."

"Are you?" Her eyebrows raised. "Well, I never. Had she realised?"

"Yes, I am. And no she hadn't." She paused for a moment. "Is this going to be a problem?"

"N...no. No problem at all." Catherine gave a slight stutter. She had never had to think about this before. "You don't look like I would expect a lesbian to look." Catherine laughed, "I got this image of that actress in the old black and white version of Miss Marple. Wearing brogue shoes and a twin set. I know it's wrong but I've never met any lesbians before."

Georgina shook her head to disagree, "You've met plenty."

"Have I? How do you know. I've only known you a week."

"Exactly. Think back to this past week in the coffeehouse."

Catherine pulled her eyebrows together in a frown. Georgina gave a smile, "Bren."

"I forgot about Bren."

"And there is the walking group. The woman with her little boy, who has a cup of tea before going to pick up her daughter. The one who always has a latte and a danish. The two who always argue over whose turn it is to pay. I could go on."

Catherine stared. Her mouth forming an oh. "How do you know?"

"By talking. You can also pick up the nuances, the little things."

"Well, I never. So was Laura a lesbian?"

"Yes. A very reluctant one."

"So you two were an item?"

"We were at one time." A smile played on Georgina's face as her eyes twinkled with distant memories.

"Spill the beans. You looked delightfully happy as you thought back. So was it love at first sight?"

"Not at first. Not for quite a while. As I said we spent our university years in a shared house. We then shared a flat for a couple more years.

"So how did you get together? Become lovers?"

"I'm going to blush now. We went to a party. and I got so drunk all my inhibitions went out the window. I kissed her.

Not a peck on the cheek but a proper full-blown kiss. Tongues and all. She kissed me back. I was so drunk. She led me back to our flat and I pounced on her."

Georgina blushed, at the memory, "I don't go around pouncing on people. We lived together as a couple for the following ten tumultuous years. In between, we were saving up for this place."

"Sorry if I'm being nosey so why didn't it work out?"

"We tried our best to live together without killing each other. But I wanted more than she was prepared to give. And even though we had the same close circle of friends. She would be off playing the field whilst I went home to the cat."

"That's a shame."

"Falling in love with Laura was so much easier, than being in love or staying in love with her. I wanted to hold on to the best thing that had happened to me but Laura wouldn't allow it. She went out of her way to drop me from her life."

"You have to realise that the person you fell for may never have been ready to catch you. So no matter what you did, however much you let them know, they may have let you fall and you would have ended up hurt."

"She hurt me all right. Not physically. She never laid a hand on me. But she played with my emotions." Georgina set her face with a grim determination. "After one particularly bad row, we decided that we, the relationship, the living together thing, couldn't go on. So we took out a second mortgage, split the flat from the coffeehouse, which enabled me to buy a little place about two streets away. We made sure we worked opposite shifts. We only came together when something needed to be decided with the business. Over time things between us settled down and our working relationship got back on track. We might not have been together anymore but we were always each other's best friend."

"That must have been hard for you." Georgina sighed,

"It was. But that happened about twenty years ago."

"And everything turned out fine? What did any new girlfriends think of the closeness between you?"

"Never saw anyone with Laura though I knew she had loads of flings."

"Do you think her lifestyle is why my Mum and she had that massive argument?"

"I honestly don't know. Even when we were together, she never spoke of family. She was an extremely private person. I wish she would have been more open. Mind you back then it was hard being a lesbian. It's much easier today."

"Have you a significant other?"

"No." With a voice filled with sadness, she replied, "I never had another long term partner."

"I'm sorry."

"I always loved your aunt and any girlfriend could see my heart wasn't truly in it. Over the years your aunt and I became friends with benefits. It worked for us, but she would always be the one to instigate it. She would turn up at my house, never the other way around. And I could never resist her. She still had a hold over my heart."

Georgina sighed, "A few months ago I invited myself up to her flat. And for once she let me make love to her. I told her that I still loved her. That I had loved her from the moment we had first met and I had never stopped loving her. I have never seen anyone move so fast. She went absolutely ape shit. The way she was, took me back to when we were young. I thought her feelings had changed and she felt the same, but obviously, for all those years she was using me. I've never felt so stupid or so humiliated in all my life. After that, we made sure our paths at work rarely crossed. At work, Rachel was the buffer between us. We were civil but the closeness had gone."

She stared into space, thinking of her memories, "A month before she died, she turned up on my doorstep and for once I pushed her away. I felt in control of my life, my future. I wish I knew then what I know now. I would never have pushed her away. At the Will reading, I found out that she was dying. Of what I have no idea."

"That's awful."

Georgina snapped, "How was I meant to know if she didn't tell me."

Catherine shook her head. "That's not what I meant. I meant that it was awful she kept you in the dark. I'm so sorry that you didn't know, that she didn't let you know, that she blocked you out."

"No. I'm sorry. If I've snapped at you or made you feel uncomfortable, I didn't mean it. I think she was going to tell me that night, but I didn't let her. I feel guilty for what happened."

"It's understandable. But you shouldn't feel guilty."

"But I do. What if..."

"Don't you dare go down that road? It wasn't your fault. What you have said sounds as if she treated you badly."

"But..."

"No buts."

"I feel completely out of sorts. My whole world has been turned upside down."

"Understandable. Firstly to lose your best friend, then to realise that she hadn't told you she was dying, and then to find out I've had been given her share in the business. If I was in your shoes, I would be absolutely gutted."

"I was. But watching you work I couldn't wish for a better person to have to work with me."

"Thank you. That's very kind of you to say. As you mentioned work, shall I get us another drink and then we can discuss my research on the new till."

Catherine came back and placed the drinks on the table. She sat down and took a slurp of her drink. She licked her lips in appreciation. Georgina felt a jolt flow through her. Oblivious to the disconcertment she was causing, she placed the drink down and started talking.

"Concerning the point of sale, cash register. I found out there were four companies in the surrounding area which will provide some, if not all, of the services we require. The one we rent from also includes sales and provides assistance, which I'm sure you know. Another of them only rents the equipment but does not provide service. Another company only provides the after-sales service for a variety of registers. And the last one not only offers sales but also after-sales service. The prices are similar rent wise, sales-wise and after service wise. So I suggest no matter what, we stick with the company we already deal with. You told me that they are always reliable, and they know us and we know them."

"How much extra will it cost?" Georgina asked. "And what are the actual benefits."

"It is a bit more expensive than the system we have now but the benefits are all that you would expect and more. The normal Z Report. A summary of all the sales for the entire shift. A breakdown of sales by tender. You know, cash, debit or credit card, and phone." Catherine smiled on the word phone.

"You think that is the way to go." Georgina pushed

"I do."

Georgina nodded.

Catherine continued, "You can also program it to show returns, discounts, bank drops, and change pay-ins. So we can tighten up on our wastage and our profit margin. And it will also help with the stock."

"You mentioned something about emails addresses." Georgina shuddered. "I hate all this technology stuff."

"I've gathered." Catherine nudged her shoulder and again laughed. "We'll bring you kicking and screaming into this year."

"But what if I don't want to go there?"

"Then the business will start to die a slow death."

Georgina baulked. "Do you think?"

"Yes. I do. The multinationals are hovering down the road. The first impressions of this part of the street are that the locals want to encourage independents but they also want the ease of payment. They don't want to carry cash."

Georgina nodded. "Explain how we would use the emails."

"Our customers would be able to receive their receipt through either the usual, printed receipt or via their email. It will be their choice. I know it will take a little while to collect all the emails but it will be worth it. Once we have our customers in the system's database, we can send out promotions and other marketing emails. We can produce surveys to send out so we can design and tailor our promotions to our customers."

Georgina slowly nodded, "Okay. Let's call the company and have someone bring a POS register here and get them to show how easy, or hard, it will be to use. See whether they can do a deal."

"See. You're even using the lingo. POS register." She smiled, "and I'm not making fun." She paused, "Well maybe a little."

Georgina nudged her as she joined in with a smile. Catherine continued, "When's the best time to set up a meeting with the two of us."

"Tuesday late morning."

"Okay. I'll phone them tomorrow and set up a meeting."

CHAPTER TEN

Old friends and truths

Sue sat in one of the comfy seats flicking through a magazine. Sue looked up and smiled at her friend as Catherine perched on the arm of the chair. "How was your trip over?" she asked. "Sorry I couldn't speak when you arrived."

"I saw that you were a bit busy. The trip was good. Two hours twenty minutes door to door. Not bad." Sue looked around appraising the place. "I can see why you like it here. Everyone seems so friendly."

"They are. I feel as though I'm a part of a community. I have been welcomed by the locals and the rest of the staff with open arms."

"Rachel seems nice."

"She is. And her husband. She's a real people watcher. I thought I was but some of the things she notices, makes me shakes my head in wonder. She seems to know everything about everyone but I have never heard her ask a deep question. She might ask innocent questions like how's your husband, wife, child, and people tell her their life stories."

Catherine smiled whilst shaking her head, "If you want to know anything, she knows who to recommend for what. Where's the best place to go? What has the best discount? She is a real font of information."

"So have you told her your life story yet."

"Not much to tell."

Sue laughed, "You so have."

"I might have told her one or two things." She swatted Sue's arm. "Now stop teasing me and let me get on with my job." Catherine looked up at the clock. "Do you think you'll be okay for the next hour?"

"What more can I ask for. A comfy chair. A lovely cup of coffee. Magazines to read. But the thing I'm especially enjoying the most is watching my best friend work. An unusual sight in itself."

"Very funny. But you should be careful or I'll have you on dirty mugs and plate collecting duty."

Sue laughed, "I'd like to see you try."

At that moment Georgina walked through the door. Catherine beckoned her over.

"Georgina. I'd like you to meet my good friend Sue. Sue this is my business partner Georgina."

"Pleased to meet you." Georgina held out her hand and gave her a sweet smile.

Sue shook the proffered hand, saying, "And you."

Georgina started to walk away. "Hopefully we'll have the chance to talk again. Will you excuse me, I have a few things to do before my shift starts."

"I'm sure we will," Sue said as she watched the retreating back. As the door to the office closed, she continued, "So that was the infamous Georgina."

Rachel sidled over, "Don't mind her. She can be a little curt when she has things on her mind. She'll snap out of it soon enough. She's one of the nicest people you can meet."

"I'll take your word for it," Sue replied.

Catherine swatted at her arm, "She could have been a real bitch to me but she hasn't. She is a really warm person."

"Okay. Okay. I believe you."

As they walked towards her flat quite a few hours later, Catherine asked, "A cup of instant upstairs or some proper coffee downstairs?"

"Some proper coffee. And this morning I was eyeing one of those danish you sell. I hope there's still one which has my name on it."

"We're going to the Turkish restaurant soon. Don't fill yourself up on cakes."

"But that danish has been calling to me all day. I can't let it down."

Laughing Catherine pulled Sue into the coffeehouse. "Afternoon Molly. This is my best friend Sue. Sue, this is Molly who helps out after school and at weekends."

"Hiya Molly."

Molly shyly smiled.

"May we have a frappe, a mocha," she looked at Catherine for confirmation, "and a... oh no... where's the danish?"

Molly grimaced slightly as she apologised, "I sold the last one about half an hour ago. Sorry."

"Ha." Catherine exclaimed, "Serve you right for trying to spoil your evening meal."

Sue huffed and spoke to Molly, "May I have the tart instead? What about you Slim?" she asked as she turned to Catherine. "Are you having anything?"

"No thanks, Miss Piggy. I'll wait."

Laughing, Molly replied, "Go and sit down and I'll bring your order over when it's ready."

"Thank you, Molly." Sue nodded.

"Oh hi, Georgina," Catherine noticed the woman sitting

working at the single table. “What are you working on?”

“Hi Catherine, Sue.” She smiled at the women. “I’m ordering next week’s stock. Nothing exciting. This is the time I usually restock. It’s quiet. What have you been doing all afternoon?”

Sue held up her arms. A big smile plastered across her face. “Shopping.” Sue beamed.

Catherine groaned, “And my feet are killing me.”

“I don’t see any bags in your hands.”

“Perhaps because I didn’t waste my money.” Catherine laughed.

“Don’t let me keep you from sitting down. It looks as though Molly has finished your order.”

“Come on Miss Piggy, let’s sit down and allow you to stuff that tart into your delicate mouth.”

Sue tried to swat Catherine's arm but the bags got in the way. They sat down laughing into their seats. Molly placed the tray down on the table and took her leave.

Sue held the iced tart with a cherry on the top directly in front of one of her boobs. “What do you think babes? Do you want a nibble or lick of this?”

Catherine was grateful she had only taken a tiny sip of her hot coffee as she spurted it out in laughter.

“You’re such an evil cow. I can’t take you anywhere. Behave yourself.” Catherine retorted as they both dissolved into more fits of giggles.

Georgina looked across the room at the women. They looked so comfortable in each other’s company. She could see the love and mutual respect between them, even when they were taking the mickey. She smiled at the laughter that was flowing from them.

Sue caught her eye and Georgina looked away quickly. She kept feeling her eyes drawn to Catherine, and every time Sue saw her looking over. After a while, with the ordering still not completed, Georgina was finding it difficult to concentrate, difficult to not feel sad. She packed up the laptop and turned to Molly saying, "Buzz me if you need me. I'll be in the office."

"Will do."

Georgina noticed that her business partner and her friend was looking at her. She waved to Catherine and Sue and walked into the office.

When the door to the office closed, Sue let out a small scream as she grasped Catherine's arm.

"What?" Catherine asked shocked. She hadn't expected to be manhandled.

"Yep." Sue was grinning from ear to ear.

Catherine rolled her eyes, "What do you mean yep?"

"I've realised something."

"Oh for goodness sake. Am I going to have to play twenty questions?"

Sue laughed, "If you want to."

"Alright. I'll go along with you for a moment. What have you realised?"

"She fancies you."

Catherine rolled her eyes again and swatted her friend's arm and said, "Don't be daft."

"I tell you she does."

"Now what makes you think that?" Catherine shook her head at her friend.

Her face screwed up with laughter as she recounted, "The number of times I caught her looking at you."

Catherine shook her head. "No."

"She has. And it seemed like a little bit of jealousy was creeping in. That I was monopolising all of your time."

Catherine disagreed, "Georgina's not the jealous kind."

"You know her that well in just a couple of weeks."

"No... I didn't say that. But she has never appeared jealous. She opened her arms to me even though I was taking over half the business. She realised I could do things she couldn't. That doesn't strike me as a jealous type."

Sue nodded in agreement, "But I think she sees me as a threat. Do you think that was why she was a bit off earlier?"

"She wasn't really. As Rachel said she must have had something on her mind."

"No, I think she definitely fancies you." Sue continued nodding.

"No. I don't see it. Don't feel it."

"I do. It's the way she looks then pulls away when she thinks someone is watching. I've been quietly studying her. I'm sure she has looked more at you than she has the screen of her laptop."

"No. I don't believe that." Catherine shook her head. "I do think she's very lonely and needs to replace what she has lost. Don't forget not only her best friend, and sometimes lover, has recently died. She's also been worried about this place, trying to make it work smoothly whilst my aunt's estate was sorted. Then she found out that this new whippersnapper has to come on board. It a big change. I don't know if I would have coped so well."

Catherine blew out her breath and continued, "And then you are here. And we are carrying on as though we have not a care in the world. Wouldn't you want a part of that?"

"I suppose so." Sue grabbed a hold of Catherine's arm and said, "So let's invite her to eat with us tonight. In that way, she will see I'm no threat to either her or the business."

"Okay. I'll go and invite her." She got up and walked into the office.

When Catherine came back, she noticed that Bren was sitting next to Sue. She wandered over to them looking puzzled.

"Hi, Bren. Has my friend Sue introduced herself?"

"Yuh... yes, she has, thank you. Mol... Molly mentioned my name and your friend asked me if I was an author."

Catherine gave Sue a questioning look.

Sue smiled, "I was telling Bren that I enjoyed 'Did she?'. And I was about to ask her when her next book was coming out."

Both women looked towards Bren, whose cheeks blushed in shyness. "I... I'm going through the final checks now," she stuttered. "I... I have got a date in my head for next month."

"That's brilliant news. Where are you thinking of having the launch party?" Sue asked. "And you'll have to keep a signed copy back for when I next come down."

"L... l... launch p... party." Fear clouded Bren's face. "I... I'm... I'm not having a launch p... party."

"Why ever not?" Catherine asked.

"N... no one will want to come to a launch party."

"Who says?" Sue frowned at the shy woman next to her.

The terror, that she had hidden for years, rose in her as she gulped then stuttered, "M... me."

Sue replied, "If I was here. I'd come."

Molly butted in, "And me. I'll come."

A couple of women at an adjacent table spoke up, "We would as well. We love your books."

At that moment Georgina came out of the office. Catherine called across to her. "Don't you think it would be a good idea if we host a launch party for Bren's new book coming out soon? You said she has lots of followers who come in here. I'm sure loads would jump at the chance of getting a signed copy and have a photo opportunity."

"What a good idea." Georgina enthused. "We'd be happy to help. We could move a few tables around. You could set up your signing station where the comfy chairs are."

"I'll design a few different flyers to advertise it. Did I see a print shop up the road?" Catherine butted in.

Georgina smiled, "Yeah. DP Print Services. Dani runs it. She usually comes in with a friend on a Wednesday at lunchtime. I'll ask her if she will print stuff off for us."

"I'll start to post some teasers on our social media sites." Catherine nodded. "All settled. It's a shame we haven't our new till, otherwise, we could send emails out to all our customers on there."

Bren sat open mouth.

Catherine continued, "Ooh. Don't forget the salesman is coming Tuesday late afternoon to show us a demo." She turned to Molly and asked, "Did you find out if you could get away?"

"I can at the moment."

"Good. We can all be there at that time."

Glad that the focus had shifted from her Bren asked, "Do... do you want me to be around? S... so I can look after the counter."

"That would be so kind of you. Thank you, Bren." Georgina smiled. "You're always stepping in for us. Are you sure you don't want a part-time job?"

"N... no. You're alright. I... I quite enjoy helping when I can. B... but my writing will always come first."

Georgina nodded understanding.

"Right. Now, all we need is the title of the book and a launch date from you." Catherine commanded.

"D... don't I have a say in this." Bren's fear had abated slightly. She shook her head with a small smile.

"Obviously not." Sue laughed. "Go on. Embrace it."

Georgina touched Bren's arm. "Knowing you as I do, you don't think you're good enough for a launch party. I, for one, think you are. So I don't want any excuses. We are doing this for you. Okay."

A look of terror flashed by quickly before Bren nodded, "kay."

Sue apologised, "Sorry Bren, I just thought you would be having a launch party. Now it looks like I railroaded you into one."

"Th... that's okay ." Bren smiled and again blushed. "I... I know they c... care for me."

Changing the subject Sue asked, "Which of your other books do you recommend? I'd like to take home a signed copy if I may."

"Th... they are all my b... babies. I don't like to have favourites" She thought for a moment. "Per... perhaps 'Secrets of Fernwood Manor' might be one you would like."

"Can you get me a signed copy before I leave tomorrow?"

"I... I'm sure that can be arranged."

Catherine spoke, "Hey Bren, Georgina is joining us over the pub for a bite to eat this evening. Why don't you join us?"

"Yes, join us." Sue urged.

"Great idea." Georgina nodded. "What time shall we meet? You didn't give me a time."

Catherine looked at Sue. "We were thinking about seven-thirty. Both of you fine with that."

Bren nodded. "I... I'll bring the book."

"Brilliant." Catherine gave Bren a big smile.

Georgina thought, "That should be plenty of time to go home, have a shower and get back. Works for me. I'm looking forward to it."

CHAPTER ELEVEN

The launch

The tables had been stacked to the side and the chairs were in rows. Catherine continued to sit down in the different rows checking the legroom. She wanted to maximise numbers but not at the cost of comfort. She walked the path from the office door to the area of comfortable seating, adjusting a couple of the chairs along the way. She nodded her head and sat on one of the bar stools behind the counter.

Catherine looked around the room with a critical eye. She studied the table encased in a blue tablecloth. The name of the author proudly displayed along the front. The chair behind was draped in one of those white covers that you see at weddings. The blue and the white complemented each other.

A banner proclaiming a book launch was proudly displayed behind the table beneath the poster of the author's smiling face. Promotional material showcasing the new book cover formed a halo around the aforementioned face. Smaller flyer versions of the promotional material adorned each seat.

An adjustable microphone stand hovered over the chair, ready to divulge the secrets of the written word.

Liking what she saw she nodded her head. She got up and pressed a switch. She wandered to the mike and flicked it on.

"One, two, one, two," she spoke into the mike.

Satisfied she flicked it off and glanced at the clock. Fifteen minutes before Bren was due to arrive. She let out a sigh of relief. The room was looking perfect. Catherine allowed herself a smile and, after picking up her tablet, she started taking pictures of the room from every angle.

She sat back down on the stool and downed her now cold cup of coffee with a grimace. She heard a gentle tap on the door and expecting Bren, she was surprised to see Georgina's smiling face looking at her.

Catherine reached up and pulled back the bolt.

"Hi. I wasn't expecting you." Catherine said as she opened the door. "Well, not just yet."

Georgina replied as she walked in, "I couldn't let you have all the fun. And I thought you might need some help behind the counter. I promised Bren I'd be here supporting her."

"I know. But I could have managed."

"But there is a difference between managing and enjoying the experience. You've put so much effort into this. Persuading everyone to get on board. From the printers, photographers, local radio... Wow. Bren looks stunning in that publicity photo." Georgina pointed towards the large poster. "She looked lovely before, but that... Wow."

"Jak restyled her hair and make-up. Reina took her to her studio for a photoshoot. Althea worked her computer magic and Dani printed the result. Quite a team effort. You should have heard the moans from Bren when I told her what I had set up."

Georgina laughed, "So that was what all the noise was, I thought I heard kicking and screaming earlier." A gentle knock sounded on the door. Georgina opened it. She smiled and said, "You look lovely." She paused before she asked, "Nervous?" Bren gave a bashful smile and replied, "Extremely n... nervous."

"Do you need a hug?" Georgina asked.

Bren nodded silently.

"Is your Dad coming?"

A sadness replaced the anxiety. "No. He said he would never support this nonsense. That it was bad enough I was living in his house let alone flaunting my sexuality as I am tonight."

"At least you still have a roof over your head. And you can come here to write." Georgina replied tightening her hug. "You are amongst friends here."

"Th... thank you."

"You're welcome."

Bren looked around the room. "The room looks good. You've put a lot of chairs out. I doubt whether even a quarter of them will be used."

"I don't know." Georgina gave Bren's hand a reassuring pat. "You might be pleasantly surprised."

"I doubt it."

Georgina continued, "I hear Catherine had to drag you kicking and screaming to get the publicity photos done."

"I wasn't that bad, was I?"

Catherine looked over at her, shook her head and smiled.

Bren allowed a small laugh to escape, and answered herself, "Well maybe just a little."

Georgina again squeezed her hand. "They did a good job. You look stunning."

"I didn't realise the poster was going to be that big. I feel as though I'm a movie star."

Georgina wrapped her arms around Bren and said, "You are better than that. You are our beautiful author."

"Thank you. Don't make me cry. I don't want to have to try to touch up this makeup. I'd never make it look so good."

Catherine looked at Bren and thought, '*She may be nervous but she has hardly stuttered at all. And she is standing taller. Per-*

haps all she needed was for someone to believe in her'. Out loud she said, "Some of your boxes of books are under the table. The others are in the office. I didn't know how you wanted to set the table up so I let it be. You'll find bits and pieces you can use, some matching blue cloth, stands and boxes underneath, arrange it as you like. Also, there's a box with pens, in case yours runs out. When you're done, I'll put all the extras in the office. I'm going to have a quick wash and change and will be back down with you shortly."

"Okay," Bren said as she started to arrange the tabletop.

"Georgina, will you do one more round with the tray then take your seat. I can finish off with any stragglers that may come in. Ten minutes to kick-off. I think it's going to be standing room only soon."

"I think you're correct. I'll have a quick check on Bren before I take my seat. I bet she is nervous as anything."

Catherine pressed the dishwasher for the last time before Bren was due to give her reading. She turned to the customer standing at the counter. "Yes, please. What can I get you?"

A few minutes later Catherine walked up to the microphone. "Good evening ladies," she cast a quick glance around the room and clocked two men, "and gentlemen. Thank you all for coming. I will ask you all to start taking your seats. And a gentle reminder that no more coffee or tea will be served until after the reading. Soft drinks will be available in the meantime. Those of you standing, may I ask you to either stand along by the windows or over there." She pointed to the opposite corner. "Please leave gangways clears."

Someone caught her attention. "Yes. Sitting there is fine." She gave a smile around the room. "Thank you again for coming to support Bren and the launch of her latest book. Don't forget, when you have read it, to support her even more by writing a review. They are the lifeblood of any author."

Bren stood up. “Th...Thank you for coming. I can honestly say that I am blown away by the number of people who are here tonight. I’d like to thank ‘The Perfect Blend’ for allowing me to launch my latest book in my favourite coffeehouse. Especially C...Catherine who pulled everything together. Rachel and G...Georgina, who would let me rant and then would issue me with the right amount of coffee to calm me down.” She looked at each one in turn and smiled. “Thank you, ladies. Thank you, my friends.”

She turned back to the audience. “I’d like to thank my editor and beta readers. I know they could not be here tonight but their input has been invaluable.”

Bren waved her arm and encompassed the display behind her. She looked and acknowledged each of the people as she spoke their names, “I’d also like to thank J...Jak and Faith from ‘Mane Tamed’, Reina of ‘Focus Photography’, Althea from ‘Bytes and PC’s’ and Dani from ‘DP Print Services’. Without them, none of this wonderful display would have been achieved. You’ve made me look fairly attractive and presentable. Thank you.”

The four women nodded the response.

“I...I know you are expecting M...Maddie to read the excerpt. You might not know but I have been working c...closely with her, and I will attempt to do the reading by myself. She is ready to step in if or when it is necessary. Th...Thank you, M...Maddie for your time and encouragement in giving me the confidence to try to do this. If I get through this, I will be forever in your d...debt”

She nodded to Maddie who put her thumbs up in support. Bren took a deep breath. She again looked at Maddie.

Maddie had made her believe that everyone struggles to one degree or other to get their words out sometime. She made her realise that there are levels of fluency in everyone’s speech, and, to some degree, all fluency is flawed.

Bren, through Maddie's inspiration, had tried some mindfulness meditation, breathing, relaxation and other exercises. Each exercise was known to reduce anxiety and stress, and to help with the stutter.

They had started reading the excerpt together so many times. Maddie had spoken slowly and deliberately. Bren mirrored the pace Maddie set and had gradually become almost word perfect.

She rolled her shoulders and tried to relieve the tension she felt building. Again, buoyed by the wonderful smile Maddie greeted her with, she took a deep breath. "*You got this,*" she said to herself.

After another deep breath, she spoke, "And now I'd like to read an excerpt from chapter three of my new book, 'F...Falling for you, again'." She smiled around the room. "It is ten years after Elle disappeared from Liv's life. Now both women have moved to the big city with their respective jobs. While out j... jogging Elle has literally stumbled and fallen into Liv's arms."

Bren cleared her throat and started reading, concentrating solely on the words in front of her.

When the clapping died down, Bren looked across to Maddie who, with a massive grin spread across her features, again gave her the thumbs up.

Bren smiled and said, "Th...Thank you everyone for bearing with me. I did it. Thank you, Maddie, for all your hard work."

Whoops and hollers greeted her words.

"You won't believe how nervous I was."

"We do," someone yelled back.

Smiling Bren said, "Finally, I'd like to again thank you for coming. Anyone who would like to buy any of my books, please see G...Georgina over by the office. Give me a few minutes to go to the loo then I will be back to sign and dedicate them. Rachel has taken over coffee duty if anyone would like more coffee and tea."

Catherine stopped her on her way back to the table. "Could you answer a couple of questions from David and Marie? Dave writes for the bi-monthly local freebie and Marie is from the local independent radio station."

Marie looked as though she was in her late thirties. She was of medium height and build. Dressed in black jeans and a jumper, underneath a leather jacket. Curly red hair framed an oval face. Her lips curled as if she was mocking people in her vicinity. Her almost black eyes had held the gaze of those who dared look at her.

David was six foot tall. Short blond hair and blue eyes. Designer stubble adorned his chin. His whole demeanour displayed confidence and empathy. Almost making you divulge your deepest, darkest secrets. His round face was graced with a willing smile.

David replied, "I'd like two pictures. One standing behind your table with all of your books. Another sat down behind the table, with you signing a copy of your new book. My first question is:- where do you get inspiration for your characters?"

Bren was used to observing those around her in a casual silent way. Trying to memorise every small detail and compartmentalising them in her brain.

"Easy. I mainly write in this c...coffeehouse. It's called 'The Perfect Blend'. So many people from different walks of life come in and pass the time, how could I not get inspiration here. I look at people and make up different stories about them."

"So in your latest book are any of the characters based on anyone who frequents this place?"

"Not really. One of the main c...characters is a conglomeration of three or four different people."

"Will they be able to recognise themselves."

Bren laughed, "I... I hope not."

"Phew. I was beginning to get worried for a moment." David grinned.

Marie did not join in the laughter but instead placed a mike in front of Bren. "I notice all your female characters are strong and in control. Why is that?"

"I think strong women, especially older women are under-represented in l...literature and I am trying to do something that will redress the balance."

"Would it be correct to say that not everyone would enjoy reading your books? You do write lesbian romance."

Bren smiled sweetly, almost daring Marie to interrupt what she was about to say. "My latest book is about two people f... falling back in love and the journey they have taken to realise their love. Their chance meeting should have been over as soon as it started. Neither woman has anything in common with the other. One loves the outdoor lifestyle. Going camping, swimming, skiing and hiking. The other enjoys everything cosy and homely. P...Preferring to read about adventures than take part. And yet they are both drawn back towards the other. Will the ten years apart scupper any chance of happiness and are the obstacles be too big to overcome? Will they finally acknowledge the mutual attraction they still feel? Will love find a way through? You'll have to read it to find out all the answers."

Bren looked Marie squarely in the eyes and held her stare. "But going back to your question. I do not know of one book that has ever been p...published that everyone will enjoy reading. Even those that are considered c...classics. I indeed write about women loving women, but love is love, no matter who is loving whom. Why does love have to be categorised? My novels can be read by everyone. I try not to define who my books are for?"

Persisting in holding Marie's stare, Bren continued, "My books are about strong women characters. Is that a c...crime? Not in my eyes. My followers are made up of all genders, gay, straight and everything in between. I know they will not be everyone's cup of tea but show me a book that is."

David and Catherine both grinned at her and gave her a thumbs up.

She gave a nod. Marie stood open-mouthed. Bren turned to move back towards the sanctuary of the table, "Okay. If that is all the questions, I would like to start meeting my readers."

As Bren walked behind the desk David asked her to pose for a photo. She sat down and again posed with her pen poised.

"Thank you, Ms Blankley. I hope your sales go well. You will get a very favourable write up from me. It's not often I meet an author. Especially a funny, charming one, like yourself."

"Thank you, D...David. May I interest you in a copy?"

He laughed, "My wife is already in the queue for your dedication."

Bren smiled as he moved away. The first person in line moved closer and the signing process began.

David turned to Catherine and said, "She handled herself well."

"That she did. I've never seen or heard her so confident. It's like a complete transformation has occurred. Thank you for coming and covering this."

"My pleasure. If you are doing anything else you think our readers might be interested in, let me know."

"Will do. We have plenty of ideas in the pipeline."

Catherine stood in front of Marie as she was packing up her equipment. "I hope you are going to portray our resident author in a favourable light as you seemed to be pushing for controversy."

"Just doing my job. Asking questions our listeners want to hear."

"Do you get many gigs?"

Marie shrugged and answered, "Enough. I don't have to like everyone and everyone doesn't have to like me. I report it as I see it." And then under her breath, she muttered, "And as I'm told to see it."

She picked up the small case and walked out the door.

"Stuck up cow," Catherine muttered to herself.

David had walked up behind her and heard her last comment. "Don't worry about her. Her listeners are dwindling by the week. She delights in trying to wind people up. I'm pleased Bren gave as good as she got."

"And me. And me." Catherine said, the second time with conviction. "Will you excuse me. I have to mingle."

Catherine worked the room. Chatted with various people sitting around or in the queue. A woman she recognised as a weekend patron stopped her.

"That went well."

"Thank you. I'm really glad for Bren's sake. I think she's found some new followers."

"I hope so."

"You're Sharon aren't you. You usually come in late Saturday morning with a dark-haired woman."

"Yes. But everyone calls me Shazz." Sharon agreed. She studied the other woman. "Did I hear Bren correctly? Your name's Catherine?"

Catherine nodded.

Sharon continued, "My better half is called Natalie or Nat as she likes to be called. She will be gutted she missed tonight. She was so looking forward to supporting Bren with the launch. She has spent many an hour talking books and literature with

Bren. I'll just have to get this one signed for her." Sharon said holding up her book. "I know she wanted to buy one of the others but for the life of me, I can't remember which one."

"If you phone or pop in and let me or one of the others know which book it is and the dedication you want in it, I'll get Bren to sign and leave the book in the office for you."

"That would be a wonderful surprise. Thank you."

"Any reason Nat can't be here?"

"She is on call, but she was hoping to be back in time." She glanced at the clock, and disappointment played in her eyes. "But looking at the time she wouldn't be coming now."

Sharon's phone pinged. She glanced at the text and sighed.

"Bad news?"

"Nat can't make it at all. The dog she went in to look at needs an emergency operation. She doesn't know when she will be home."

"So she's a vet?"

"Yes. At one of the local practices." Again she sighed. "I'm going to drown my sorrows at her having to work and have decided to go over to the pub for a quick drink. You can join me if you want to."

Catherine's cheeks turned pink as she realised what she had been asked.

Rachel sidled up behind and said, "She's straight so behave yourself."

Sharon laughed, "I always do."

"Yeah, yeah. Anyway. It's great seeing you back in here again."

"It's good to be back. And don't you dare say it, I know." Before Rachel had the chance to say anything she continued, "You didn't like my previous girlfriend."

Rachel held her hands up in surrender and backed away.

Sharon turned back to Catherine and said, "I don't bite. And I can hear a wine calling out my name. Will you join me?"

Catherine took a moment to ponder, then grinned, "When I've tidied up here. I'd love to. So you have a horrible ex as well. I think we should exchange notes."

CHAPTER TWELVE

Heart to heart

The rush had died down and any dirties had been collected. Georgina looked around the room. The hiking group has recently arrived and had taken over their favourite corner. A man appeared to be doing either the Times or Telegraph crossword. Bren was sitting in her normal seat chatting with a couple. A young mother was on one of the comfortable chairs quietly reading to her young daughter in her lap. Two women in their twenties were looking doe-eyed at each other in one of the booths.

Georgina smiled.

The sights in the coffeehouse filled her with joy. Everyone looked happy, which made her happy. This is what she dreamed of all those years ago when all this was still a flight of fancy. Hard work and sleepless nights had brought her to this. A feeling of accomplishment ran through her.

"You look pleased with yourself." Rachel's voice cut through her musings.

"I am," Georgina replied, giving Rachel an even bigger smile. "I looked around and thought. I help to create this tiny oasis of calm. This place of sanctuary, security. And my heart bursts with pride."

"And so it should." Rachel smiled back. "People enjoy the service we provide. They feel comfortable in here. You make everyone welcome. You care about them."

She pulled both stools out and beckoned for Rachel to join her. "I try. Now let's both sit down whilst we have a moment."

As soon as Rachel sat the bell above the door dinged

"I've got this." Rachel smiled over to her boss. "No peace for the wicked."

After serving a takeaway latte to a businessman in a suit she sat back down next to Georgina.

Georgina still had the contented look on her face. "I never thought I would say it but Catherine has been a breath of fresh air. A jolt in the arm to help me realise the little gold mine we have here. The changes she has made have been spot on."

Rachel let out a loud laugh that startled Georgina a little. "You should have seen your face when she first started proposing things. I know you slapped down some of her ideas, yet she didn't let you talk her out of her main vision. Are you glad you went along with some of the suggestions?"

Georgina rolled her eyes. "I never thought I would embrace social media but here I am. Putting myself and this place out there. Well, not me putting this place out there, but you know what I mean."

"I noticed," Rachel laughed as she continued, "Ms Technophobe has a Facebook page. But you are going to have to change your profile picture."

"Why?" Rachel grinned, "All you need is a set of numbers running along the bottom."

"I don't understand." Georgina knitted her brows as she said this.

Rachel grinned even more. "If the prison further down the road wasn't men only, I'd be worried."

Georgina continued her frown.

Rachel laughed out loud. "You look like an escaped convict who has been cornered."

Shaking her head, Georgina replied, “Oh very funny. It was the best I could do. I want to know how do you hold out your tablet and make sure you’re in the shot? Then keep it steady, look semi-human and press the shutter. In some of the pictures I took, I could see either up my nose, or my double chin was the prominent feature. Or else it was so close up I could see some whiskers on my upper lip and chin.”

Rachel roared with laughter as she inched closer to Georgina’s face, placed her hand under Georgina’s chin and said, “You do have a few.” She pointed, "There and there and..."

“Thanks.” Georgina slapped her hand away. “How to make someone feel good about themselves.”

“You know I love you.”

Georgina harrumphed, but a smile played on her lips.

“Go and sit over there,” Rachel indicated one of the tables. “Take a coffee, give me your tablet or phone and I’ll take a few pictures.”

“You can’t.”

“Why ever not?”

“My tablet is at home and my phone is only a basic one.”

“Let me see?” Rachel asked as she held out her hand.

Georgina pulled a phone out of her pocket and handed it to Rachel, who burst out laughing.

“I think this belongs in a museum. Does it still work?”

“Of course it works,” Georgina replied. Then in a quieter voice, “When I remember to keep the battery charged up.”

Laughing even harder Rachel said, “Okay bring your tablet next time we’re due to work together and I’ll help you change it. Alright.”

“Okay. Thank you.”

Georgina thought for a moment then said, “I fought so hard against having this new cash register but even I wouldn’t be without it now. It's so much quicker. Who would have thought I'm trying to embrace new technology?"

"Someone had to bring you kicking and screaming to the present."

The two women sat in silence for a few moments. Georgina spoke, "Your Simon did a wonderful job for us. It seems strange not having him around the place."

"He said he enjoyed working here and was glad to help out. He said anytime we need extra hands, and he's available, he'd step in."

"That's good to know. And I'm also pleased we've been able to take on another member of staff. And that she has settled well into the team. Maddie seems lovely."

"She is. She spent her whole life caring for people and that shows in how she talks. Her empathy shines through all the time."

Georgina nodded, "It was a big step for her to retire from her job and move in with Alison. I know she was virtually living there but still." Grinning at Rachel, she said, "I'm glad you overheard her telling Alison that she would only retire from the care work she was doing, and move in with her permanently if she could find a part-time job. And it was a good shout taking over our advert to her before taping it to our window."

"Yeah. It worked out well." Rachel nodded her head. "She was keen as soon as she read it."

"And it was another good call suggesting she try out a shift to see if she would enjoy it before making up her mind."

"When is she coming on board properly?" Rachel asked.

"Her contract comes to an end next week but she has some leave due. She said she needs to sort out her own house and get that rented out. Then she can do more than a shift here and there."

Rachel smiled, "I think we're getting a really good team together. A bit different than all those years of just me, you and Laura."

"That's true."

Georgina was quiet for a while as she stared into the distance. She shook her head and spoke her thoughts. "I never dreamed that Alison was ever going to get into another relationship. Especially after that psycho ex of hers. I thought she had given up on trying to form some sort of a dalliance and was destined to a life of living alone. Well, that's what she said to me. And then she goes on that cruise and comes back all loved up."

"The two of them look so well suited. You watch them interacting and you see the love radiating between them." She looked at her boss and hoped that one day she would find the love she deserved. She nudged Georgina's shoulder. "See there is a chance of love a second time around."

"I didn't say there wasn't. I just said I couldn't see it happening for me"

"Why?" Rachel asked, a look of concern for her friend, showed on her face.

"I don't want to put myself in that situation ever again. I've hankered after someone for too long, over half of my life. I can't put myself out there again."

"But what if the feelings were mutual. What if your feelings were reciprocated? Wouldn't you like to have someone to love you as much as you loved them? Wouldn't you like to go to bed with someone and wake up with that person every day? Wouldn't you like to have someone you could share the good times with?"

Georgina looked sad. "Yes. I would. But what if they don't love me as I love them. What if they don't want to go to bed with me and wake up with me. What if the good times are on their terms?"

"Not everyone is like Laura. Not everyone takes and gives nothing back. Your past will not give you any new answers. You will have to make a new conversation."

"You don't stop loving someone just like that." She snapped her fingers.

"True. But you must learn to live without them."

"It's hard." Georgina's voice hitched

"I know it's hard. Everything worth doing is hard. But you must allow a space in your heart for someone else. You don't have to find that person today, tomorrow, next week, next year. But if that person is right for you, they are worth waiting for. Change is not a process for the impatient. How does the saying go? Good things happen."

"To those that wait. Yeah. Yeah." She shrugged. "It seems as though I've been waiting my whole life."

"Then be content to wait a little while longer, even though I know you are not looking. You don't have that weight around your neck anymore so you can be yourself in every aspect. You are free to do what you want, with whom you want, and how you want, without any guilt dragging you down. Now is the time to grasp with both hands a different life, a new life. As I said start a new conversation with someone, don't regurgitate past dialogues. There are plenty who come in here who are worthy to begin a discussion."

Georgina shrugged then a smile played on her face and she looked off in contemplation. She wasn't sure when it happened but she knew that the crush she had for Catherine had turned into a feeling of something akin to love. How did it start? One moment they were strangers, and then what? Friends? And yet she felt a hint of something more.

She took a deep breath and let out a sigh. She suddenly wanted to be forever in her company. She knew she had a touch of jealousy when Catherine's gregariousness took her close to the various customers. Especially when she sat down for a chat. She realised she had fallen hard and wondered if she could keep her emotions in check. She didn't want to do anything that would harm the budding business partnership. She was brought out of her reverie by Rachel's voice.

"Ah-ha," Rachel exclaimed. "Who are you thinking of. Someone special by the way your face lit up."

"Don't be daft."

"Go on. Spill the beans. Who did you think of?"

Georgina huffed. "If you must know it was Catherine."

A gasp escaped, "Catherine? You mean business partner Catherine?"

"Yes. Catherine." Georgina replied. A look of exasperation crossed her features.

"Oh."

"What do you mean oh." Georgina's eyebrows creased into a frown.

"Nothing. I don't mean anything by it." Rachel shrugged as she thought for a second. "I'm surprised that's all."

"Why are you surprised?"

"Don't get me wrong. I like Catherine a lot. She is lovely, funny, charming, intelligent. Too intelligent for me. The way she takes everything in her stride. Some of the ideas she has had have been perfect for this place. She's been, as you said earlier, a breath of fresh air." Rachel studied Georgina, looking for any hints. "So, you like her? Do you like her more than a workmate, business partner? The 'I want to get to know you better' like her?"

"I think I do." A shy smile began to light up her face. "It felt as though I had an immediate connection. I felt drawn to her from the first moment I saw her. And every day the connection seems to have got stronger."

"Okay," Rachel said dubiously. "I know and have seen you gawping at her. I thought you just liked the way she looked. I didn't know you'd started having feelings for her."

Georgina shrugged, "Every day I feel something more for her. It has been different from anything I had ever experienced before. A feeling so strong."

"You know she's not a lesbian"

Annoyed Georgina replied, "Of course I do."

"So why do you do this to yourself?"

"What do you mean?"

"Pick a woman to become infatuated with who doesn't share your feelings."

Georgina's face crumpled as she replied, "Perhaps I like the idea of being close to someone, but deep down am scared of getting close."

"Oh, Georgie. That's sad." Rachel wrapped her arm around her friend and pulled her into a hug.

"I know I cannot and will not act on these impulses. But damn, I think she's who I've been waiting for all my life."

Rachel shook her head in an understanding way.

Georgina looked at her friend and said, "Don't worry. I'm not going to jump in. Not even a little hop. I promised myself many years ago I would never look at a straight woman, let alone go out with or feel anything for one. I'm going to admire from afar and enjoy the friendship we are building."

"Catherine does know you are a lesbian?"

Georgina nodded her head. "I told her almost straight away. when we were in the pub."

"Do you know for sure she is straight?"

"She's been married, for goodness sake."

"So am I." Rachel smiled.

"And I know she's only been with men. She hasn't ever been with a woman." Georgina's voice took on an exasperated tone.

"She's told you that," Rachel asked.

"Not exactly but the only relationships she has ever mentioned has been men."

"That's true, but that doesn't mean she hasn't dabbled in the past."

Georgina nudged her. "Like you, you mean."

"Yeah. Like me. She might be bi."

"I don't think she is."

"Ask her." Rachel encouraged.

A look of shock made Georgina stutter "I... I can't do that?"

"Why not?"

"I just can't."

"Chicken." Rachel smirked, paused for a moment then said, "Then I think I will ask her for you."

"No. Don't you dare."

"Daring me now, are you? You know I don't back down from dares." Rachel's smile became cheekier, "Shall I will say something along the lines of Georgina fancies you like crazy and wonders if you are a lesbian."

"You wouldn't."

Rachel laughed, "Your face was a picture. Of course, I wouldn't say that." She grinned. "I'd say. Are you up for it? Because Georgina wants to get you naked and make wild passionate love with you."

As Rachel laughed out loud, Georgina slapped her leg and said, "You're my friend because..."

Rachel replied, "Who else would talk to you like this?"

"True."

"So tell me. What is it about Catherine that you like? I can see she's attractive but she isn't my type."

Georgina sighed, "From the moment we started talking I knew I wanted the conversation to continue. Every time she looks into my eyes, I feel like she's holding onto my heart. And when she smiles at me, I think she likes and accepts what she sees, and I love the way that makes me feel."

Rachel looked at her friend and said with sincerity, "So what if you think she is straight, love is love. Why don't you dip your toe in and test the water?"

"There's a big difference for her to know I'm a lesbian and for me to hit on her."

"So you are continuing to admire from afar?"

"Yes."

"That will drive you crazy."

"She has already. She's like a song that I can't get out of my head. It goes around and around on a loop. The words become faint but the melody plays on. Sometimes the song goes away, then I look at her and the words and melody start up again." Georgina sighed. "Do I want to hear the song again or hope for another one to take over?"

"I think *If I Can't Have You* by Yvonne Elliman must be the one in your head. You should change it to that Adam Ant song." Rachel started singing, "*Ant music lost its taste so try another flavour. Ant music (Oh, oh, oh, oh, oh, oh, oh, oh)*"

Rachel ended the singing as though she was about to have an orgasm.

Georgina swatted her arm. "Behave yourself."

"I always do behave. Sometimes like an angel. And sometimes," Rachel smirked, "as if I was a degenerate."

Rachel slapped Georgina's backside and scooted out of reach. "But honestly Georgie," Rachel asked as she shook her head. "How do you get yourself in these messes? Perhaps you should find a willing recipient and get all your built-up frustrations out of your system."

"I don't do that."

"Then maybe you should give it a try for once."

Georgina shook her head. "No. Not going to happen."

Rachel thought for a few minutes then said, "Okay. Next time you go out for a drink with Catherine, why don't you drop some subtle hints about how you're feeling."

"How about something similar to this? What drink would I like? How about I sample your juices when we make wild passionate love? Or I don't need to look at the menu. I know what I want to eat. Your pussy. "

"Now you got it" Rachel burst out laughing. "Yes. Subtle like that."

Georgina sighed a long, loud sigh.

Rachel locked her eyes with her friend and asked gently, "So what are you going to do? Pout and sulk from this day onward."

Another sigh escaped Georgina's mouth as she blew out her cheeks in frustration. "That's exactly what I'm going to do. I can't risk the business over an infatuation."

"I think it is more than an infatuation," Rachel replied. "But I do think there is someone out there who will steal your heart. They may not be completely perfect for you. They might, however, be perfect enough to be worth fighting for. You might find that your flaws complement each other."

"Chance will be a fine thing." Georgina realised what Rachel had said, "Flaws. I don't have flaws. Cheeky mare." She smiled, "Okay perhaps one or two."

"You never know," Rachel continued. "You might have already met that person who is exactly right for you, but you both might not realise it yet. Or it might be the next person who walks through that door."

The bell above the door chimed.

"Good afternoon Rachel, Georgina."

Georgina felt her cheeks reddening, "Afternoon Catherine."

Rachel laughed, "Hiya Cat, we were just talking about you."

"All good I hope."

"More than good. Georgie was telling me how much she enjoyed the drink the other day and wondered if you were up for a meal tonight. Weren't you Georgie?"

Georgina's cheeks got even redder as she frowned at Rachel. "I was?" She turned back to Catherine. "I was."

"I was going to ask you the same thing. I have some ideas to run past you. What do you fancy?"

Rachel smirked and gave Georgina a wink.

CHAPTER THIRTEEN

Pun time

Catherine stood by the comfy seating area and looked out to the sea of faces and said, "Welcome to the inaugural creative writing session. It's good to see so many faces, both old and new. I promise I will try to learn all your names. I would like to thank Bren, who has kindly offered to run our Tuesday evening sessions. If you don't know Bren, she is our resident author. Bren would you like to come here and introduce yourself."

Bren made her way towards Catherine and spoke to the expectant crowd that filled the seats.

"Hi. My name is Brenda Blankley, and I have published six novels. Most people call me Bren. You might have seen me helping behind the counter. Writing at that table over there." She pointed to her usual table. "Or at my book launch a week or so ago."

Quite a few people sat around the tables nodded and murmured in recognition.

"May I ask you, if you didn't when you arrived, to sign the paper and give me your email address or similar so I can contact you easily." Bren passed the clipboard to the person on her right. She looked around the room at the expectant faces and spoke.

"What qualifications do I have to do these sessions I hear you ask. Well, I have a degree in English Literature. And before writing full time, I was an English teacher in a secondary school in Devon for eight years."

She continued quickly, "I will be running the sessions every Tuesday of each week. The timetable is as follows, so hopefully, everyone will find something they will enjoy. The first Tuesday of the month will be a book club. Where we will discuss a variety of genres from science fiction, to thrillers through to romance. Any genre the members are interested in. The first book we will be reading I will choose and it will be displayed on the notice board over there." She pointed to the brand new notice board that was already festooned with a variety of flyers and cards.

"The second Tuesday will be a free writing session, mainly prose. You will not be expected to write more than 150 words. I will give a different topic heading each session. For example, I might say water. You can write however you want on whatever you want within that topic. To me, water means a babbling stream, or waves crashing against the shore, even a dripping tap or a torrential downpour." Bren giggled and said, "Ha, I'm a poet and didn't know it." She paused before saying, "To you, it might mean something completely different."

She looked around to see if everyone was still on board. "As you see, plenty of scope to let your creative juices flow. Towards the end of the session, I will ask you to share with your fellow writers, so they can give you positive feedback. If sharing does not appeal you may keep your musings to yourself. But remember, positive feedback can help develop your writing."

"Will we get the topic heading before we arrive?" A woman at the back asked.

"And your name is?"

"Paula. Paula Burns."

"Good question Paula. I hadn't intended to do that. I wanted to allow you all to let the juices flow, without any preconceived idea, for you all to simply start writing. Every story, poem, song and blog, starts with one word. And to this one word, another can be added, until a sentence, paragraph, and passage is written. I want you to write, not think. I want you to realise that anyone can write and it doesn't have to be perfect to be important. Don't worry about getting it grammatically correct straight away. You can spend time later perfecting it and changing it."

Paula and others nodded, deep in thought.

"The third Tuesday will deal with memoirs. Again I will give topic headings. For example, your favourite toy, a smell, the first day of school those sort of things. You might want to write it as a blog, text messages, in fact however you want to write. Everyone has stories of days gone by, that would be of interest to your children, grandchildren. Memories that future generations might be interested in. You never know where these memories might lead."

Bren could see a few head nods and others in deep contemplation. She continued, "And the fourth Tuesday continues the same sort of lines but this time all about poetry, jingles, songs, in fact anyhow you want to write. Rhyming or not."

She looked around the room "Any questions thus far?"

"Do we have to come every week?" A man at the back put up his hand.

"Your name please."

"Steve, Steve Williams," he replied.

"Well Steve, the simple answer is no. But you can join as many of the different sessions as you like. I just would like for you to each week register your interest through text or email so I have a rough idea of how many and who is coming and I can plan accordingly.

"Fair enough," he agreed.

She looked around the room and not hearing any more question she continued, "Occasionally there will be a fifth

Tuesday and they will be one-off activities. When there is a fifth Tuesday in the month, we will be doing something completely different. Again I will put it up on the notice board. And today is one such day. We will come to what we are doing in a moment."

She took a drink of her water, smiled and proceeded, "First I want us all to go around the tables and tell us your name and a funny or embarrassing incident that has ever happened to you. Or if you haven't one of these perhaps something only a few people know about you."

A few people squirmed in their seats or caught another person's eye.

Bren pressed on, "As I told you, my name is Bren, I go by the pronouns she, her. Only a few people know this but," she paused for effect. "My middle name is Cleve because I was conceived down the road in Clevedon."

She continued, "My embarrassing or funny story is this. When I was walking through a muddy path one of my shoes got stuck in the deep mud and was sucked off my foot. Before I knew it, I had placed my stockinged foot into the squelchy mud. Yuck. The mud had gone between my toes and felt horrible. I had to go down on my haunches and delve into the gooey mess with both hands to try to retrieve it. I lost my balance and ended up sitting in it. I think I ended up with more mud on me than was on the path. I was visiting friends, and we were walking together at the time. By the time we got back to their house, it had caked solid. I left a trail with every step I took. I had no choice but to strip down to my underwear before I could enter their house. Was I ever embarrassed?"

After the laughter died down, she looked around the room to see if anyone appeared to want to share their story. She overheard a woman whisper to the woman she was sat with, *you ought to tell them about the bee stinging you,* so Bren asked, pointing to the women, "Perhaps this table would like to go first?"

One woman nudged the other and said, "Go on it's funny and embarrassing."

The other woman glared at her and through gritted teeth said, "Funny for you and embarrassing for me."

"Go on," the woman said and started laughing.

"Okay," came the reply. In a stronger voice, the woman said, "My name is Anya. Do you want me to say the pronoun I like to use?"

"Yes please, if you would."

"Okay. I like to use the pronouns she, her." She took a breath. "Well," Anya started the story. "This is so embarrassing." She shook her head and looked at the woman next to her and grimaced.

The woman waved her hand in the time-honoured, get on with it, motion. "Laney and I." Anya pointed to the woman sat next to her. "We decided to go to the seaside on a really hot day. The sand was boiling. We found two deckchairs and I took off my trainers without undoing the laces. I pulled my socks off and placed my feet back onto the top of my trainers. I had tried just standing on the sand but the sand was so hot. I had stepped out of my shorts. I did have my bikini bottom on." She nodded around the room to see if she had their interest. "Again placing my feet back onto the top of the trainers."

She closed her eyes at the memory. "I sat down in the chair but unfortunately I must have sat down on a bee or a wasp as my backside started to sting like crazy. I jumped up but the sand was so hot on my feet. I was hopping around not knowing what to do. My bum hurt and my feet were burning. So I ran as fast as I could down the beach, swearing and cursing all the way. The relief was wonderful when I ran the few yards and reached the shallows. I stood there laughing and crying at the same time. My feet thought they had been cooked over a barbecue and a spot on one cheek of my ass was throbbing and swollen."

Laney butted in and between laughs, she said, "I had no idea what was going on. All I saw was this demented woman screaming and shouting something about being stung by a bee." She giggled. "Well, the word she used began with a 'B."

"What happened next?" someone asked, chuckling.

Laney started laughing again and Anya swatted her arm.

"Laney brought my trainers down to the water's edge and through her mirth, asked me what was going on. I turned and showed her my swollen backside."

The words hardly decipherable between chortles, Laney continued, "I helped her into her trainers. I tried to stop laughing, but I couldn't.

Anya began laughing as well. "You try putting your feet into trainers that still has the laces done up, with burnt feet and a sore ass. Eventually, we managed it."

Laney butted in again, "I told her to go back to the chairs and disappeared off."

Anya grinned at Laney and said, "When she came back, she was holding three ice lollies. She made me sit on one and we had one each to eat. Gradually it cooled my bum down."

"Wow," Bren exclaimed when the laughter died down. "I didn't expect anything as exciting as that. Thank you, Anya and Laney. Can anyone beat that? Don't worry if you can't."

A tall woman stood up. She was dressed in tight leather trousers and a buttoned-down short-sleeved shirt. She had striking blue eyes that begged to be obeyed. She had a commanding presence. A presence that at first glance said don't mess with me. She had a piercing on every conceivable part of her face. Her neck was covered with a navy coloured tattoo, which needed a closer study to pick out the intricate design. Both arms displayed full sleeves down to her wrists. and said,

"My name now is Sandy Smith. The pronoun I use is they, them. My original surname was Dowe. My parents thought it would be funny to name me Dill."

She abruptly sat back down. The woman who sat next to them grinned and hugged them. Soon laughter, rolling eyes, explanations and grins filled the room.

Bren nodded to her with a grin. "Thank you, Sandy, for sharing. Who's the next victim. I mean volunteer?"

Gradually most people around the room had introduced themselves and told a short story with a varying degree of embarrassment or amusement. Bren spoke to the few who hadn't regaled then yet with an anecdote, "Don't worry if you do not have an amusing story et cetera. An introduction will suffice and hopefully, in the future, you will feel comfortable and confident to share." She turned to one of the women who hadn't yet given their narrative. "Paula. It was Paula, wasn't it? Would you care to share?"

Paula grimaced and nodded her head. "I haven't anything amusing or humiliating to say, so I will let you know the nickname only my family calls me by." She gave a small wince. "They call me Paups because my Nephew couldn't say, Paula."

"That's cute." Another woman exclaimed.

Paula laughed, "Don't let him hear you say that. He's embarrassed enough as it is when we all remind him of it."

"I like it when I hear unique nicknames. It makes them special," another woman replied.

After a while, all introductions were completed and Bren said, "Well we have all been introduced and most have told something about ourselves. Now to do what is the purpose of tonight. Something creative." She paused for a moment. "What I want you to do is think of a pun for any of the drinks that The Perfect Blend sell. We are running a little competition. Catherine," Bren turned to Catherine. "Do you want to say more?"

Catherine stood, swallowed and cleared her throat, "A storm in a teacup is coming and trouble is brewing."

A groan vibrated around the room.

"I know. I know. Truly groan-worthy. I spent hours trying to think of something clever and witty and all I came up with was that." Catherine laughed with a shrug. "So do you think you can do better? We are giving the interior of this place a paint job. We are putting a hard border going all around the room at table height. We would like to have puns written in script above it, and other strategic places on the walls as well. I thought that perhaps the best pun ideas people come up with from this group could be used."

Catherine hesitated and Bren jumped in. "So today's session is, fun time is pun time. There are ten free cups of beverage for the winner. Isn't that right Catherine?"

"Yeah. Coffee, tea or chocolate."

"I will give you about ten, fifteen minutes to think of some puns by yourself. Then we'll join with another person to share ideas. Then in groups of four or if more of you are sitting together, your table. I want each group to pick your favourites."

Catherine gave a smile, "At the end of the session I would like to have about five ideas to take away to Georgina, so we can decide the winner. We will use as many puns as we can, and the winning one will have pride of place. We have yet to decide where to put them."

The group started to work furiously and laughter and groans permeated the room. "Okay." Bren stopped them, after the requisite time, clapped her hands and brought the room to order.

Before Bren could continue proceedings Catherine butted in and said, "May I also say that everyone who has taken part this evening will be entered into a secondary draw for five free beverages."

Bren nodded. She looked around the room and asked, “Can each table nominate a spokesperson to say your four best puns? And then when all the tables have had their go, we will between us pick the five best ones to go forward. Don’t forget when you speak to the whole group to say your name. Which table would like to start?”

Paula put her hand up. “Shall we start?”

Bren indicated for her to continue.

“Dot, myself, Gaynor and Jo came up with these. Here’s our four:- Rise and grind, Mugs and Kisses, Don’t Be Chai and What's Sumatra with you?”

Each pun was met by groans of varying loudness. Soon every table had shared their ideas.

“Okay. Let’s do a show of hands for our favourites” Bren instructed. After a show of hands Bren counted them off on her fingers, “So definitely Everything I brew, I brew it for you. Is it tea, you’re looking for? Don’t worry, be frappé, and It’s a grind of magic.” Catherine nodded. “And a tie between Deja brew, and Blends, with benefits.”

Catherine replied, “I’ll take all six to Georgina as they are all good. I’ll post the winning pun and the winner of the ten and the five free beverages during next week’s session. And may I take this opportunity to thank Bren for all her organisational skills and for agreeing to oversee these Tuesday evening sessions. And to thank everyone here for joining in and making the first literature and creative writing session a success.”

She started clapping and soon everyone was joining in.

CHAPTER FOURTEEN

Chats and spats

"How did it go last night?" Georgina asked Catherine in a quiet moment. "I see that quite a few drinks other than coffees were served."

"Seeing it was the first one I think it went very well. A lot of faces I would have expected to see. And others I've never seen in here before. Hopefully, they will join our growing band of regulars. I've put their emails into the system so we'll be able to include them in our promotions." Catherine shook her head in slight disbelief. "We served more soft drinks and water than I expected. I did ask a few people why and they said they don't drink caffeine after a certain time. I think we might have to research other decaf drinks to offer."

Georgina nodded in accord.

Catherine continued, "We began to run a bit low and had to get more for the stock. We'll have to count that in when we're inputting our next order."

"How was Bren?"

"Oh my goodness. She was in her element." Catherine gushed. "Her stutter was almost gone. She seemed so confident and full of herself. You can see she used to be a teacher. She was a far cry from the shy young woman of a few weeks ago."

Georgina agreed, "She has blossomed so much from the launch of her book. It's as though a butterfly has emerged from the chrysalis. She has been radically changed. It's been brilliant to see. I wonder what caused her to leave the teaching profession? She obviously has the knack."

"I don't know. Maybe one day we'll know why she suddenly turned up on our doorstep and took over that table. Now all she needs is for her to believe there is someone out there waiting to sweep her off her feet. I hate seeing people sad and lonely especially when they have so much to give." She pointedly looked at the woman who was busying herself around the counter.

Oblivious to the sardonic observation, Georgina asked, "What makes you think she is sad and lonely."

"Well," said Catherine, "she spends most of her time sitting in this coffeehouse drinking her coffee, watching the world go by."

Georgina shook her head in disagreement. "You know she gets her inspiration from the little snippets she hears or the small interactions she sees. We're her office of inspiration."

"Be that as it may, it feels rather strange to come in here nearly every day, sit by yourself and write."

"We don't know anything about her home life. She might not be able to write when she is at home. I heard she lives with her dad."

"Yes, she does." After a short while, Georgina resumed "I think I'll ask her to come to the pub sometime."

"Good idea."

A comfortable silence settled over the two women. After a while, Georgina asked, "How were the puns. Were there many?"

"There were loads of them. Some were a lot better than others. We narrowed it down to six. Have a look over them when Rachel comes in."

"Any good ones? Ones that you think should be the winner?"

"There were plenty of funny and groan out loud ones. I think everyone enjoyed doing it. A lot of people were reticent to share but Bren manoeuvred around that with ease. I heard plenty of laughter and silliness. But I'm not going to sway your judgement."

"Spoilsport."

Catherine laughed which turned into a yawn. She turned serious for a moment. "I'm struggling to do this early shift though. All I've done is cover my yawn with my hand. Lots of people wanted to hang around and chat after the session had ended. As long as they were drinking coffee et cetera, I didn't mind. But it's catching up with me now."

Georgina scrunched up her face. "Sorry, I should have thought when I did the rota."

"I didn't pick it up either."

"I'll put it on my to-do list. I'll cross your name off every Wednesday morning."

"Thank you. Appreciated."

"Save you hanging around after your shift, why don't you tell me them now and I'll decide my favourites. Then if we get time during our shift together tomorrow, we'll decide our winner then."

The door opened and the bell tinkled. Catherine gave the woman a wave in acknowledgement. "Okay. You serve this customer and I'll get the stuff from the office."

Georgina nodded and turned to the woman who had entered, "Yes please."

"A cappuccino and a jam doughnut please."

"Eat in or takeaway."

"Eat in please."

Catherine re-entered the shop from the office as the woman was taking her seat. She went over to her.

"Hi, Paula. Did you enjoy last night? I was just going to tell Georgina the six best puns that were picked."

"I enjoyed it. I didn't think I would. My best friend dragged me along. Not quite kicking and screaming, I didn't want to come. There was a programme I wanted to see on the telly. But I enjoyed it. I haven't laughed so much in a long time." Paula gave a winning smile. "I'll be definitely be coming to book club and last night whetted my appetite for writing, so I'm thinking of doing the free writing session as well."

"That's good to hear. So if I don't see you before, I'll see you next Tuesday."

Georgina studied the interaction and felt the stirring of jealousy rise from inside.

"Welcome to the inaugural book club meeting," Bren said to the waiting gathering crowd. "I see some of you have brought the paperback with you, and others are armed with their e-readers. But before we start the session so many of you have asked who won last weeks fun time pun time competition. Drum roll please."

Everyone started banging on their tables. She cut her hand through the air and the noise abated.

The winning pun is Everything I brew, I brew it for you, closely followed by Is it tea, you're looking for? Congratulations to everyone who took part, but especially to Anya for winning ten free beverages of your choice. Anya, stand up please."

Anya stood and Bren passed her an envelope saying, "Congratulations."

"Thank you," Anya replied with a grin.

The others on the table she was sitting at gave her their plaudits and congratulations.

Bren spoke to the room again, "The person who will receive

the five drinks is Paula. Congratulations," she said.

Paula stood and was handed a different envelope.

A round of applause filled the room.

"Again thank you all for taking part. And now down to business. Does anyone want to start by saying what they liked about the book?"

The bell gently sounded and David quietly sneaked inside and made his way towards the counter.

"Thank you for coming in," Catherine whispered.

"My pleasure," David replied, as quietly

"They are due to finish in about five minutes then I'll take you to the two winners."

He nodded.

"And thank you for the brilliant article of Bren's launch. She's sold loads of extra books because of it."

"Again my pleasure."

"May I get you a drink whilst you wait. I'm sorry it'll have to be a soft drink because making the hot drinks is too noisy whilst this meeting takes place. But if you want something hot, I'll prepare it when they've finished."

"Any type of soft drink will be fine."

Bren's voice could be heard above the general hubbub. "So we've decided on next month's book. I will think of questions I would like us to discuss and send those out by the weekend."

She formed her next words carefully, "I think the following sessions we will divide into two groups, as we seem to have two distinct groups. I will tailor the questions we are pondering to both books. That way you can read one, either or both books. You'll also be able to swap between the two groups depending on whatever book you decided to read and discuss."

There were a few nods around the group. She hoped she had nipped any future discontent in the bud, and she wasn't alienating and losing any members. She didn't want exclusivity, she wanted everyone who enjoyed reading to feel comfortable.

She spoke again, "Thank you all again for coming. And finally, Paula, Anya will you meet me at the counter in a moment."

Bren went to sit down but instead continued, "Oh I forgot. I've extra homework for you all. I want you all to email me what songs you thought of when you were reading our next book. Don't worry if you don't think of any. I know some people won't. I will make up a playlist for next weeks background music whilst we discuss them."

Bren began tidying all her notes and Catherine busied herself making a variety of drinks, as conversations about the book they had been discussing continued. Bren moved towards the counter and greeted David.

"Thanks for the write-up. It made me look good." Bren shook his hand.

Smiling at her, he replied, "Nothing more than you deserved."

"Perhaps you could tell the woman on the local radio that."

Bren's sales locally had been good, whether that was due to her burgeoning following or the adverse attention her latest book received due to the radio show, she neither knew nor cared. The ratings coming in were better than she expected, and the positive feedback made her heart sing. And she also knew she couldn't please all of the people, all of the time. But she cared about pleasing her loyal followers and new ones she was collecting along the way.

"Why don't you tell her yourself?"

She huffed, "I might."

"And you might be surprised at her response." David smiled as though something more was being played out.

Frowning, Bren gave him an inquiring look, and asked, "I

wonder why it took so long to be aired. The launch happened a few weeks ago now."

"Ask her," he replied as he passed over a business card from the radio station.

But before she could ask anything else Catherine stood in front of her with a steaming mug held out.

"Your usual." Catherine placed the mug down. "Do you want any nibbles? Crisps? biscuits? cake?"

"No. I'm good, thanks."

"David, I've finished serving for a moment. Do you want to take some pictures and talk to the winners?"

"I'll go and bring them over." Bren got up. "Where are you going to want them?"

Catherine butted in, "I have two large versions of the winning vouchers. Bren could hand these over for the photo opportunity."

"Good idea. If Bren gives the winner theirs and you give the runner up theirs, and you are all standing in front of the counter. I think that will work."

Soon all the questions had been asked and the requisite photos, with the overblown vouchers, were taken.

"Time for me to greet my wife and take her home," David said as he finished the last of his soda. "Don't forget to keep me informed of any new developments and I'll see you again at the next event. Take care."

"And you, David. Thanks for coming."

He raised his hand in acknowledgement as he walked over to a woman sitting patiently by the door.

"Will you put me through to Marie, um," she looked at the card David had given her the previous day, "Marie Laporte."

"Who's calling please?" The voice on the other end of the

phone replied.

"Ms Brenda Blankley."

"One moment, please, Ms Blankley."

Bren heard bubblegum music in her ear and a sickly sweet voice kept interrupting the music, 'Thank you for calling Radio Bris. We value your call. Please hold the line.'. After the cycle replayed itself five times, she shouted to the automated voice, "Oh for goodness sake."

A voice interrupted her tirade. "Marie Laporte speaking. How can I help."

"Ms Laporte. I'm insisting you retract the comments you said about me, and I demand an on-air apology."

"Hang on a minute," Marie interjected.

"No. I won't hang on. You will give me an on-air apology and show me the common courtesy of not spreading lies on your show."

"I'm sorry. But who are you?"

"My name, as I told your receptionist, is Brenda Blankley."

"Oh..."

"And as I said earlier, I expect a retraction and an on-air apology, for slander and homophobic comments..."

"Brenda. I can call you Brenda?"

"No. It is Ms Blankley to you. Only family, friends and acquaintances may call me Brenda. As you are none of those things, I won't allow it."

"Ms Blankley," Marie again tried to speak.

"On what day are you going to retract your comments and apologise. I would hate to have to sue both your radio station and yourself for defamation of character and homophobia."

"Ms Blankley, I will have to get back to you after I have spoken to the boss." She sighed quietly, "I promise I will get back to you as soon as possible." Marie let out a more audible sigh. "But before you take this further, please may we have a face to face meeting. Just the two of us, no bosses, no lawyers, just me and you."

Gone was the cocky assuredness from the day of the launch, replaced by something akin to hesitation and doubt, almost pleading. Bren noticed the change in her voice and instead of refusing the request straight away, she hesitated.

The silence was broken when Marie asked, "Ms Blankley, are you still there?"

"Yes, I'm here," Bren replied, in a tone that began to voice inquisitiveness rather than anger and hurt. "But I'm not coming to the radio station."

"And neither would I expect you to. How about somewhere neutral? Perhaps a pub." Marie answered, again with a hint of pleading.

Bren wondered what a face to face would achieve. It was more than likely to give her a personal apology. But what she wanted, and needed, was more than that. She needed some sort of redemption. This time she wasn't going to sit back and allow the darkness to happen, she had already walked that path. This time she had friends to back her up, to rely on, to give her background support. This time she wasn't ploughing a lone furrow. This time, someone was going to be held accountable for the lies, and the abuse these could perpetuate. This time she had the confidence to take on the opposition. This time she wasn't going to be run out of town. This time she was going to win.

"Where and when?" Bren asked in a voice full of confidence.

"Any evening and a place of your choice."

"I'll meet you at The Cat and Moon. Seven o'clock tomorrow. Don't be late."

CHAPTER FIFTEEN

Not everything in the garden is rosy

Catherine and Georgina stood side by side behind the counter. Each doing their job proficiently. Each ignoring the other. They had not exchanged one word after their disagreement.

Rachel finished clearing the tables and said, "I'm fed up with the pair of you. You are turning the milk sour. Now go into the office and sort it out. We can't be having the pair of you putting the customers off. I will be able to cope better without you both anyway. Now go and sort it before I walk out and decide not to come back."

"You wouldn't dare." Georgina gasped.

"Try me," she said as she picked up her jacket and walked to the exit.

"Okay." Georgina panicked and stopped what she was doing.

Catherine huffed and made her way to the office, followed closely by Georgina.

They stood either side of the room with their arms crossed. Neither making the effort to sort out the differences.

"Well." Catherine suddenly said. "What have you got to say for yourself. It had better be good."

Georgina was speechless. Her mouth gaped, "Me. What have I got to say?"

She stared at the woman opposite for some time. Hurt was etched on Catherine's face. Georgina felt her mouth go dry. She licked her lips and swallowed. She realised at that moment that what she said was wrong, but knowing she was wrong and doing something about it was two different matters. She looked away embarrassed.

She glanced back and promised herself that she would put it right. After all, it was her foolishness that had started this spat.

Georgina spoke in a voice made soft, breaking the silence and awkward tension between us. "I'm sorry."

Catherine's face remained placid as she stayed quiet for a moment. "Excuse me?" she replied as if she hadn't heard her properly.

"Please find it in yourself to forgive me."

A frown creased her brow as Catherine again wondered if she had heard correctly, she had been expecting another tirade of angry words but was greeted by a soft apology. An apology that sounded heartfelt.

"I said, I'm sorry." Georgina continued apologising. "Please find it within yourself to forgive me."

Catherine looked at Georgina in disbelief. Did she think those words would make it better, but the softness and the sadness of Georgina's voice began to penetrate the barrier she had placed around herself. She shrugged her shoulders and replied, "What you said really hurt."

Emotion was building inside Catherine. She looked down and avoided Georgina's eyes. She needed a few seconds to compose herself.

"I know." Georgina looked over at her. "It was completely unacceptable, totally hurtful, not true and I'm sorry," Georgina said earnestly.

Catherine pursed her lips as if in pain and nodded. When both of them stayed silent, an awkward tension took hold of the air. Not of anger, but something else. Something equally as powerful. Georgina had felt it before with her, but this time it was much stronger. As though a major storm was brewing. As with all storms, would the tension in the air be cleared, or would there be irreversible damage?

Catherine shook her head. She didn't want to show her weakness, didn't want to give her an easy way out, she needed to rebuild her inner strength which would take a moment longer. She took a couple of deep breaths then raised her head, stared directly into Georgina's soul. Trying not to let her voice give her away she simply said, "Tell me why you said it. I'm sure your reasoning will be worth listening to. Then I'll know whether to laugh or cry."

Georgina cleared her throat but didn't know where to start. She shook her head. Georgina saw a side to Catherine that she hadn't known existed. A side that was so delicate, so sensitive. A side she wanted to get to know better. She seemed to have been overly affected by the unfairness of Georgina's words. As though they had mingled with a previous hurt and manifested themselves.

"Well?" Catherine again asked, her jaw set firm, her eyes piercing through the armour Georgina had wrapped around herself.

Georgina opened her mouth but no words would form. Conflicting emotions played on her features. Georgina had always wondered what Catherine's reason was for moving across the country. Did she want to take over completely? Perhaps it was personal and it was always meant to be. Perhaps her own feelings of betrayal were closer to the surface than she thought.

Catherine continued to appraise Georgina and swallowed hard. She had a good understanding of people. She could read the nuances and she knew how stubborn some people were. And as they aged, the more stubborn they became. Did she push too hard to implement the changes she had planned in her head? She knew that there could be sticking points to reach the outcome she envisioned. But after all the other things that had been implemented, she didn't think twice about the last suggestion.

Georgina had needed someone with whom she could vent. She was emotional, angry and frustrated. It could have been anyone and yet her sights had unfairly rested on Catherine. As soon as the words had left her mouth, Georgina quickly came to her senses, but they had already been spoken aloud. She should have told her back there and then, her true feelings. That she couldn't deal with the feelings she had bottled up inside. Instead, she pushed against them, pushed Catherine aside with uncalled for, harsh words. She didn't want to relive the same feelings she had for Laura with Catherine. Why couldn't she find someone to love her?

Catherine knew Georgina was proud. Was she destroying her pride? She had indeed embraced change, but she was too stuck in her ways for this last suggestion. Had she chipped too much away? Had she pushed too hard? If so, she was sorry, but Georgina's outburst was just cruel. She studied the woman opposite her.

Then Georgina's face softened as she gave Catherine a look. A look very few people had given her, and it started to dawn on her what Georgina's intentions were. Catherine had always felt this slight frisson between them. A different look came into Georgina's eyes for a fleeting moment and in that millisecond, Catherine suddenly realised that this was more about them than the coffeehouse. The running of the coffeehouse was secondary to everything that was going on, or not going on, between them.

Georgina gestured to Catherine to sit as she moved and lowered herself into her chair. Catherine slowly perched down on hers. She smoothed her top and trousers as she sat opposite. They both held their counsel. And the silence dragged.

Catherine wondered whether Georgina was ever going to

open up and explain what and why she said what she did? She looked at the woman opposite her and saw a myriad of emotions.

Suddenly, inexplicably Catherine apologised, "I'm sorry. I've been too quick to try to bring in all my ideas. I've run roughshod over your feelings. You and Laura ran this place successfully for years, then I arrive and threw everything up into the air. It is no wonder you blew a gasket. I'm sorry."

"No. I'm sorry. You are only doing what Laura and I talked about. You have implemented a lot of other changes but they have all been for the good."

"So what happened this morning? Do you want to talk?"

Georgina breathed in. Her breaths caught in her throat as though she was on the verge of tears. "I didn't mean what I said. I was so frustrated and angry with the situation and I thought you were Laura."

Catherine didn't expect that.

"Laura?" She questioned.

Georgina nodded.

Her breath again hitched. "You may not look exactly like her but there is a family resemblance. Your mannerisms. The way your hands move when you're excited. The way your eyes blaze when you want to put your ideas across. The tone of your voice." She paused. "It doesn't usually bother me."

"So what changed earlier?" Catherine asked with a touch of sympathy in her voice.

Georgina shook her head. She didn't want to say. She didn't want to hurt. And yet she knew she had to say. She knew she had to hurt if they were to overcome any more obstacles that landed in their path. If they were going to work together as equals.

"It was the dismissive way you reacted when I had the opposite viewpoint. Laura did that to me all the time. She disregarded me with no thought for me or how her words were hurting. There is a limit to what you can handle."

Catherine grimaced, "I'm sorry if you thought I dismissed you out of hand. Sue says it's one of my not so good traits. All I was doing was trying to put across a different point of view."

"I was so angry with you, yet all I saw and heard was Laura disparaging me again with her scathing insults and petty point-scoring. And I blew it. For a split second, you were Laura, and all my anger and unrequited love spilt out."

"I would never disparage you. And I don't think I insulted or tried to point score. Why would I."

"You didn't. But in my anger, my mind said you did." Georgina admitted.

Both women were quiet for a moment.

Catherine squinted her eyes at Georgina and said, "Unrequited love? I know you loved her, but I thought she loved you back, well at least in her own way."

Georgina sighed, "For thirty years I loved her. For thirty years I tried to get her to love me. But I think she only truly cared for me about three of those years. The only person she cared about was herself. Now she is dead that opportunity to get her to love me is gone. I will never be able to persuade her to give us a try." Georgina said in a quiet voice as she felt tears gathering in her eyes. "She didn't even let me say goodbye to her properly."

Georgina rubbed at her eyes with her knuckle. "And I hate myself for feeling this way. I look at you and you remind me so much of her. I know you are not her." Georgina scrunched up her face. Emotion pouring out of every pore. "I took all my inner frustrations out on you. I'm sorry."

"That's okay."

"No, it's not okay. You are a lovely, warm, funny human being and you didn't deserve to listen to my wrath being directed at you. It was unfair and uncalled for. What I said I didn't mean. You are not selfish, a bitch, or any of the other things I remember calling you." Georgina held her head in shame.

Catherine went over to her and crouched down in front of her. She placed two fingers under Georgina's chin and lifted her head to look into her eyes.

Catherine smiled and said, "My mother said to me once, and her words have never left me. She said, *"You don't need to push your way to the top with little concern for anything or anyone else. Be humble and admit when you have made a mistake. Don't try to be perfect, be the best you can, but not to the detriment of others. When you act out of love, compassion and kindness you are showing your true colours."* I want to show you my true colours. I'm sorry I did or said anything wrong. We are a partnership and I want us to treat each other as such."

Georgina's voice caught as she continued, "I know you are not trying to take this business away from me. I appreciate that you are trying to improve turnover, and the steps you have already implemented are working. I understand what you have to do to honour the contract you were forced to sign. Well not forced, but you know what I mean."

"No. I wasn't forced into signing." Catherine smiled at Georgina. "I signed because I thought it was achievable. I signed because I saw the potential. I signed because I thought we would work well together."

Georgina lowered her eyes. She wasn't able to look at Catherine. She knew if she looked at them, she would be pulled into their depths. That the distance she had maintained would disappear and she would say something, not in anger, but equally deep in feeling.

Instead, she said, "I suppose I just felt worthless again. That my opinion didn't count. That I was a failure in your eyes because I didn't understand or want to understand some of the new ways of working. I just felt so inadequate."

"Oh Gee," Catherine replied, feeling the sadness in Georgina's words. She squeezed Georgina's hand to show support. "You will never be a failure. You are not worthless or inadequate. So what if modern technology has passed you by. It doesn't matter. What does matter is that we work together to get through any problems? I think we make a good team. You have honed your skills over many years and it would be remiss of me to dismiss your worries out of hand. I'm sorry if I caused you pain. I know I have pushed you, from the very first minute, into places you didn't want to go. And I also know that you have not had any time to grieve your loss."

Catherine heard a strangled cry and gentle sobbing, as tears flowed freely from Georgina's eyes.

"Come here," Catherine said as she stood and pulled Georgina into her arms. "Let it all flow out. We're a partnership. Let me help."

She pulled Georgina into a tight hug, and she stepped into her embrace, Georgina felt herself melting right there in her arms.

Catherine was also being drawn in and she felt herself falling. Her stomach was suddenly full of butterflies, and each flutter was making her body temperature soar. Her heart was going haywire and started pounding in her chest.

Catherine puffed out her cheeks and steadied herself as she realised something unexpected. She had unexpectedly found out that she enjoyed wrapping her arms around this woman. She had unexpectedly found out that she truly cared what Georgina thought and felt. She had unexpectedly found out that this felt more than friendship. She had unexpectedly found out that the butterflies that danced around in her stomach were because of this woman in her arms. And she had unexpectedly found out that it had all happened at a very unexpected time.

And all the while Catherine stood there, cradling Georgina

to her chest, rubbing at her arms and back, pressing soft kisses to her hair and tear-streaked cheeks, whispering soothingly into her ear, telling her she was going to be okay, to let it all out, telling her she was sorry she was going through this, emotions within her began to grow.

Catherine's mind let out a silent laugh as she shook her head in disbelief. Georgina moved slightly in her arms and the butterflies in her stomach danced again, closely followed by a nudge of confusion and uncertainty. Georgina moved her hand and slipped into it into Catherine's, holding on tight as if her life depended on the contact. Catherine's breath grew shallow. Her heart seemed to beat out of her chest, and her legs quivered.

Catherine couldn't believe that these sensations could be happening. Was she also on a rebound? Did moving away from all things dear, make her question everything. Who she was, what she wanted, why she wanted it and how she was reacting?

Heat swept through her body. She felt a thousand things all at once, and not one had raised its head before. The awareness of being this close to Georgina made her body and soul come alive, her sweet scent creating wild butterflies in her stomach.

They clung to each other for a moment, nose-to-nose. Georgina's face was in front of her. Their eyes locked and something seemed to shift between them. The tension in the room grew agonisingly dense. As if all the air had been sucked and had dissipated through the cracks. Catherine found that she wasn't sure what was transpiring but couldn't look away from the eyes that, even with her tears, held a unique quality.

The sobs subsided from wracking sobs to silent tears. Suddenly, Catherine wondered what it would be like to just kiss her. Catherine found herself drawn to the full lips which slightly parted at the intensity of her gaze. She wanted to bring her lips to hers and find them open and willing. She felt herself being pulled towards them. Adrenaline filled her veins, and the disagreement was forgotten.

Georgina pushed away slightly, and the spell was broken.

Catherine blinked a few times as though she trying to understand what had occurred. Her face scrunched up in thought. Surely the loneliness and the lack of physical closeness of someone, anyone, had affected her more than she realised. She needed to think this through. To talk this through. To compartmentalise her thoughts into fact and fantasy, reality and romanticism. But now was not the time. Nor was Georgina the person. Perhaps Rachel. Rachel was wiser than her age suggested. But she was Georgina's friend. It wouldn't be fair to impose.

What she needed was her best friends perspective. She nodded her head. She would phone Sue this evening. She would know what to say. She would tell her tht she was being daft. Having decided in her mind her plan of action she held the gently sobbing woman even more tightly, giving comfort as best she could.

Georgina asked, in fear, "Are we good?"

"Yeah, we're good." Catherine squeezed Georgina's hand. "Why don't you stay in here for a little while and let the puffiness around your eyes dissipate. Give yourself as much time as you need. This past year has been a pretty emotional time for you and I think you have been pushing yourself too hard. And I haven't helped by all the changes we've implemented. I'll go back out there and see what chaos Rachel is dealing with."

Georgina looked hopeful and said, "Sure?"

"Sure" Catherine gave a small laugh and joked, "We don't want you putting the customers off their food and drink."

Georgina sat back down, "Thank you." She answered, too exhausted to come back with a retort.

Catherine placed her hand on Georgina's shoulder and

squeezed it. “We’re good. I promise.”

CHAPTER SIXTEEN

Admitting her feelings

Later that night Catherine picked up her phone and punched the button for Sue. Without preamble, she asked, "Hey babes. Do you fancy coming over this weekend?"

Sue answered, "What's wrong."

"What makes you think there is anything wrong?"

"You sounded desperate." Sue laughed.

"I'm not desperate. I just want to see you." Catherine replied with a smile. "It's been a while since we met up. I know we've talked on the phone but it's not the same."

"You must be desperate if you want to see me. Now, are you going to tell me what's wrong?"

How does she do that? She seems to instinctively know when I've got something on my mind. It's not as though I don't invite her down often. "Nothing's wrong," Catherine answered, still smiling.

"Okay. I won't push at the moment but I expect the whole story when I'll get there."

"John won't mind, will he?"

Sue laughed, "No. but he did say like he'd like to visit sometime. He's always wanted to go there."

"Perhaps not this time."

"So there is something on your mind?"

"Maybe."

"Hah. I knew it. But don't worry about John. He'll practically push me out the door this weekend. I think he wants to play golf with Stu. He started to mention a tournament a couple of days ago." She laughed, "Tracy had already told me all about it. He's being extra nice to me so I know he's been building up to asking me if he could take part."

Catherine could hear the smile in Sue's voice.

"I'll let him stew whilst he plucks up the courage to ask. Then when he does, I'll tell him that as he's leaving me for the weekend, I'll come over to see you."

Catherine chuckled, "Cruel and naughty."

"You've got to keep them on their toes." Sue continued to chortle, then asked, "Are you free all weekend?"

"No. I have to work for an hour on Saturday teatime when the football finishes. And they pile in for hot takeaway drinks. Apart from that, I am free."

"Do you want me to try to wangle off a couple of hours on Friday and drive up during the evening?"

"No. You don't have to do that."

"I know I don't, but my friend needs me by her side to tell me some important news so I will."

"It's not important."

"Don't give me that. I know you. And I can tell by your tone of voice that something or someone is concerning you." She laughed. "I'm hoping for good juicy gossip."

"I don't think you will be disappointed," she laughed back.

"Good that's what I want to hear. I hope it's risqué, and the racier the better. See you Friday. If anything changes, I'll text you."

The line went dead, allowing Catherine no come back. She smiled and shook her head.

Sue looked at Catherine, and smirked, “Well, we've talked about my drive over, what tournament John is playing in, and the new colour scheme looks stylish.” her mind was visualising the room downstairs.

A smile played at the corner of her lips as she continued, “Oh, the border, with the different puns painted in the black script above, stands out. But the ornate wooden board above the counter is pure genius. The gold script on the dark work is a thing of beauty.” She paused before saying, “I think it is very impressive and very eye-catching. Well done. I'll make an interior designer out of you yet.”

“Thank you. It does look good, doesn't it? Your idea of a border to break the room up was also a good one.” Catherine asked, “It's not too much, is it?”

“No. Not too much. It looked classy.”

“Anything you would change?”

Sue thought and pictured the room downstairs again in her mind. After a couple of minutes, she replied, “Perhaps change the soft seating area. Get rid of three-seater loungers and replace them with two-seater ones. And if they weren't quite so bulky and with a bit of rearranging you could get a couple more doubles and some single seats as well. I think the ambience would be better. Most of the time the middle seat is never used.”

“Come to think of it, I noticed that was the case but it hadn't fully registered. But it all costs money and at the moment I don't think it will change our profit margin.”

“True. But you did ask what I would change.”

“One idea for the future then.”

“So there is going to be a future here?”

A huge grin spread over Catherine's face, she then spoke as embarrassment affected her voice, “I truly hope so.”

Catherine looked away and Sue grinned as she noticed a tinge of colour had spread across her cheeks

"Anyway," Sue said as she started counting off their conversations again. "We've also talked about the weather, how the twins are, in fact, everything including the price of fish." She grinned at her friend, "All are very interesting but not the type of conversation that will go with this delightful bottle of wine." She picked it up. "Which we have almost finished. So are you going to tell me what's on your mind? You've been fidgeting and wringing your hands ever since we sat down. Now spill."

A look of panic showed in Catherine's face as she turned to look at her best friend. She quickly blurted out, "I almost kissed Georgina."

Sue's eyes grew wide, her mouth fell open. She was expecting that a man had come into her life and she had taken it a step further, but not what she heard.

"Excuse me. What did you say?"

Catherine looked downward and in an as quiet voice as she could produce, she mumbled, "I almost kissed Georgina."

She covered her hands across her face and peeked through her fingers. She wanted to see Sue's reaction but at the same time, she didn't.

Incredulousness made Sue draw out the next word, "No..." Shock showed on her face. "Oh... my... days... you made a play for Georgina... Georgina? Really? No... Never..."

Catherine leant back in her seat as her hands still covered her face. A deep blush could be seen emerging through her splayed fingers, as she groaned into her hands.

"When?" Sue responded in disbelief. "How? Why? Where?"

Catherine groaned again as Sue studied her.

"But more importantly, why didn't you?" Sue asked as she shook her head.

The moan that emitted from Catherine was longer. She kept on peeking through her fingers at Sue. She could feel embarrassment flowing out of every pore. “The day I asked you to come for the weekend.”

Sue exclaimed, “Wow. No wonder you were so flustered. What happened? How did you get to the stage of nearly kissing her?” She grinned and with a slight chortle asked, “But I’m still more interested in why you didn’t.”

Catherine gave her a look before letting out her breath in a steady stream. She gathered her thoughts and started the narrative in a louder, clearer voice, although she still hid her face behind her hands.

“We had this big disagreement about a change I wanted to make. We weren’t talking. Giving each other the silent treatment. I could see that Rachel was getting annoyed with us. But I did nothing to alleviate the bad feeling. I knew that if I apologised it would work itself out but I was too stubborn. My pride was getting in the way. Eventually, Rachel gave us a piece of her mind and pushed us into the office to sort it out.”

Taking a deep breath Catherine shook her head at the memory. “I did not come out of it very well I’m afraid. We were staring at each other. Not getting anywhere. She had said some hurtful words, but deep down I understood where she was coming from. Then Georgina suddenly broke down in tears and all this baggage came gushing out. There were tears and snot and everything. She looked so vulnerable. I began to feel like a real shit. I did the only thing I knew what to do and pulled her into me and held her tight. And all these butterflies started dancing in my stomach.”

“And.” Sue prompted. “Is that when you tried to kiss her,” Sue smirked knowing from her body language that Catherine was in discomfort with the retelling of the story.

“No, it was not.” Catherine sounded indignant.

“Go on. Tell me all about these butterflies and how they

managed to find their way into your stomach."

Taking her hands away from in front of her face Catherine smiled at the feelings her thoughts had made resurface. Sue smiled her encouragement

Catherine continued, "Even though I was holding this blubbering mess. I could feel her soft skin in my arms, could smell her subtle perfume on her neck, could hear her heart beating in tandem with mine, I could almost taste her."

She took a deep breath as the scene played around her.

"Her full lips were only inches from mine. Begging to be kissed. Her eyes locked on mine. Something happened inside of me as the butterflies turned somersaults in my stomach and sensations flooded other places." Another blush crept from her neck upwards.

Catherine sighed as the memory came flooding back and the feelings these memories were evoking.

"And at that moment, I wanted to kiss her. To kiss her so badly, my legs felt weak. I was meant to be holding her in my arms, but I didn't know who was doing the supporting, me or her. I could see the pain in her eyes and wanted it to stop. She was suffering and I wanted to be strong for her. To love her as no one had before."

She let out a long sigh, "But what I wanted to do was kiss her."

"So why didn't you?" Sue asked gently.

Shaking her head Catherine answered equally as gently, "I don't know. Georgina stirred slightly in my arms and the moment passed."

A look of sadness flashed in her eyes before she closed them with another sigh.

"And now. Do you still feel like that? As though you want to get naked, get laid and have the biggest orgasm possible?"

"Crude and rude." Catherine sloshed Sue's arm.

"Well? Do you?" Sue ignored the slap.

Catherine knew she was to say no. But that would be a lie to both herself and her best friend and it was something she couldn't do.

She took a deep breath. And as her body was telling her to say yes, "No," came out of her mouth.

Sue raised her eyebrows. Catherine knew what she said was a lie, and that Sue knew it as well.

"Okay. I don't know. Yes. I suppose." Catherine shook her head. "No. No, I didn't."

All the conflicting emotions scrambled her thoughts. Sue placed her hand on Catherine's knee and gave it a squeeze of encouragement. "Go on. Ramble on as much as you want. You might work out what is important to you."

"Okay. Now. Right at this minute. No. I can't even imagine kissing her or me doing anything more than that."

"Why?"

"Because she's the other co-owner of the coffeehouse, for goodness sake," she tutted, as though that was the only answer she could give. "I still have the rest of the year to get through and that magic five per cent number to reach. I cannot do anything to jeopardise that."

"But what if you had nothing to jeopardise?" Sue put across a counter-argument. "What if Georgina felt the same way?"

Catherine took in another deep breath and admitted to herself that no one had ever made her feel like this. The truth was she had feelings for a woman. Not any woman. She fancied Georgina. She shook her head. She wasn't a young kid anymore who flitted from one person to another and experimented. She was getting on in years. She was meant to be mature. And yet these sensations made her feel young again.

She sighed. How far did she want to take it? How far could it go? Was it possible to start a deep and meaningful relationship? Could she find love in her later years? Please let that be the case. Would Georgina want only companionship and friendship? Both their lives had been a mess on the relationship side. Would this be what she had always craved but was forever just out of reach? But was this what she truly wanted?

"Yes. Maybe."

"Why only maybe?" Sue prompted.

"Because..."

"Because what?" Sue asked encouragingly. "I can see lots of thoughts flickering behind your eyes. Thoughts you are still trying to get your head around. But what is your biggest worry?"

"That I won't be able to satisfy her." Catherine huffed, "There I've said it. I want to make love to her but I've never been with a woman before."

Sue frowned at Catherine's remark and asked, "And that matters because?"

"I'm not gay."

"Why are you putting a label on your emotions? You have fallen in love, well perhaps not love, but definitely in lust with someone. You wouldn't have this hang-up if it was a man, so why because it's a woman. Love is love. No matter who it is with. No matter what form it takes.

A blush again appeared on Catherine's face. "I wouldn't know what to do."

Shaking her head in amusement, Sue replied, "Don't worry about that. You would do what comes naturally to you. Answer this question. How many women have slept with a woman before they actually do?"

Catherine made a face.

Sue gave Catherine a look back and continued, "Everyone has to start somewhere. It's never too late to do what is right for you. I see the way she looks at you, and the way you look at her."

"I don't look at her like that."

Sue scoffed.

"But it's not natural to me. I'm not like that, not really. For a few minutes, I had those feelings. Emotions I had never experienced before. Yes. Georgina is lovely and I feel blessed to have made a friend of her. But nothing more."

"If you say so." Sue nodded in disbelief.

"I do say so."

Sue smiled a knowing smile, "So your stomach didn't do a flip when you held her? And you didn't want to hold her, protect her and keep her safe in your arms? You didn't smell her perfume and want to taste her? You didn't want to nuzzle your head in her neck? You didn't want her to embrace you in her arms? You didn't want to get lost in her kiss?"

Catherine gave her a rueful smile. "No. Not really."

But even as she said the words, she wondered how true they were. She blushed, and Sue saw the colour rise in her cheeks.

"Hah."

"What do you mean hah?"

"I mean your blush has given you away. I bet you wanted to do all those things."

Catherine felt her blush deepen.

"Talk to me. What are you feeling now? You can tell me anything."

"I know." Catherine paused before saying, "Perhaps for a fleeting moment, I did want to kiss her and get close to her."

"And now."

Catherine shrugged, not saying anything.

"Will you own up to your feelings?" Sue asked.

A shocked look came over Catherine's features, "Good grief no."

"She likes you," Sue replied.

"And I like her." Catherine shook her head. "More than like her."

Catherine knew there was no way she would act on her feelings. They were, as she had told Sue, a fleeting moment. All the emotion of the disagreement with Georgina, and her obvious distress brought out these instincts. She wasn't going to kiss her. In her heart, she knew she wouldn't. She'd had similar affections in the past and she had dismissed them quickly. It wasn't as though her heart ached until she could see her again. She was only affected like that when they were in very close proximity, so she would make sure that closeness wouldn't happen. She couldn't afford it to happen. There was too much at stake. And yet it hovered in the background.

She shook her head, trying to put all thoughts away. "But I'm not going to do anything about it. I am not gay."

She could hear the eye roll in Sue's voice. "And yet you have feelings for her."

"Yes, I do. But they will go as quickly as they came." Catherine said in a voice that was trying to convince herself.

"Do you want to fester away? Become all dry and shrivelled?"

"I'm that already." Catherine retorted with a pained look on her face.

"There's ways around that as you know. We all need physical contact." Sue's tone sounded annoyed.

"It's better than being hurt again." Catherine owned up. "I am not hankering after Georgina." she reiterated trying to distract herself from the thought that flashed through her mind, but also remembering the sensations she felt. "Anyway, I have my favourite toy."

"You need more than that. Everyone needs a hug."

Catherine ignored Sue's last remark, "It has always served me well, " she smiled, "much better than the real thing."

Sue looked at her sceptically.

"It has."

"Okay. It might be that you haven't met the right person." She again squeezed her friends knee. "But please be strong enough so you don't hide away from your feelings. Either those you are feeling now or other ones further down the line. Know that you can love again after the hurt."

She looked deeply into Catherine's eyes and said, "Some people cross your path and force you to change the path you are on. Allow that to happen. Don't step out of the way. See where that path takes you. You never know, you might be destined to walk beside them and share the journey."

Sue got up. "I'm going to leave you to ponder all that we've discussed and go get us both a coffee, okay?" she said, walking out of the door

Catherine and Sue walked down the back stairs into the coffeehouse. Rachel was behind the counter. They greeted each other warmly.

Catherine asked, "Is Georgina in the office?"

"Yep. She's gone to look something up."

"Is she okay? I'm sorry about the other day. I didn't mean to drag you into our disagreement. I know it wasn't professional and I promise it won't happen again."

Rachel nodded her head in acceptance of the apology. "Georgina comes across as a strong woman, but under the surface, she is full of vulnerabilities. And you were correct. I don't think she has given herself time to grieve. But at least she recognises that now. I don't know what you did or said in that office but she seems to have her mojo back."

"Good." She paused. "I think I might have pushed a tad too hard. I'll hang back a little."

Rachel nodded her agreement. "It might be best for the moment."

"Morning Catherine, Sue," Georgina said as she opened the office door and saw them. The women greeted her back. Georgina continued, as she touched Catherine's arm, "And no you haven't pushed too hard. Thank you for letting me vent my anger, hurt and irritability on you. It was something I needed to do. And perhaps you were correct. Perhaps I didn't take enough time out for myself. I've changed the rota a little next week and have emailed everyone a copy. It's half term next week. Molly said she'd do some more shifts and Maddie will take up the slack. I've booked a little place down by the sea in Cornwall for a few days."

"Blimey, Georgie." Rachel exclaimed, "I've never known you to go away before. Are you alright?"

"I'm fine. I need some time to reflect and recharge my batteries, and where better, than the seaside."

"It was nothing I said or did was it. I'm not forcing you away," asked Catherine with a mixture of dread and sadness in her eyes."

Georgina squeezed her arm, "No silly. You brought things into perspective. You were right I do need to grieve, to contemplate my past and consider my future."

Catherine gasped in a breath.

"No nothing like what you are thinking. I've been alone for so long and hankering over someone I couldn't have. Perhaps by allowing myself the time I can put my life back into a new frame of mind and get a better work-life balance. All I do know for sure is that I need my friends," she looked pointedly at both Rachel and Catherine, "more than ever. Your hug yesterday made me realise the closeness I have been missing."

A blush worked its way to Georgina's cheeks. Catherine came out in sympathy. Rachel looked between both women as a slight frown creased her brow. Sue suppressed a smile.

Catherine felt flustered so did the only thing she could think of and pulled Sue towards the exit. She turned to Rachel and Georgina and said, "Bye. We're off now. I'll see you after four."

When the two women were on the pavement outside the coffeehouse Sue burst out laughing. "I don't think you could have made it more obvious if you tried. You obviously fancy her and she does you. Georgina couldn't take her hand off your arm." She laughed again. "And you. All you did was look doe-eyed at her all the time. If I didn't know better, I would be thinking you were having an illicit affair."

Catherine huffed and swatted Sue's arm. "Are we going into town or what?"

Sue continued smirking as they crossed the road to the bus stop.

Rachel watched as the two women walked away and turned to Georgina and said, "Would you like to tell me what's going on?"

"Nothing's going on."

"Right." Rachel nodded. "What was with all the touching and feeling and looking lovingly into each other's eyes."

Georgina frowned. "I didn't fondle her arm. I might have brushed it once when I was thanking her. That was all."

Rachel shook her head and smiled, "You fancy her. You have from the first minute you saw her. Remember I told you to stop gawping. Well, you were gawping again just then. Even Sue noticed and was smiling."

"I didn't."

"You did."

"Humph." Georgina was saved any more embarrassment by the doorbell tinkling.

"I'll get you to tell me. Don't you worry?"

"Humph." Georgina turned towards the customer and asked, with a smile in her voice, "Yes please, and what can I get you?"

CHAPTER SEVENTEEN

Talking to Rachel

"Do you know what?" Rachel asked Georgina, as there was a lull in the early morning footfall.

"No. But I'm sure you are going to impart whatever thought has just come into your head."

"Damn right I am."

A few seconds past and nothing was forthcoming.

Impatient Georgina asked, "Well?"

Rachel smirked as she said, "I thought you'd never ask."

An eye roll and a shake of the head from Georgina followed the words. "Come on if you're going to say it then say it. I haven't got all day."

"Good. Now I've got your undivided attention I will tell you."

Georgina gave another eye roll.

Continuing, Rachel said, "You never know what life has in store for you until you turn to the next page and a new chapter awaits you. I suggest you get stuck into that new chapter and see what it has to offer."

Georgina frowned at her. "Very profound but what do you mean by that? Is it something to do with it being book club tomorrow night?"

"Oh come on Georgie. Stop acting coy. I've seen you looking

at her. How long ago since that argument? Two weeks? Three weeks?"

"Three weeks." Georgina owned up. "And by her, I take it you mean Catherine."

"Hah. See. I don't mention anyone and Catherine is the first person on your lips."

"We do work together. And she's the only one I've disagreed with." She paused for a moment. "And I don't go around looking at her."

"No. It's more like sly glances when you think no one is watching. And I've heard the sighs."

"I don't sigh."

"Do too."

Georgina sighed.

"See. There you go." Rachel nodded with a satisfied grin on her face. "You're doing it now."

"But she isn't here. So it's not a valid point as you don't know why I'm sighing."

"But I know you were thinking of her."

"How do you know that."

"Because you get this dopey look on your face." She nudged Georgina's shoulder. "Just like the one you have now."

Georgina smiled, "Okay. I admit it. But it was only because you put her thoughts into my head. No other reason."

"And the dopey look?"

"I always look like this."

Rachel narrowed her eyes and nodded, allowing the grin to stay in place. "You should ask her out. Not a drink over the road, you do that often enough. But go into town, go watch a film, see a show, a fancy restaurant. Do something special. Pining away is not doing your cause any good."

"I'm not pining."

"You are."

Catherine was now firmly ensconced in the forefront of Georgina's mind. She thought the feelings she'd had for Catherine had gone away, but they were still there. They swamped her, pressing into every cell, into every drop of blood, to every inch of her body.

She could imagine her standing close by with her charismatic presence. And she felt comfortable. A comfort, unlike anything else. Something she'd searched her life for but never quite found.

Even without her being nearby the butterflies fluttered as she thought of her. The fibres of her body responded in a way that no other person ever inflicted on her before, not even Laura. Catherine could always put people at her ease. And Georgina was not immune to her magnetic personality.

Rachel brought her out of her musings by asking, "Why Catherine?"

"She saw the pain in my eyes whilst everyone else saw the smile on my lips."

"Tell me how she makes you feel in here?" Rachel pointed to her heart.

"Earlier I looked in the mirror and I was smiling. Do you know why I was smiling? It was because I was thinking of her." Georgina let out a contented breath.

She closed her eyes and when she reopened them, she smiled and said, "She makes me feel like the woman I've always wanted to be. She has always made me feel more alive than she had the day before. And now, I'm in a happy place. She speaks to me in that alluring voice of hers, and my knees go weak. I feel that even though the change has been gradual, everyone has noticed it. I've noticed the change in me and for that, despite everything, I am grateful."

Georgina closed her eyes again and Rachel didn't interrupt, allowing whatever thoughts Georgina had to run their course.

Georgina reopened her eyes and continued, "She makes me feel fearless because I think she is ready to catch me when I fall. When you know there's someone there to catch you, being fearless is the easiest thing in the world. She has made me push myself out of my comfort zone. I'm sure I will do things which might precipitate, perhaps not a fall, but maybe a stumble. And I know she has the safety net out for me in case I trip up."

"So what is holding you back from telling her how you feel?"

"I'm scared where this could lead. I'm not going to lay myself bare again. I'm going to keep my feelings under wraps. I can smile at her, I can laugh with her, I can feel comfortable in her presence, but I'm scared. I don't think I can act on any of the feelings I've described."

"Why not?"

"There's a massive question which I cannot answer."

"And that is?"

"Can I trust her with my heart," she took a deep breath, "because we all know what happened when I did that before."

"Not everyone is like Laura."

"I know."

"You can't live like a nun for the rest of your life."

"But I can and I will." Georgina reaffirmed her intention. She spoke to a mother and child as they exited. "Thank you. Come again."

Georgina walked over and cleared the table.

As Georgina was putting the dirties into the dishwasher Rachel said, "I'm so pleased that you have fallen back in love with yourself."

Georgina frowned, "I've never stopped loving myself."

Rachel raised her eyebrows.

"Okay, I fell out of love with myself a little bit."

Rachel raised her eyebrows again.

"What do you want me to say? Because I wasn't loved by the person I wanted to love me I didn't feel worthy of loving myself? There I've said it."

"You were always worthy of love and of loving yourself. You lost sight of it for a while." Rachel touched Georgina's arm and said, "And it's great to see you blossom back into the person who had lain dormant for so many years. You are back to the person I first met all those years ago. You are smiling, laughing, talking more to the customers again."

"I've always talked to the customers," Georgina said indignantly.

"I know. But you're talking to them differently. Like you used to. You're friendlier. You find out about them. You ask after them and their families. You act as though you truly care."

"I've always cared," Georgina said defensively.

"I know you have. But because of the barrier you put up, it didn't always come across as you did. The self-confidence you have acquired again recently makes you more approachable. You are almost back to the one hundred per cent loving, laughing, caring Georgina I first grew to love. Now you need to find yourself a playmate so those missing percentages can be reignited."

Georgina groaned.

Rachel didn't let up, "So if it's not going to be Catherine, find yourself another woman. Find a special someone to share that love with. Not another woman who is out for what they can get from you. I believe there is that someone for everyone. I'm just saying, don't be surprised who that person could be. I don't think I will be."

"Humph."

"Go and find someone who appreciates you for who you are and will give you their heart."

"Easier said than done at my age. I could never do those dating sites or anything like that. I'm too old to go by myself to the gay bars in town. And although we have loads of lesbians using this place, no one has taken my fancy."

"So ask Catherine out on a date. You don't even have to call it a date. You can always say it's a friendship dinner, show, whatever. Take her somewhere new where you are both slightly out of your comfort zones. What's the worst she can do. Knock you back. She knows you're a lesbian, so there's is no shock there. You've become friends. So nothing new there. She has already made an imprint on your heart, now make an imprint on hers. Make her feel special. You know and I know she has some sort of feelings for you."

Georgina smiled at Rachel, and then, slowly but very surely, nodded, "I think she does and here we are in an in-between state. And wherein lies the problem. I vowed many years ago to never get involved with a straight woman. Once bitten twice shy."

"But is she? Is she one hundred per cent straight?" Rachel said, with a wink.

Rachel was finishing the split shift which she hated. But at least she had two full days off. She hoped that the weather would stay fair so that she and her husband could get away as planned.

"May I ask you a question?" Rachel turned to Catherine.

"If you must," came the reply as both women wiped the tables and lifted the chairs on top.

"We've known each other six months, haven't we?"

Catherine frowned at the question, wondering where the conversation was going. She answered. "A tad longer but yes, almost seven months."

"You know I'm bisexual, don't you?" Rachel admitted as the questioning frown stayed.

"Is that your question?" Catherine laughed as she shook her head.

"No. Don't be daft." Rachel smiled back and laughed as she said, "Bear with me, I'm working up to the question I want to ask."

Catherine smiled a winning smile. "Yes, I know you're bi."

"And you also know that Georgie is a lesbian?"

Catherine gave a slight frown but nodded.

"And a lot of our regulars are also on the LGBT+ spectrum?"

She studied Rachel as is looking for clues. She again nodded and answered, "Yes. You got me intrigued, where are you going with this?"

"I was wondering." Rachel paused and scratched her chin trying to form the next question.

"What? You were wondering if I was uncomfortable at all."

"Well not really, sort of. No." Rachel jumbled up her thoughts.

Rachel creased her brows, "That's not what I was thinking. After all this time that would have been obvious if you were truly uncomfortable. No one is that good at hiding their feelings."

Catherine gave Rachel an inquiring look but said nothing.

"As I said, I was wondering," Rachel resumed, "seeing as I am bisexual, Georgina, Bren and Maddie are lesbians. Molly, I think is working through all the emotions, teenage years bring. So..." she dragged out the word and looked at Catherine.

Catherine continued looking back at her, not saying a word. She instead started smiling and raised an eyebrow in question.

"You are not making this easy for me, are you?" Rachel squirmed

"I've never seen you squirm before." Catherine laughed out loud. "And I don't exactly know what you are trying to ask me. I'm good, but I'm not a mind reader."

Rachel huffed. "Alright, I'll just come out and say it."

"About time." Catherine chortled.

"Are you gay?"

"Has Georgina put you up to this?"

"Goodness no." Rachel gasped and hid her mouth behind her hand. "She would be mortified if she thought I had asked that question. Mind you, I am curious that you thought Georgina put me up to it. Why not me." Rachel eyed Catherine and asked, "Is it that because you have feelings for her?"

"Tosh."

Rachel peered closely into her eyes. Catherine looked away quickly, her cheeks reddened slightly.

"Tosh yourself. I've seen how you look at her."

Catherine drew in a breath. "I don't know what you mean. We are friends and that's all there is to it."

"Yeah. That's why I see you sneaking looks at her when you think no one is looking. That's why the air crackles between you both when you are in the same room. That's why you blush when Georgie has said something a bit risqué. Do you want me to go on?" Rachel gave her an enquiring look. "So are you?"

Catherine gave a shy smile, "Yes I agree, I do look at her sometimes. She has something special about her, something I cannot put my finger on. I think she is a warm, funny individual. But no, I have never thought about any woman in that way. And yes, for a fleeting moment I felt something pass between us." A blush spread through her cheeks as her thoughts went back to the office. Where she had held Georgina in her arms and the feelings that flowed through her in that touch. "But I've only ever fancied men, been with men, wanted to be with men," Catherine spoke emphatically. "I'm not a lesbian. Does that answer your question?"

"If you say so," Rachel looked at her and smiled.

"I know so?"

Rachel raised her eyebrows, continued smiling and nodded. "So are you bisexual?"

"Honestly?"

"Honestly."

"I have no idea. You tell me. Does having a moments attraction to Georgina make me one? I don't think so." Catherine shrugged her shoulders.

"So you admit you have had feelings for Georgie?"

"I've already said for a fleeting moment I did. And that's all it was." Catherine shook her head, turned her back on Rachel and carried on with the end of day clean up.

She wasn't going to say any more on the subject. Or even think about wanting to kiss Georgina. She'd done enough of both over the past few weeks and she felt drained. She hadn't realised Rachel had noticed so much. She thought she had hidden her feelings quite well. She had hoped all these feelings were all in the past. She shook her head in disbelief and thought, *who am I trying to kid?*

CHAPTER EIGHTEEN

The date but not a date

Georgina and Catherine had gotten into the habit of meeting after work one night a week. Their relationship had become easy and they had started calling each other nicknames. Georgina had suggested a few days ago that they should spend an evening in town instead of going over the road for a quick drink. To dress up a bit instead of their everyday clothes. To do something special, something different. Catherine had agreed readily.

"So are you going to tell me where we are going tonight Gee?" Catherine asked as she sat down on the seat next to Georgina.

The seats in the bus weren't designed for too much comfort and she found their shoulders and thighs pressed against each other. She felt the heat radiate where their bodies met. The bus lurched forward and the two women were pushed closer together.

"Sorry," Catherine said as she tried not to squash Georgina against the window. "These seats seem to be made for skinny things. Not people of average height and weight." She scooted over a fraction. "Is that better?"

"You're fine, Cat. At least you're not some big fat hairy bloke who takes up half of my seat as well as his own and smells as though he has drunk the whole cider farm. Then proceeds to belch and fart the whole journey."

Catherine nodded, "Or the resident nutter, who has the pick of the whole bus, but comes and sits next to you."

"Yes." A wicked grin spreads across her face as she says, "Who virtually sits on you, then starts a conversation and you haven't a clue what they are rambling on about." Georgina looked pointedly at Catherine, feigning horror and annoyance. She giggled into her hand.

"Oi. Rude." Catherine slapped Georgina's thigh.

The two women burst into laughter

When their laughter died down Catherine asked, "Do you have a place in mind, or are we seeing where the fancy takes us?"

"I thought a wander around Millennium Square and the surrounding streets and plazas first off. Soak up a bit of the atmosphere, the hustle and bustle. Have a look at the different pubs and restaurants. See if any place took your fancy, either to eat or drink. What do you think Cat?"

"That works. I've tried a few places along the watershed but nothing further back. Is there anywhere you would recommend?" Catherine asked.

Georgina shook her head, "I only usually come here when one of the many festivals are on. And then it's too crowded to find anywhere to sit down, let alone eat. I have to admit that I have no idea what any of the places are like these days because it's years since I've eaten down here."

"Why ever not?" Catherine asked.

Georgina's mannerisms changed from confidence to shyness, "It's a bit lonely going out to a restaurant by yourself. It's a bit different eating in the pub opposite. I know them and they know me. I don't feel if I am out by myself."

"So you never go into town," Catherine asked

"I didn't say that. I said about going into a restaurant."

"Okay, Gee. So which of these pubs have you tried?"

Georgina shook her head, "Again none of these."

"Why ever not? I thought you implied that you come into town. You must have drunk in at least one of these."

"Honestly I haven't. I often pop in for a drink in the old city area after I've wandered around St Nicks or the covered market. Then that's usually the Three Graces. But if I was coming into town just for a drink I would go to Fairies, its proper name is The Lord Fairfax. They are both predominantly gay pubs."

"Oh." Realisation dawned and Catherine said, "I forgot you were gay."

Georgina laughed. "Well, I am. And that's a good thing you forgetting that, isn't it? It means you are comfortable in my company. Thank you. I didn't suggest us going to either place because I didn't want you to feel uneasy or on edge. I wanted us to have a pleasant, relaxed evening."

"I would have if you wanted us to go there."

"Thank you, but for our first d..." Georgina stopped what she was going to say and hurriedly continued, "but for a night out I thought going to a gastropub or restaurant would be better. More convivial for talking, eating and drinking. So let's decide which one we want to try."

Soon the bus arrived at the city centre and the two women made their way across the bus lanes towards Millennium Square. They wandered around the different squares and plazas. They dipped their fingers into the wall of water feature, goofed around having selfies with the Cary Grant statue. They sat for a while watching youngsters and those not so young splashing in the water, and at the sporting event that was being shown on the big screen.

"Do you like Italian?" Catherine asked. "That restaurant over there has taken my fancy."

"Yes." Georgina replied, "but we haven't looked at the

menu."

"I expect they will have the usual fare, Bolognese, Carbonara, et cetera, but I'm fascinated by the building. Amongst all this new stuff this old grey stone building seems to have survived. I bet it has a story to tell?"

"I expect it has." At that moment Georgina's stomach rumbled. She laughed. "My stomach is telling me it's time to eat. Let's go grab an Italian."

"What? By his arm?" Catherine asked with a smile

Georgina replied laughing, "No. On her bum."

Catherine studied Georgina perusing the menu. Her brow creased. She fought to understand the feeling she was experiencing. She looked around the room. She noticed the subdued lighting, the quiet background music, the waiters hovering discreetly out of the way. The screens and distance between tables offered intimacy.

Georgina reached across the table and placed her hand on top of Catherine's and asked, "What would you like to drink?"

"A house white is fine by me."

Georgina nodded and smiled a dazzling smile, which lit up her whole face. She beckoned a waiter over and gave their drinks order.

Again they were left alone. The light of the candle between them threw shadows over its immediate surroundings. Georgina's face glowed in the light it cast out and sparkled brightly in her eyes. Bringing them to life. Making them feel more alive than she had seen for ages. The dull tiredness had been eclipsed by this shining light. She looked beautiful and serene.

Catherine felt her stomach do a flip. She stared at the woman opposite. Her eyes travelled over her whole face. Everything she had ever wanted in a person was in front of her. She was honest, honourable, humble and most of the time happy. Her kindness, generosity and intelligence shone through. She made everyone who stepped into the coffeehouse feel welcome and special. Not in a false 'have a nice day' sentiment but in a 'how's your Bob doing' type of enquiry.

Catherine gaze halted on Georgina's eyes and she let out a tiny sigh and a sense of sadness hit her. Georgina cared about people and how they were feeling. And yet she didn't care enough for herself. She was always putting herself down, portraying the fact that she thought herself unworthy. How could anyone with a personality as beautiful as hers, ever have those doubts?

Again the feeling of wanting to protect this woman settled in her heart, and she smiled at the thought. She saw Georgina's lips move. She knew she had said something but she hadn't heard the words, so wrapped up was she in the emotions of the minute.

"Pardon. I didn't quite catch that." Catherine replied.

Georgina again placed her hand on top of Catherine's and laughed, "Nothing profound. I said, are you ready to order?"

Catherine looked at Georgina's hand, she heard the kindness in the words, she felt the warmth of the touch. It felt as though she was on a date.

Was this a date? They both had dressed up as though they were on a date. Did she want to be on a date with Georgina? She couldn't truthfully answer that. Everything felt good but everything felt wrong. But why was it wrong? Her thoughts went to a myriad of places. Each place arguing with the previous. She gasped but didn't remove her hand.

Georgina heard the gasp. "Don't worry I don't date straight women."

Feeling unsure of herself, Catherine gently removed her hand and looked at the menu.

"I think I'll have the Carbonara," Catherine answered.

"I was thinking the same." Georgina nodded her agreement.

Catherine picked up her wine glass and took a sip as Georgina ordered for both of them. Catherine again studied the woman and smiled.

Georgina turned to her and said, "What are you smiling about?"

"You," Catherine answered truthfully.

"Why? Is everything alright? Have I done something wrong?"

"No. Not at all. It's the complete opposite. Everything is fine." Catherine paused for a moment then asked, "Have I told you how beautiful you look tonight."

Georgina's face turned red as she blushed deeply. "Don't be daft," she said as she fidgeted with her dress, smoothing it down.

"You do. You look gorgeous in that dress. The colours suit you." Catherine complimented her.

Georgina squirmed slightly in her seat and said, "You look lovely as well Cat."

Catherine lifted her glass and said, "Here's to good company, a wonderful setting, and hopefully an excellent meal. Cheers."

Georgina clinked their glasses together. "

Catherine said to the screen as Sue's face appeared, "You'll never guess what?"

"We're not doing that twenty questions thing again, are we? I need more of a clue than you'll never guess what."

"I think I went on a date. It felt as though it was a date. But maybe it wasn't. Perhaps it was just a meal and a drink. But it felt more than that. At times it felt like a date but at other times it felt like I was going out with a mate."

"Stop." Sue held up her hand. "I think I'm going to need a

wine."

Sue shouted off-screen, "John, will you bring me a glass of Prosecco, please. Bring the whole bottle. I could be here a while."

Catherine heard a quiet voice in the background. "If that's Catherine say hi. If it's one of the twins tell her to wait until your next get together."

Sue turned back to the screen and said, "John says hi."

Catherine laughed, "I heard. Tell him hi back."

"Catherine says hi."

"So what mischief did you and the twins get up to." Catherine continued as though the interruption hadn't happened.

"Just the usual." Sue waved off the question. "What I'm more interested in is this date but not a date."

Catherine felt herself become embarrassed.

"So?" Sue prompted.

"Well," Catherine started. "You know we've been going over to the pub about once a week for a bite to eat and drink."

"Yes..."

"Well..."

Sue rolled her eyes and tutted, "For goodness sake get on with it."

"Patience is a virtue, you know," Catherine replied, haughtily.

"And as you know, I'm not very virtuous. Now get on with it." Sue laughed.

"Where was I?" Catherine asked herself.

"Not even at the beginning," Sue mumbled into her drink.

Catherine pouted at her and continued, "A few days ago Gee asked whether I fancied going into town to have a meal down there instead. So I jumped at the chance."

"So you're calling her Gee now are you."

Catherine huffed and said, "Are you going to continue interrupting me or can I get on with the story."

Sue did the get on with it gesture.

"We caught the bus into the city centre and wandered around the Harbourside area. We came across this Italian and decided to eat there."

"Sounds like something me and you would do. What makes you think it felt like a date."

"I don't know, it just felt like it. The ambience was lovely, not too dark, not too bright. The tables were far enough apart that we could talk without anyone listening. She kept on reaching over and touching my hand. I know I squeezed it back. The way she looked into my eyes. And the conversation rolled along and the wine flowed. I didn't want the night to end. It felt perfect."

"And how did you leave it?"

"I didn't. Guess what I suggested?"

"You didn't," Sue gasped. "Spill the beans. Did you go to your place or hers?"

"No. Nothing like that." Catherine rolled her eyes. "Is that all you think about?"

Sue thought for a millisecond and replied, "Yes," as she laughed.

"You are incorrigible."

"If it wasn't that then what? I'm afraid you're going to have to tell me because I have no idea."

"I suggested we go and have a drink in a gay bar." Catherine looked embarrassed.

Sue nearly choked as she spat out her wine. "You did what?"

"It's called The Lord Fairfax but the locals call it Fairies. She mentioned this bar earlier in the evening and I thought why not suggest we go to a place where she feels completely comfortable."

"So did you go?"

"Yes. And I knew a couple of people from the coffeehouse there. We did only stay for one drink as it was a bit loud."

"You poor old thing." Sue waited for a moment then asked, "So? Would you go again?"

"Why not. It was just like any other pub."

"And are you going to suggest another not a date, date?"

"I think I might."

CHAPTER NINETEEN

Christmas Eve

The weeks flew by and the routine was similar each week. Occasionally Catherine and Bren would go to the pub across the road for a drink after the Tuesday session. Georgina and Catherine would go out on their weekly date but not a date. And before they knew it Christmas was upon them.

They had closed earlier than normal along with all the independent shops in the vicinity. And all the staff had gone home to get ready for the celebrations.

Georgina and Catherine were going to throw a small Christmas Eve party that evening for all their workers, and local shopkeepers and suppliers with whom they had worked closely.

Georgina looked around the room. She nodded pleased with the result. She had quickly put up a small tree and had scattered presents underneath, making the place more Christmassy. The tables were pushed to the side allowing room for dancing in the middle.

Cushions were scattered on the floor between the soft seating and a variety of age-related games, puzzles and magazines were placed on a low lying table. The doorbell dinged and Catherine came in carrying a box of wine.

"Need any help?"

"Please." Catherine clicked the car fob and opened the boot. "Have a look at what I got and see if you think it's enough."

Georgina walked over to the car and had a quick look. She lifted out a case of beer and carried it into the coffeehouse.

"There's plenty there. Well, I hope there is." Georgina acknowledged as she dropped off the beer.

Catherine nodded. They continued bringing in the different boxes and cases of alcohol and placed them on the counter.

When it was all lined up on the counter Georgina asked with a laugh. "Blimey. Are we catering for the whole block?"

"If it's not drunk tonight, I'm sure we will find a use for it."

"I'm sure we will, as long as it's not only the beer that's left."

"So who is coming to this shindig? How many replies did we eventually receive?"

"Molly is bringing her new boyfriend," Georgina laughed. "If she is as loved up as she was yesterday, we won't see much of them."

Catherine laughed, "Loves young dream."

"Maddie is coming with Alison, as soon as Alison gets back from work. Bren is coming with someone. She won't say who she is bringing. She said that we would be surprised."

"More and more interesting. she hasn't mentioned anyone." Catherine scrunched up her face in thought, then she smiled, "She has come out of her shell since her book launch. You hardly ever hear her stammering now. Her confidence has grown exponentially. I'm pleased for her."

"Who do you think it may be?" Georgina contemplated, "I think it may be Laney who goes to creative writing."

"It could be. Or even her mate Anya."

Georgina thought for a moment then asked, "What about the woman who won the free coffee?"

"You mean Paula? No. It's not her."

"I've no idea then," Georgina shrugged her shoulders. "It's obviously someone we know. The sly old fox. She's kept it quiet that she's seeing someone."

"She knows that you would take the mickey."

"As if." Georgina tried to look innocent but failed miserably.

Catherine laughed. She asked, "So apart from our lot who else did you invite?"

"I invited David from the local rag, with his wife, I still don't know her name. To thank him for the couple of articles he has written."

"It's Meg."

"How do you know that?"

"I asked her. She comes to book club."

"Oh." She paused for a moment. "I've also invited our new cleaner Kelly plus one. I don't know whether she will come. She has three children under six."

"Nah. She's not." Catherine agreed. "When I spoke to her this morning, she said she would have her hands full but she might be able to slope off for half an hour. I doubt whether she will though. Who else?"

"I've invited our accountant, Niki, and a couple of our suppliers. Jak, Faith, Reina, Althea, Dani and their other half or plus one. They all said yes but we'll see who else will arrive. Jakob and Zofia next door, said they would pop in if the party was still going when they finally close their shop for the holidays."

"This will be a nice crowd if they all make it."

Georgina took hold of one of Catherine's hands and said, "It's a shame all your friends live on the other side of the country."

"Yeah." Catherine said wistfully, "That's what I miss from being over in the West Country." Catherine forced a smile, as a hint of sadness and online played with her emotions. "My friends love a party, as do I."

"Right," Georgina nodded, not knowing what else to say. She continued, "Let's have a double-check that we got everything we need."

Catherine surveyed all the wares and ticked off an imaginary list in her head. Satisfied she nodded, then suggested, "If you would take the turkey upstairs, I'll move the car to the side streets. You might as well shower and get ready. I'll finish off down here then join you upstairs."

"You don't mind me using your place to get ready. I could easily go home." Georgina asked, feeling slightly unsure and shy.

"I wouldn't have offered if I didn't want you to. Now go upstairs. Have a shower, put your feet up and relax for," Catherine looked at her watch, "about an hour."

"If you're sure."

"I'm sure."

Catherine returned from safely parking the car in the side street. She was putting the finishing touches to the room. They had borrowed some glasses from the pub and she was arranging them next to the correct drinks. Nibbles were strategically placed around the room. She had taken out a few of the light bulbs so the room would be more conducive to a party atmosphere. She stood in the corner of the room and surveyed the effect of their endeavours. Pleased with the result, she ensured the entrance was securely locked and switched off the lights.

As she paused outside the stockroom her thoughts wandered to the present that was hidden in the shadows. A smile, followed quickly by concern, flashed over her face. She hoped Georgina would like it. She shook her head and thought *too late to do anything about it now*.

She entered her flat and was about to speak when she noticed Georgina wrapped in her towel, asleep on the settee. She smiled at the sleeping figure. Her face looked so serene and at peace. She pulled the blanket off the back of the settee and gently laid it over the sleeping woman. Georgina stirred slightly as gentle snores were heard.

Catherine turned away from the sleepy woman and made her way into her bedroom. She showered quickly and dressed in a pair of tailored trousers and a plain, long-sleeved purple blouse. She picked up the shoes she was going to wear and carried them into the living room. She placed them by the side of the settee which still held the sleeping body of her business partner.

Catherine cooped down on her haunches and spent a few minutes admiring the figure so innocent in her slumber. Her relaxed features had all but extinguished the lines around her eyes. Her lips were slightly parted and the corners of her mouth turned up in a smile. As though she was dreaming happy thoughts. Georgina twitched slightly and a gasp caught in her throat as though she knew she was being studied. Catherine held her breath and stayed very still, then the rhythmic sound of Georgina's breathing again filled the air.

She felt the butterflies in her stomach start to build, as she was drawn towards kissing the lips she was staring at. Desire started to pull her downwards. She leant over and as their lips were about to touch, Catherine suddenly pulled back, as though the realisation of what she was about to do dawned on her.

She wouldn't take advantage of a sleeping woman no matter how those lips asked to be kissed. No matter how much she wanted to kiss her. And how she wanted to kiss her. What was wrong with her. Never before had anyone affected her like this. She shook her head and took a couple of deep breaths.

She reached out an arm and gently shook Georgina's shoulder, and spoke quietly, "Gee. It's time to get yourself ready."

Georgina shot upwards. The blanket and towel fell off her.

Catherine gasped and at the sudden movement fell backwards onto her backside. She looked up and was greeted by the sight of Georgina's boobs in all their glory.

Georgina gasped and frantically pulled the blanket back around her. "Shit," she said in a voice louder than normal. "You scared the living daylights out of me. And stop gawping at my boobs."

"I'm sorry. I'm sorry. I didn't mean to. I didn't expect you to jump upright and flash at me. You scared the living daylights out of me as well." Catherine's shocked face morphed into a smile. "And, by the way, they are very nice boobs to gawp at."

Georgina pulled the blanket tighter around her.

"Good job you had some knickers on." Catherine teased. "Otherwise I'd have seen you in all your glory."

"Humph. You'd have been so lucky. And what are you doing, still sprawled on the floor? Haven't you got a party to get ready for?"

As Catherine tried to rise from the floor, using the arm of the chair, she groaned as her knees cracked, she said, "I'll make us a coffee whilst you get yourself presentable." Catherine turned towards the kitchen.

Clutching the blanket to her chest, Georgina got up and started to walk towards the guest bedroom. "You can add a sugar to mind seeing the shock I've just had," she pouted, but the corner of her mouth turned up slightly.

"I think I'm the one who needs the sugar. At least no one flashed at you. That's a criminal offence you know."

"It's not." Georgina paused then asked, "Is it?"

"Nah. Just teasing," Catherine grinned. "You're okay, you're not in a public place."

Catherine heard Georgina mumbling as she closed the door to the bedroom. *Watch out*, and *own back*, could be heard. A smile spread across her face and a joy invaded her mind. She felt happy and fulfilled. She was looking forward to Christmas for the first time in years. She let out a huge sigh of contentment.

CHAPTER TWENTY

The party

Georgina greeted the first arrivals, by giving Rachel and Buwan a hug, saying, "Hi, the drinks are on the counter help yourself to whatever you want and to the nibbles."

Georgina looked at their two children. She ruffled both Ramil and Brando's hair, and said to them both, "Happy Christmas. My, you've both gotten tall. How old are you now, I've lost track of your ages?"

Rami answered, "Happy Christmas Aunty Georgie, I'm fourteen and he's twelve."

"Wow." Georgina replied, "You certainly have grown. Your soft drinks are at the end of the counter. I see you have your phones with you but I've brought out some games and puzzles if you want to play with those."

Rami replied, "We'll be alright Aunty Georgie." He looked at the older woman and asked, "Does help yourself apply to us as well? Especially if we get to sample a glass of wine."

Georgina nudged the teenager's shoulder, "Oh yeah. Since when did you turn eighteen. Soft drinks only for you young man."

Rami gave a winning smile, "It was worth a try."

Brando said quietly, "Happy Christmas Aunty Georgie." She ruffled his hair again, "And to you Brando."

"And if Rami manages to wrangle a drink I will have," he

looked along the counter, "a lager, I think."

"In your dreams buddy." Rachel butted in. "Now go and make yourself scarce over there."

"Okay Mum," they both replied.

Buwan wandered off to get the drinks and was soon engrossed in a conversation with Catherine.

Rachel turned to Georgina and said, laughing, "I wonder how long until he realises he has my drink in his hand as well. If he's not back within five minutes I'll give him a piece of my mind."

"You could always get yourself your own glass," Georgina suggested.

"Nah. That would be too easy on him." She laughed, "He'll owe me. And I will claim my compensation later." She wiggled her eyebrows, grinning.

Georgina shook her head at her friend.

Rachel turned serious and asked, "Can everyone make it this evening?"

"Your Simon, Jean and the twins will be here later. Simon said he has to work until half-past five. He said he'd get here as soon as he can."

"I'm glad the twins are coming at least my two will have others their age to react with. That's if they will get off their tablets and phones for a few minutes."

"I could be cruel and turn the router off."

Rachel laughed, "Aunty Georgie. You wouldn't dare. And you are their favourite Aunt."

"Their only aunt. And not even a proper one."

"Sometimes those are the best sort." Rachel said bumping shoulders with her friend.

"Thank you." Georgina grabbed hold of Rachel's hand and squeezed it.

"I'm looking forward to tonight. You haven't hosted a Christmas party for a few years. Should be good fun."

Georgina nodded, "Laura stopped wanting to do it. She said it was too much trouble trying to be nice to everyone. She said she had to do it every day at work. Why would she want to do it in her own time as well?"

"It was a shame. Did you give Catherine a choice, or did you tell her it was going to happen no matter what?"

Laughing, Georgina said, "I gave her the choice. She was well up for it."

Rachel suddenly remembered, "Didn't Catherine said something about karaoke tonight?"

Georgina groaned. "My worst nightmare. But yes. She's borrowed a monitor and some mikes from one of the customers. The one who runs the second-hand goods."

"So it's true. Brilliant. Love it. And the kids will too."

Georgina groans even louder. "I stopped her when she suggested flashing coloured lights and a disco ball."

Rachel burst out laughing. "I can imagine the look on your face when she suggested it. I bet it was priceless." When she stopped laughing, Rachel asked, "I'm going to get my wine. Do you want anything?"

Georgina rolled her eyes, "Bring me back a case. If we're doing karaoke then I'll need it."

The door pinged and Alison and Maddie entered. Maddie held a bag in front of her. "I have got a few presents." She looked around the room and asked, "Shall I put them under the tree with the others."

Georgina nodded and said, "You didn't have to buy anything."

"I know. But they are only silly bits and pieces. Things I saw that I couldn't resist."

“Thank you.”

Over the next half an hour most of the others, who said they would attend, were there. Music played through the speakers. Occasionally the improvised dance area was filled with people dancing and being silly. During the break between two songs, the doorbell jingled and everyone looked towards the door, awaiting the newest arrival. Bren entered and was followed closely by a redhead. There were gasps as some people drew in their breath.

“Good evening Georgina. I don’t think you’ve met Marie. Marie this is Georgina, the other co-owner of this establishment.”

From the gasps that accompanied her entrance, she realised that this was a total surprise to some of the gathered crowd. She wondered who she was and what had she done to receive such a reaction.

Georgina shook Marie’s hand. “Pleased to meet you. Help yourself to drinks and nibbles. I think Catherine will be getting the karaoke going soon. So you might need some Dutch courage. I think she’s expecting everyone to take part in some way.”

Under her breath, Marie muttered, “I need Dutch courage but not for karaoke.

Catherine returned to the room after a swift sojourn upstairs and came face to face with the redhead.

“What the fuck are you doing here?” Catherine spoke through clenched teeth whilst she grabbed hold of Marie’s arm, open hostility and her anger pouring out of every pore.

Marie looked down at the hand on her arm. Catherine took her hand away but continued her steely stare.

“Well,” she asked as quietly as she could. Trying to control her temper and not create a scene. “You’ve got a fucking nerve.”

Marie put her hands on her hips and returned the glare. She

replied in an equally quiet and controlled voice. "I'm here to support Bren."

"Support Bren, my fucking ass." Catherine was trying hard not to raise her voice. "Just like the support you gave her on her book launch. Just like the support you gave her on your radio show. So I'll say it again. What the fuck are you doing here?"

"C...Catherine."

Catherine turned towards the voice.

"C...Catherine, will you come with me please."

Shooting Marie more daggers she followed Bren into the corridor. "I thought you'd be pleased for me," Bren asked as they stood near the fire exit. "You've been trying to set me up with all and sundry since almost the first day you stepped through the door."

Catherine showed her agitation as she paced a step in each direction until Bren took hold of her hands and looked directly into her eyes. Catherine lowered her gaze. They had become firm friends since the launch and the Tuesday evening sessions.

The mutual arrangement had worked well, and the coffeehouse was always full. Catherine had seen her blossom into the confident woman in front of her. The funny, kind and caring side of her personality shone through like a beacon. She didn't like to think of Bren being taken advantage of.

A couple of other women had joined her at her usual table and a small writing group had grown up, giving each other reciprocated support. She hoped that Bren would have got together with one of them. To say it was a shock to see Bren walk through the door with Marie was an understatement.

"I am pleased to think you have someone," she said. "And yes, I admit I have been steering people towards you. I thought you had got it together with Dot. But not her." Catherine nodded her head toward the room. "Why her? She painted you and your kind of books in such a bad light on her radio show. She couldn't have been a bigger bitch if she tried. Why in the world would you bring her here, tonight. You knew she wouldn't be wanted."

Bren smiled at Catherine. "Thank you, Catherine. I know you are trying to look out for me and I understand your misgivings, but we sorted it out a couple of weeks ago. She explained why she did it."

"Hah," Catherine exclaimed, "there is no excuse for what she did. It bordered on homophobic abuse."

"I agree with what you are saying. And yes, I was livid when I heard it. You knew how I was feeling."

"And yet here she is."

"Yeah, here she is."

"But you could have brought anyone. Why did you bring her?"

"Because after I phoned the station and demanded an apology and retraction, Marie explained everything to me over a drink. We found out we had a lot in common and sort of hooked up. We've been seeing each other since."

"You've kept that quiet."

"Why do you think that is?" She looked pointedly at Catherine. "I knew your feelings ran deep and I wanted to see where it was going before upsetting the apple cart. As we've been seeing each other for a little while now, and are on a firmer footing, it's about time we let our friends know."

Catherine nodded and smiled at her friend, then asked, "What I do want to know is why she did it?"

"Now that's a conversation for another day. Not Christmas Eve, when we're all out to have fun. I'm going back to rescue her from anyone else's clutches. Will you behave yourself if I leave you alone with her?"

Catherine nodded, "If you think she's alright then she must be. I trust your judgment. You will have to tell me the whole story when we next go out for a drink."

"No. I'll let her do that," Bren answered. "However, the first thing you are going to do is to apologise for swearing. I have never heard you swear like that before."

Catherine laughed, "Oh I can swear like a trooper when riled. And seeing that woman."

Bren gave her a look.

"Sorry. Seeing your girlfriend waltz in here without a care in the world made me see red. For that, I will not apologise. And she will have to gain my trust. I will not accept her completely until she has done that. But I promise I will play nicely from now on. I may not like it but for you, I will."

"Thank you. That's all I ask. "

Catherine spoke into the mike, "Happy Christmas everyone. Thank you for coming. If you have any requests for music then let me know. As some of you have already realised there should be enough space for dancing. I've placed around the room some sheets with the different karaoke songs I've managed to download. Please write your name and the song you want to sing on the request slips."

She continued, "So that you know the standard of singing I expect I will start it off. I'm sure most of you have told me to shut up sometime over the nine months I've been here. Help yourself to drink and nibbles and let the party commence."

She turned the music up, grabbed hold of Georgina and started swinging her around the dance floor. Georgina threw back her head in pure enjoyment and abandoned all inhibitions. Others joined them on the dance floor as the party started in earnest.

A few songs later the dancers sat back down to enjoy their

drinks. Catherine got back on the mike.

"Okey dokey let's have some karaoke. As promised, I will start by murdering 'Eternal flame', followed by Buwan and Rachel doing the classic 'I got you, babe', then Jax with 'Girls just wanna have fun'."

She checked that the three of them were okay with doing it. She then continued, "Don't forget to put your music choices in, and some more karaoke requests before I start twisting some arms. Are you ready for my singing? Don't say I didn't warn you," Catherine laughed.

The wines and beers continued to flow. Everyone either volunteered or was volunteered to sing karaoke to various degrees of proficiency. The presents under the tree were given out and everyone was having a good time even the teenagers who joined in the karaoke with gusto. A few hours later the party started to wind down and the only people left were Georgina and Catherine.

Catherine closed the door behind Rachel. She turned to Georgina and said, "That was a good idea of Rachel's to give each table a bin bag to put their rubbish in. It made it so much easier. I only have to plonk them in the bin out the back"

Georgina nodded with a silly grin on her face.

"You're drunk," Catherine said in disbelief. "When did you become drunk?"

"I think it was the last bottle." Georgina hiccupped. She started to walk towards the brush that was leaning against the wall but staggered into one of the tables and giggled.

Catherine rolled her eyes. She had never seen Georgina drink more than two glasses of wine. She dreaded to think how much she had imbibed.

Catherine guided her to a seat and sat her down, "You sit down here whilst I load the dishwasher and sweep the floor. I'll walk you home after that."

Georgina rose to her feet and staggered, "Let me help." Catherine put her hands on Georgina's shoulders and pushed her back down. "You will help more if you sit still."

"O...Kay," she giggled.

Catherine made short work of the glasses and swiftly wiped down the table. She swept the floor and noticed Georgina's head had now rested on her arms and she heard gentle snoring emanating from her. She smiled. She quickly mopped the floor to get up most of the sticky spilt alcohol.

She dashed upstairs and picked up a coat, going back downstairs she retrieved Georgina's coat from the office. Waking her up she gently pulled Georgina to her feet so that she wouldn't topple over. She guided her through the door and after locking up she walked her a couple of streets to her house. She manoeuvred her carefully onto the settee and covered her with a blanket.

Georgina looked at Catherine and said, "I love you."

"And I love you too," Catherine responded but Georgina was already asleep. "I'll see you sometime tomorrow when you've sobered up."

CHAPTER TWENTY-ONE

Christmas Day

She tugged the blankets off the back of the settee and threw one of them to Georgina. She wrapped the other one around herself and plonked down next to her. Georgina stretched, then allowed her arm to rest over Catherine's shoulder. Catherine dropped her head and snuggled in. Wrapped in her friend's arm brought a comfort that Catherine never knew before and there was no other place she wanted to be.

Her eyes moved down Georgina's face to her full lips and back up to her eyes. "I think you are beautiful."

"Thank you," Georgina replied, putting a hand on Catherine's bicep and giving it a gentle squeeze.

Her touch was always gentle, and Catherine loved the way it made her feel, blushing at the heat Georgina's gaze was causing in her body.

"I enjoy being around you. You're a sincerely caring and loving person, and I love that about you."

Georgina hugged her tighter. "Thank you again."

"Hold that thought." Catherine disappeared and came back carrying a small gift. She placed it in Georgina's lap. "A little something to say thank you for encouraging me to succeed in this venture. Without you pushing me and gently guiding me,

I'm sure I would have given up like I have done so many times in my past."

"You shouldn't have," Georgina replied, as she picked up the gift.

"You don't know what I've got you yet." Catherine smiled at her friend and business partner.

Georgina read the words on the label.

'Memories are the things you make,

With people, you want to love,

They stay within, inside your heart

And fit you like a glove'

xx Catherine

"That's lovely." Georgina wiped a tear away with the knuckle of her hand. "Look what you've made me do."

Catherine smiled and squeezed her hand. With surgical precision, Georgina carefully untied the ribbon and took her time peeling back the Sellotape. She unfolded the paper surrounding the item. She recognised the logo which adorned the box and gasped.

"You remembered."

"I might have done." Catherine smiled.

She opened the box and a Bristol Blue Glass earring and necklace set was beautifully displayed.

Georgina burst into tears, and between the sniffles, she said, "It's much too much. Especially after the measly present that I gave you last night."

"No. Gee. You asked me what I wanted, and you got me what I wanted. And it was perfect."

Georgina leant over and gave her a hug and kiss on the cheek. "Thank you. Thank you so much. It goes perfectly with this dress."

"That's why I asked if you were going to wear this dress today."

"No wonder you seemed upset when I was said I was going to wear the other one you said you liked." She turned her back and lifted her hair from her neck. "Would you do the honours?"

"I thought you'd never ask." Catherine smiled back.

"Let me go and replace my earrings, then we can snuggle down to watch the film.

As Georgina was about to get up Catherine asked, "Are you sure you want to watch the Sound of Music?"

Georgina sat back and laughed, "The Sound of Music reminds me of Christmas during my childhood. It was always on and it was about the only time we all sat down together." She laughed again, "Usually after about ten minutes Mum, Dad and Grandpa Jack would be snoring by then and I would be the only one awake."

She sat holding Catherine's gaze, she kissed the top of her friend's head. Then a long-lost memory of Laura on their first Christmas watching it together began to play in her head. Georgina let a slight shudder vibrate through her. She nodded her head ever so slightly, acknowledging the feeling before shaking it away from the image. She needed to build new memories.

Catherine oblivious to the turmoil of emotion that had invaded Georgina's thoughts asked, "Before we snuggle down properly to watch the film, do you want something else to drink? Some wine or maybe a coffee?"

"We're not open tomorrow so another wine please."

"I'll nip downstairs and bring up a couple more opened bottles we didn't finish yesterday. It would be a shame to waste them."

"Are you trying to get me drunk again?" Georgina asked

with a smile.

"Last night was all your own doing. I expected you to be late getting here this morning with a sore head. I was so surprised when you arrived on time looking chipper."

Georgina shrugged her shoulders, "I suppose I'm lucky. My head was a little fuzzy but a couple of paracetamols did the trick. And it was Christmas morning. I couldn't let you do all the prep."

"You were funny last night. I thought you didn't want to have the karaoke. But you kept dragging everyone up to sing off-key with you. And at the end, why did I have to be Kenny Rogers to your Dolly Parton? Why couldn't we sing something like 'Dancing Queen' or anything by Blondie."

"It seemed apt at the time and I was drunk." came the reply, a slight blush crept into Georgina's cheeks. "Now go and get that wine and I'll change my earrings."

"Okay bossyboots." Catherine scooted away laughing.

Georgina made quick work with the jewellery and whilst she was gone, she had a closer look around the room. A snow globe caught her eye on the table near the door. She went over, picked it up and shook it. The swirling storm of glitter made her smile, knowing that no matter how much it was shaken up it would come to rest and be peaceful again. She smiled at the memories it evoked. She continued walking around the room examining various ornaments. She turned towards the door as she heard Catherine return.

Catherine hesitated in the doorway. A sudden nervousness gripped her as she looked at the woman in the figure-hugging blue dress. Holding the two bottles in one hand Catherine nibbled on the skin by her thumbnail of the other. She shook her head at the thoughts rolling around in her brain. It was as if Georgina were a force that made her forget how to breathe, how to speak. She tried to push these thoughts down. They were going to be spending the rest of Christmas together so she needed to stay in control of these alien emotions.

Georgina walked slowly the short distance to Catherine and ran her hand from her arms down to her hips. She leant in and gently kissed Catherine's cheek. "Thank you for dinner and for cooking it. Nobody, since I left home, has ever cooked me Christmas dinner before. And thank you especially for these," she shook her head and the earrings wobbled side to side. "And for this." She lifted the necklace.

Georgina took the bottles out of Catherine's hand, walked over and placed them on the coffee table.

Catherine stayed rooted to the spot. She touched her cheek where Georgina's lips had been. The kiss was so soft and considerate and it warmed every part of Catherine's body. From the top of her head to the tip of her toes. She wondered how every cell in her body could react to such a light touch. She frowned at her reaction.

"What's wrong? Georgina asked as she turned back to look at her. Catherine still hadn't moved from the spot. Georgina wondered if she was the cause of Catherine's obvious discomfort.

There was something in the way Georgina looked at Catherine that made her insides churn. Creating a stir within Catherine that she could not avoid, a need that she could not fulfil. No matter what she had told Sue about her trusty toy.

Being close to Georgina made her stomach flutter, and heat consumed her entire body. Catherine had no idea what caused this type of reaction. How could someone she considered a friend could make her entire body react in such a way?

She looked at Georgina and was overcome by something Catherine never thought she'd have again. Hope and a feeling of safety. She wanted to be in this place forever, to feel this way forever. To feel this hope building inside her as though she had waited all her life for this moment. She felt safe with Georgina by her side. A feeling that she hadn't felt in a very long time. A feeling more than female friends was supposed to feel for each other.

Georgina moved back towards her. "What's wrong?" she asked again.

Catherine took the nibbled thumb out of her mouth and wondered when she had started biting her nails. Was it out of nervous anticipation? She gulped down the saliva that had built in the back of her throat.

"U... uh... uh...I...um... N... nothing."

Worry came over Georgina's face as she took another step. And the closer she got, the more Catherine's heart began to race. She could feel her skin began to perspire. She wiped her hands down her trousers and tried to maintain some semblance of normality. And yet her head spun, her stomach flipped and she felt sick with nerves.

"Sure?" Georgina asked for reaffirmation.

Catherine let out the breath she'd been holding and answered with a smile, "I am fine."

A small smile pulled at Georgina's lips as she held onto Catherine's eyes. A quiver rushed up Catherine's spine as she watched Georgina's gaze move from her eyes to her lips.

"Are you sure?" She placed her fingers and lifted her chin. "You looked a little perplexed for a moment. And now I'm getting lost in those beautiful, expressive eyes of yours." She blushed as she said it, not meaning for it to sound so flirtatious.

"I'm sure. Don't worry about me." Catherine beamed at Georgina, her unease lifted and happiness flooded her whole being. It was as if Georgina had opened the shutters to her heart and light had flooded in. A light that had been missing for as long as she could remember. Catherine felt her breathing become ragged as she stared into Georgina's expressive face and looked into her welcoming eyes. She reached out and touched Georgina's cheek with the back of her hand.

Georgina stood frozen to the spot. She couldn't move, she couldn't speak, every nerve ending in her body was waiting to see what would happen next. Waiting in anticipation at what she wanted to happen next. She couldn't risk any movement on her part, couldn't risk upsetting the moment. She felt scared and excited at the prospect of being up close and personal. The snow globe on the table again caught her eye, and the storm was still swirling, like the sensations in her heart.

Seeing Georgina's body tense, Catherine smiled. Georgina ran a hand over her head, as was her habit. She closed her eyes to try to recover her composure, but when she reopened them, Catherine's soft gaze was caressing her face, a smile playing around her lips.

Georgina looked away before she could take her feelings further. She felt her eyes being drawn back to the vision in front of her. She could feel her resolve begin to break. None of her insecurities mattered when she looked at Catherine. She drank in her beauty. She marvelled at the smile on her mouth, the sparkle in her eyes.

Catherine reached out and she brushed her fingers over the skin of Georgina's wrist. Their eyes locked and Georgina felt a warm fuzzy feeling in her stomach as though someone was looking into her soul and fluttering their eyelashes.

What Catherine did next came as a surprise, as all rational thoughts went out of the window. Catherine shook off her reserve and smiled at Georgina. As she had been at a loss for words, and couldn't express her feelings in sentences, she did the only thing she could think of. She pressed her lips softly to Georgina's, letting the pleasure and comfort of that kiss drive the worry from her heart. And as their lips touched, nerves were woken up that she'd forgotten had existed. Her fingers drifted up into Georgina's hair and massaged her scalp. Her skin prickled with goosebumps as she moaned into her mouth.

Catherine pulled back and she touched her forehead to Georgina's. Neither of them said anything for a few minutes, and Catherine wasn't sure what to make of that silence. Her breath rushed across Georgina's face. She licked her lips, "I . . . didn't plan that."

Georgina looked into the eyes so close to hers. The silence was comfortable. She wondered whether this was a dream, a hallucination born of wishful thinking. For those moments when they locked eyes, they seemed to forget everything else even existed.

Catherine gently pulled Georgina's head down towards her. When their lips met again, she was amazed at the softness of Georgina's lips. They pulled apart to take a breath. Catherine's head swam, and it had nothing to do with the few wines she'd had with dinner. It was a pure pleasure, an undeniable lust, and like nothing she'd ever felt before.

Georgina smiled and said, "I want you. I want us to take this further. And from your blush, I can see that you want me as well."

Georgina gazed into Catherine's eyes and they were giving her permission. She stood on her tiptoes and zeroed in on a pair of slightly swollen lips. The blatant need between them was raw and primal. Georgina closed her eyes and lost herself in desire. They broke apart and she gasped for breath. They looked at each other. Both shocked at what had happened between them.

"I can't believe I did that." Catherine's face offered a silent apology.

"Neither can I." Georgina smiled, "Are you sorry that you did?"

"Good grief, no." Catherine touched Georgina's cheek. "It's just that I don't usually go around kissing women.

"Believe it or not, neither do I. Especially someone who I

know is straight."

She felt Catherine tense in her arms. "I'm sorry. That came out wrong. I felt what we have between us. It seems we've been dancing around each other for months. I didn't mean to label you. And I'm sorry if I embarrassed you."

"You didn't embarrass me. And if I remember correctly, I kissed you first."

Georgina's head was so light and spinning so fast, it was almost impossible to breathe. And yet realisation pushed its way to the fore. Georgina gently moved and held Catherine at arm's length. "Be that as it may, perhaps it shouldn't happen again."

"What if I want it to happen again."

The look of shock on Georgina's face was priceless. Catherine cupped Georgina's face and pulled her forward. Catherine's lips were soon softly on Georgina's again. She lightly brushed her tongue along her bottom lip. Georgina used her teeth to faintly tug at Catherine's lower lip before releasing her. Catherine's mouth opened in response and as the kiss deepened, Georgina's heart raced.

She couldn't seem to get enough. As Georgina nipped at her lower lip, Catherine moaned and felt as if she'd melt. She slipped her arms around Georgina's neck.

"Did that really happen?"

"Mhmm." Georgina hummed happily and locked their lips together again.

Blushing at the rush of heat she felt from the contact of Georgina's lips, Catherine suddenly felt panic rising within.

She gradually pushed Georgina away, not wanting to meet her eyes, for she was afraid her own eyes would betray her. Would show the want and need her body craved. She had to fight the urges that she felt for Georgina's touch. She could feel herself falling and again a panic rose from her depths. As the panic rose, thoughts rushed around her mind. The more she thought about it, the more she knew this wasn't right, that they were making a mistake

She was afraid. But what was she afraid of? The unknown? The future? Being true to herself?

The feelings she had for Georgina had come too soon. Could she love a woman? It felt as though she could. The kiss had shown that she was able. Perhaps not all women but definitely Georgina.

Her sensible head invaded her primal thoughts and won the battle that was raging within. She had to stay strong. She couldn't afford to let anything get in her way. She still had to reach the year mark and that was the only thing that mattered. She hoped and prayed that she could reach the magic five per cent. She couldn't envision not working in the coffeehouse. It had become her lifeblood. Her saviour. Her home. It was where her heart wanted to be. It was where she belonged.

Catherine shook her head and continued shaking her head, as she pushed herself further away. She pressed her lips together, and when she spoke again, she subtly dabbed at her eyes. "I'm sorry. No. I don't think I can handle doing anything more right now. This isn't the time. I can't," she gasped, pushing Georgina away. She continued in a whisper, "I - I'm sorry."

She quickly cleared her throat, gazing out into nothing. The sudden lump in her throat caught her off guard.

Georgina baulked at the confusing signs Catherine's face was giving off. One minute all the need and desires were on display only to be displaced by fear and trepidation, then by resolution and intent.

And the intent Georgina saw is what she feared. Her body was shouting out for more. She needed release from her pent up emotions. And yet she felt as though Catherine's shutters had come back down. Blocking out the light, putting a stop to any chance of a fledgeling relationship.

"What's wrong, I thought you wanted it as much as I did. I thought you wanted to take it further."

"I did. But I can't." Catherine let out a huge sigh. Her eyes filled with tears.

"Why? I'm not going to hurt you. I would never hurt you." Georgina's hurt was plain to see.

Scrunching her face up Catherine wouldn't meet Georgina's eyes, "I know."

"So why? Especially since you initiated it." Georgina asked, her eyes full of hurt and incomprehension. "I don't understand."

Shifting uncomfortably, Catherine folded her arms. Georgina mirrored her, folding her arms across her chest.

"Neither do I." Catherine shook her head in sorrow and confusion. "I always said I would tell the truth. I'm sorry I led you on, but the truth is I can't."

Questions came tumbling out. "Is it because I'm a woman? Do I make you uncomfortable? Do you think it's unnatural? Haven't you felt the growing attraction between us? Did I push too hard? I'll back off, I promise. Please tell me what I can do?" Georgina pleaded.

"Of course I felt it," Catherine answered truthfully, "It's not because you're a woman. And no, you don't make me feel uncomfortable. I feel so safe in your company. I felt so safe in your arms. But… And here's the big but. I don't think I'm ready for this type of intensity. I don't want to go down the path we were on, not just yet, I can't just yet. But I think I may in the future."

"I can't lose you." Georgina strangled a sob.

Catherine took hold of Georgina's hand. "You won't lose me as a friend. I want us to stay friends. I need you to be my friend. And perhaps more. But not now."

"Do you..." Her voice hitched in her throat. "Do you know when you are likely to be ready?"

Catherine shook her head, "I've no idea when that will be and I can't expect you to wait for me."

Georgina nodded, but sadness etched her face.

Catherine could feel her resolve to start to slip. Instead, her stance became firmer. "Us becoming partners in this business was fate. We then by choice became friends. And at this moment that is how I want it to stay. I'm not my Aunt. I won't keep you dangling. I sorry if I gave you false hope."

Georgina's voice stayed calm and quiet, as she admitted, "I would have been your friend no matter what. You have become my, *no matter what*, friend here. However, me having feelings for you was totally beyond my control."

Her eyes pleaded with Catherine. "Don't ask me to not have these feelings. It's been about you since the day you walked into the solicitors. And I remember what I felt like when you first spoke to me. I think back to the moment our hands met when we first greeted each other, and the shock that reverberated up my arm."

Georgina took a deep breath, "That day something clicked. I wasn't looking for anything." She shook her head. "Why would I want you here. You were likely to take away my business. I tried hard not to like you. But you gave a shy smile and my heart told me otherwise. I had no control over it, there was this chemistry straight away. I wanted to be in your company. I counted the hours or days when we would work together again. Every day afterwards, the frisson between us grew. Didn't you feel it?"

"Yes, I did." A pained look came into her eyes as Catherine agreed. "But I cannot allow myself to feel it. Not yet. I cannot let anything get in the way of my focus. And my focus at the moment has to be purely on the coffeehouse. I don't want to jeopardise anything. I have the rest of the year to increase the profit margins to five per cent and I won't let anyone or anything get in the way."

"Stuff the contract." Georgina sulked.

"That's easy for you to say. Everything I now have is riding on that contract. And remember as you said, I'm not gay, I'm a straight woman."

"You're a woman who has kissed me. Kissed me so deeply that I felt my toes curl. Kissed me so deeply that I wanted to rip her clothes off and make wild passionate love. Kissed me more deeply than a straight woman should ever kiss me."

Catherine looked embarrassed. Everything Georgina had said was true. "It's true. I did do all that and I was affected the same as you. But I can't do this right now. I have to get through the year. It's only a couple more months. You do understand, don't you?"

Georgina pulled her into an embrace and spoke. "Not really. I understand that you have to focus. It was like this when Laura and I started the business. Fully focussed on the task at hand. I think that was how the trouble between Laura and I started. We couldn't invest the time in us. And we needed to invest the time if our relationship was to survive. I know you want me. And I want you. I feel it in here." She touched her heart.

Catherine nodded.

Georgina continued, "All I ask is that you are completely truthful with me. You will be truthful with me? Don't let me hang on to half-truths and lies."

Catherine bobbed her head, "I promise."

"Whatever happens tomorrow, the next day, I will always remember those kisses we had today. And for that, I am truly grateful."

Georgina's calm voice made the blood flow loudly through Catherine's veins. She could hear the rhythmic heartbeat in her chest and throat. She could feel the throbbing pulse in her neck and see a golden sheen of sweat on her skin. The mingled smell of shampoo and soap invaded her awareness. She felt an outpouring of love that made a hot dampness puddle between her legs. She felt all these senses and more. She hadn't put a name to them before, because she hadn't wanted to believe it. Now she knew the name. The realisation of what she had just thrown away dawned on Catherine, and she burst into tears.

The embrace she was held in grew tighter. When the tears subsided, they were both standing, facing each other with no sound but the beating of their hearts between them.

Georgina asked, "Let's not say anything more. It is Christmas. Let's have some wine and watch the film."

Catherine nodded not daring to speak. She glanced at Georgina and saw, behind the stoic mask she had erected, a deep hurt. Catherine wanted to cry again knowing that she was the cause of that deep hurt.

Georgina said with a slight waver to her voice. She was angry with herself for messing up the first serious encounter she'd had since Laura. "You set it up, get yourself a tissue and I'll get the wine," she said, knowing she could shed her own tears during the film.

Later that evening Catherine her phone buzzed. She pulled it out of her pocket, took one look at the screen, Catherine's face instantly softened, a light came to her eyes, and a silly grin immediately materialised on her face.

"Hi babes, happy Christmas. Did you have a good one?"

Catherine burst into tears and between sobs, she said, "I did it again."

"What? You nearly kissed Georgina?" Sue couldn't hide her incredulity.

"No. I kissed her. She didn't kiss me. I kissed her, then she kissed me back. And it felt so good. Nothing like any of the kisses I've had before."

"And?"

"I stopped her. I told her that I wasn't ready.... Or something like that. She must think me a right bitch. I could tell I hurt her."

"So why did you stop her?"

"Because I was afraid."

Sue waited, knowing there was more to come.

"I thought she might tell me where I could shove her friendship. And it would be somewhere where the sun doesn't shine. I told her it was about the contract and not wanting anything to get in the way. She was so sweet and so kind. I must have hurt her so much."

Again Sue waited.

She threw up her hands and wrinkling her nose. "Sue," Catherine said plaintively, "I think I really like her."

Sue decided not to respond.

"I hadn't felt any stirrings, no ache, no desire until I started working closely alongside her. Gradually I get to know her, and boom. My belly, my loins, and my heart all began these flutterings. Everything I knew, I felt, I expected from my life, changed." Catherine admitted, and let out a sob. "I'm not like that."

"If you keep fighting what you are feeling you will lose her forever, then I'd bet good money you'll regret it for the rest of your life. If it's meant to be, it will happen. Let your guard down over your feelings and let yourself be in love with her."

"I'm not in love with her."

"I beg to differ. I could see it, sense it, the last time I visited. Don't be scared of the unknown. Act on your feelings. Start loving yourself and love her."

The last few words hit Catherine in the chest. She folded her hands in her lap, and shrugged, wondering when her shoulders had gotten so heavy. "What have I done? I've spoilt everything."

"Oh, babe. Not sure what else I can say. Here's a virtual hug down the phone. Now keep talking to me."

Sue continued to listen to her, talk to her, and calm her down until all scenarios had been covered and all emotions had been talked through.

"How are you feeling now?" Sue asked, "Are you okay?" "Yes." Catherine forced herself to breathe slowly and regain some kind of calm. She said with a slight wobble. "Thank you for listening. What would I do without you?"

"You'd get drunk and cry yourself to sleep." Sue's smile could be heard down the phone.

Catherine gave a small smile, "The only thing I haven't done is sleep."

"Go and put your head down. I'll phone you tomorrow."

"Thanks, Sue, for listening."

"Night, night Sweetie. Love you."

CHAPTER TWENTY-TWO

After Christmas

"What is it? You didn't seem your normal self today, Georgie." Rachel asked at the end of the day.

"It's nothing. Just feeling a bit down today." Georgina replied with a sigh.

"Anything I can help with?"

"Not really."

"You haven't been like this for ages. Over the past few months, I've seen you falling back in love with yourself. This is a bit like you were this time last year."

"Honestly, I'm fine."

Rachel frowned as she studied Georgina.

"I am," Georgina reiterated. But sadness permeated her eyes.

"What happened over Christmas?" Rachel asked. "On Christmas Eve you were laughing, joking and the happiest I think I've ever seen you. And now the day after Boxing Day you are looking sad and sorry for yourself. Are you going to tell me what's going on?"

"Nothing's going on."

"Is that the reason why you're sad because nothing's going on?"

Georgina shook her head.

"Come on. Come into the office and let's sit down away from any prying eyes.

Rachel pulled out her chair and made sure Georgina was settled before taking her seat across from her at the small table.

"Tell me what's going on? This isn't like you. Even when I've seen you at your lowest in the past, you always had that expectation of hope. You never looked this defeated. What has happened?"

She could tell that Georgina was fighting every emotion inside of her, but the sadness in her eyes couldn't be hidden. She stood and moved around the table. Rachel leant down and held her in a tight embrace and kissed her cheek.

Finally, she broke the silence, and asked, " Do you want a coffee or something stronger?"

Georgina shook her head.

"What can I do to help?" Georgina again shook her head. A quiet sob escaped.

"I can't help unless you talk to me."

"Will you come to mine? I don't want anyone to see me in case I break down."

"Of course."

"You go now. I'll lock up here and follow you."

Georgina grabbed her coat and rushed out of the office.

Some minutes later, the two women sat side by side in the lounge. They took sips of their drinks and continued to sit in silence for a while.

Rachel was the first to speak, "Have you and Catherine argued?"

"No." Georgina shook her head.

"But is it to do with Catherine?"

Georgina nodded, as she gulped in a breath.

"You know that she is so completely in love with you," Rachel said. "Most people could only dream of a love that deep. You can see it in her eyes, her smile and the way she looks at you."

A look of confusion contorted her features. She clicked her tongue, shook her head and retorted "That may be so, but she still turned me down."

"You made a move on her?" Rachel raised her eyes. "Did you? Wow. I didn't expect you to do that."

"No. I didn't make a move on her. She kissed me."

Rachel stared incredulously, "She kissed you." Rachel huffed a laugh. "Wow."

"I wish she hadn't kissed me."

"Why? I thought that's what you wanted to do. I thought you wanted a relationship with her."

"I do. But now I wish she hadn't."

"Would you care to explain?"

"Because if she hadn't kissed me, I would be in the same place as I was before Christmas. Now she has kissed me I have this gash in my heart which I fear will be difficult to close. Now she has kissed me I have this space where there was hope, and I know of nothing that could fill that void apart from her. There is this big hole where her heart should be beating next to mine."

"Georgina, I am so sorry," Rachel felt her friend's pain

"I guess our bodies and minds weren't in synch, that it wasn't our time," Georgina admitted, feeling sad, but also pragmatic. "She pushed me away. That's all there is to it."

"So how did you leave it?"

Georgina laughed a hollow laugh. "We watched The Sound Of Music."

"Oh. Georgie." Rachel shook her head as a muffled laugh escaped.

Georgina looked at her friend with disdain, then puffed out a breath, "I don't want to lose her friendship or her."

"You won't."

"I think I love her or at least have some very strong feelings for her and would do anything to be able to act on them."

"Then you have to be honest with her."

"I thought I had been," she left her words hanging.

Rachel replied, "Things are still so stressful and messy for Catherine right now, perhaps it just isn't the right time for her. Or the right time for you."

Nodding, Georgina said, "She's worried about not fulfilling her side of the contract. She said her focus has to be on that completely. That she can't let anything or anyone get in the way."

"Stuff the contract," Rachel exclaimed.

"That's exactly what I said."

"Then do something about it."

"Such as?"

"I'm sure you'll come up with a solution." Georgina sighed a couple of times then said, "I think I might just give up on us."

"No. Don't do that. There is so much mutual attraction between you." Rachel responded.

"I'm reminded all the time of how Laura treated me."

There was no reply for a moment as her heart missed a beat. she took a deep breath and looked up at her, face softening. "I know Georgie. Stop beating yourself up. It won't change a thing. Catherine is not Laura. I bet Catherine is scared of what she is feeling. The thought of loving a woman is so alien to her."

She gave her friend a squeeze of her hand.

Georgina agreed and gave a small nod.

Rachel nodded as well. "I don't believe that Laura would have wanted you to go through life like this. Stop pining for her. She wouldn't have wanted you to lock yourself away. Do you think subconsciously you are putting up barriers? You've become so good at stopping people from getting into your heart. You've been living in denial of who you are by not putting yourself out there. You've denied yourself for too long. So take that step. Start being true to yourself. Do something to prove that you are worthy of Catherine's love."

Georgina was about to interrupt when Rachel said, "No. listen to me. There's this woman we know who, I think, you can be really happy with. A woman that is crying out to be loved. Now, stop with all the drama and show that woman the reason why she should love you, not why she shouldn't. Start going on your not a date, dates again. Don't try to woo her, just be a friend. And let her know you will be there for her come what may. But take it easy, don't push it too hard. Go over to the pub. Go into town or somewhere that will be a bit of fun. Back off and stop looking at her with lust in your eyes."

"I don't lust after her." The lie fell naturally from her lips as though she was trying to convince herself.

Rachel raised her eyebrows and shook her head.

"Okay, maybe I do a little." She admitted with a small smile.

Rachel squeezed her hand and continued, "Have no heavy conversations. Don't try to kiss her. Don't talk about S. E. X."

Rachel suddenly burst out laughing.

"What are you laughing at?" Georgina frowned as she asked.

"A picture that flashed through my mind." She looked at Georgina and continued smirking.

"What now? Tell me what is so funny. If you are laughing at

me, I demand to know why."

Rachel chuckled. "I'm sorry. I imagined you picking her up and carrying her into your bed."

Georgina narrowed her eyes and clenched her jaw.

Still laughing, Rachel replied, "Come on. That thought is funny. By the time you would get her there, your knees, hips and back will be hurting so much you wouldn't be able to do anything."

Georgina's tenseness in her face relaxed as she replied, with a roll of her eyes. "Rude but true."

"I'm going to try to put that thought out of my head." Rachel swiped her hand down her face as though she was changing the picture. But straight away she started to laugh. "I'm sorry, but I can't."

Georgina huffed.

"I'm sorry," she laughed again. "But I've heard you groan when you get up off the floor, you old git."

"Thanks for reminding me. I might not be able to do the athletic acrobatics I could in my youth, but I can still satisfy a woman. But it's been soooo long."

"You have to be patient. You have to let her make the first move," Rachel's words were significant and poignant.

Georgina nodded. After she took her time to process what Rachel had said, Georgina whispered, "But what if she doesn't."

Rachel lowered her voice and said in a tone full of concern. "Then it's not meant to be. Come and hug me." She offered her hand to Georgina, who took it and let Rachel pull her to her feet.

"Feeling better?"

"I suppose. It was good to talk to someone." She nudged Rachel's shoulder. "Even if it was you."

"Good. I'm glad I was able to be of some use." Rachel smiled.

CHAPTER TWENTY-THREE

The fire

The weeks passed and most things had returned to normal. There was a slight tension as they tried to keep their distance. They tried not to look at each other, and they would look away quickly when they were caught glancing in the others direction. Their date but not a date night had dwindled as Catherine kept politely refusing any chance of becoming close. Their relationship had returned to a strictly professional basis. And both were suffering in their own way.

Rachel tried to be as supportive to both of them as she could, knowing what the other was going through, but she didn't want to get involved. Believing they would sort it out in their own time, after a fashion. She could see the love between them and was powerless to help.

During a morning shift, Rachel sat next to Catherine on one of the stools and said, "On the calendar, it says you are seeing the accountant later this afternoon. So that means it is the end of the month meeting."

"Yep. I've been here exactly eleven months. She is going to tell me how far I'm away from that magic number. So I know whether I need to implement any promotions to get me over the line."

"And will you? Need to do some promotions, I mean."

"I think I'm pretty close to reaching the five per cent already. Well by my reckoning I am. If we continue doing our normal stuff we should pass it easily. I think the only thing that will get in the way is if we have a major catastrophe. I might do one or two more promotions just to be on the safe side."

"Any thoughts on what it might be this time?"

"Not really." Catherine gave a little shrug, "I have thought of introducing a breakfast coffee smoothie."

"Sounds interesting. What are the ingredients?"

"Chilled coffee, of course. Then there's banana, unsweetened milk, peanut butter and ice. All mixed in the blender."

"Have you made one before?"

"Only for myself. I thought it was lovely and refreshing."

"Make one for me some time, and I'll tell you what I think."

"Okay. But before I even think of trying to introduce it, I will have to do all the costings."

"It sounds a good thing to try." Rachel encouraged. "You said one or two promotions. What's the other one?"

"I have no idea, but if I do another one, I want it to be the best ever. Something spectacular and eye-catching. So everyone will know who we are and where we are."

"Something small then." Rachel laughed.

Catherine smiled back. "One more month and I will, hopefully, officially be your boss. Then no more laughing at me."

"With you." Rachel countered.

"You will be at my beck and call. To fulfil all my wishes."

"In your dreams." She swiped the tea towel in Catherine's direction. "And what wishes do you want me to fulfil?" Rachel smirked, "I've been told I'm pretty versatile."

Catherine turned a bright red. "I didn't mean it like that."

"I know." Again a smirk played on her lips. "You're waiting

for Georgina to fill that role."

Catherine blushed even deeper. "I think I've blown whatever chance I had at Christmas. But I've had to put my energy into this place and trying to come up with new ideas."

"So you do have feelings for her."

"I did."

"But not now?"

Catherine shook her head, and in a voice barely above a whisper she replied, "No. I think we've both moved on."

Rachel raised an eyebrow but didn't respond. The silence between them grew. Not uncomfortable, but more like they each knew they should say something more, but neither knew what.

Rachel placed her hand on Catherine's knee and said, "But seriously, about you becoming my official boss, I'm pleased for you. You have been like a breath of fresh air. The coffeehouse has gone from strength to strength. We hardly ever get moments like this anymore where we can relax. Congratulations my soon to be, proper boss."

"Thank you," Catherine smiled, "my serf."

Rachel roared with laughter. "Yeah, yeah. Serf my backside. I am not, nor ever will be your menial. I would never agree to be in that position."

"So what position do you want to be in?"

"Oh Ms Munden, are you flirting with me again?"

"You wish," Catherine laughed.

Later that afternoon, Catherine saw the accountant, Niki, to the door, shook her hand and said, "Thank you. I look forward to seeing you this time next month. Bye."

Catherine turned around and gave a fist pump. "Yes," she called out to anyone who was listening. She started dancing, singing, and circling her hands in front of herself, "Go, Catherine. Go, Catherine."

Georgina smiled at her antics and said, "I take it went well. Congratulations. I'm pleased for you."

"Well done, Cat," Maddie called over to her.

Others who understood the importance, and some who didn't, added their congratulations.

Catherine couldn't keep the grin from her face as she turned fully to Georgina and said, "Not there quite yet, but with no hiccups, we should reach that magic number easily."

"What is it at the moment?" Georgina asked.

"4.87. We jumped from 4.17 last month. I knew we had performed well but not quite that well"

"We are so close."

"I know. I couldn't have done it without everyone pulling in the same direction."

"Do you want to go to the pub later to celebrate?" Georgina asked, unsure of how her invitation would be greeted.

Catherine grinned and said, "What a lovely idea. My treat."

Maddie came up behind her, embraced and said, "That's brilliant news. Well done you."

"It is, isn't it."

"You must be chuffed to bits."

"I can't keep the grin from my face. My cheeks are aching already."

The next day Georgina and Maddie were working the afternoon shift. Georgina was wiping down the counter as Maddie was clearing some tables.

Georgina sniffed, then asked Maddie. "Can you smell smoke?"

"I don't think so," Maddie said as she breathed in deeply. She walked towards the counter as she was sniffing.

"Yes. I can smell it now."

"I'll go and check out the back and then go upstairs. Catherine hasn't come back yet, has she?" Georgina asked.

"Not that I've seen. She hasn't come back through here but she could have used her front door."

"Okay. I'll have a look."

A short while later Georgina came back downstairs "Everything up there is fine, but I could still smell smoke. I'm going out the emergency exit to look if I can see anything out there"

"Okay."

A minute later Georgina came running back in.

With a hint of panic in her voice, she gave instructions to Maddie "Phone the fire brigade. There's a fire in the hairdressers. Sound our alarm and make sure our customers leave safely. I'm going out the back again to see if Jak and Faith need any help." She shouted over her shoulder, "Make sure you check the toilets, could you."

"Don't do anything daft," Maddie shouted after Georgina's retreating back. Her voice got louder as she shouted, "Promise me you'll wait for the fire brigade."

Georgina rushed down the corridor, picking up a scarf that she saw lying around. She ran out of the emergency exit and across the back yard. She reached the back gate, fiddled with the latch and eventually pulled it back. She flung the gate open and tried the entrance to the hairdresser. Unable to open it, she jumped up to look over the top. She noticed that their emergency exit was closed and smoke had begun to billow out from under the door.

She ran back into her yard pushed the rubbish bin towards the dividing wall. She eventually pulled herself up onto the top of the bin, scrambled over the wall and dropped down, groaning as she landed.

"Jak, Faith," she shouted as she rushed towards the exit. The smoke started to get thicker. Looking into the glass she peered through the haze. "Jak, Faith," she shouted again.

The door flung open but no one emerged. She wrapped the scarf around her face and was about to step inside when Faith fell out of the building. She gulped in the fresh air, coughing and spluttering.

Georgina pulled the scarf down and asked, in a voice that showed a high degree of trepidation and unease, "Where's Jak?"

"Behind me," Faith replied between coughs.

Georgina peered again into the smoke and saw no sign of the woman who worked next door.

"Jak," she called out and listened.

"Jak," she shouted again.

Nothing. Then she heard a moan over the crackling of the fire.

Georgina turned to Faith and asked, "Where were you? Shop, office, upstairs?"

Faith continued coughing and pointed inside. "Office," she managed to get out.

"Stay here. The fire brigade has been called. Okay."

Faith nodded, as she started to retch.

Georgina pulled the scarf tight around her mouth and nose. Keeping close to the ground she made her way towards the office. Through the smoke and fumes, she saw a shape on the floor crawling towards the corridor. Georgina crouched downward and inched herself nearer the figure.

Recognising Jak she asked, "Jak? Are you okay?"

"Leg," she coughed. "Broken."

Georgina pulled Jak to her feet. She placed a hand around her waist as Jak slung her arm around Georgina's shoulder.

"Let me take your weight," Georgina instructed, her voice muffled in the scarf. "I'll help you hop towards the exit. Okay?"

Jak grimaced an acknowledgement.

Debris started to fall around them, as they moved as quickly as they could. Then Georgina heard a creaking sound.

"Catherine. Get back here," Maddie shouted into the phone. "The hairdressing shop is on fire."

Maddie grabbed hold of the nearest firefighter. "There's at least one person out the back. There might also still be people in there."

"How many?"

"Could be two. They close early on a Monday, thank goodness, so there are no customers."

"I'll inform the boss. Is there a way to get out the back?"

"There is a service lane. But you can come through our shop to have a look and see what is needed."

"Okay. I'll be back in a moment. Step back now please."

Maddie moved back towards their entranceway. Worry was etched on her face. She hoped that Georgina hadn't done anything stupid. Her phone rang.

"Maddie? What's going on?"

"Where are you?" Maddie asked Catherine.

"On a bus, almost one stop away, but everything has ground to a stop. What's going on? What's this about a fire?"

"There are a couple of engines outside. There's smoke coming from the upstairs windows of the hairdressers. And I can see flames."

"Is Gee with you?"

Maddie didn't answer.

"Maddie. Where is Gee?" Panic was etched in her voice.

"I... I don't know," Maddie replied, quietly. "She went out the back to check and I haven't seen her since."

Catherine gasped.

"One moment, Cat."

Catherine heard Maddie and another voice in the background. Maddie came back on the phone.

"Sorry," Maddie apologised. "That was the fire chief. He's going through our back to see what's going on out there." She paused for a moment, then spoke, "I'm being moved further away."

"And you still can't see Gee."

"No. I can't."

Catherine made her way to the front of the bus and spoke to the driver. "Open the doors please Drive. I have to get off."

"Sorry love. No can do. I'm between stops."

"Open these bloody doors," Catherine screamed at him.

"Sorry," he replied.

"Open these doors or I'll tear your fucking head off."

The driver looked stoically forward. Catherine stepped down and started pulling on the handles.

"Oi. Stop it. You'll break them."

"Then fucking open them." He heaved a big sigh

"Okay. Okay. Keep your wig on."

"Hurry up."

The driver opened the doors up. She jumped off the bus as he smiled and shouted at her, "Have a nice day."

"Twat," she shouted back.

"Cat are you there? Cat?" Catherine heard the voice being

emitted from her phone.

She placed the phone next to her ear. “Yes, I’m here. I’ve got off the bus and I’m running to you. I’ll be there soon.” Catherine panted into the phone.

“Hurry.”

CHAPTER TWENTY-FOUR

In hospital

Catherine sat quietly in the chair, mesmerised by how attractive Georgina was even when she was asleep. She looked at her serene face and her body hooked up to the beeping machines. She wanted to tell her that she would lay down her life for her. She'd only told Georgina that she loved her once and that was when she was asleep drunk, too out of it to remember. Catherine hoped she would be able to tell her again soon.

She started to become agitated because no one was telling her anything, except that they were monitoring her condition. Each beep sounded like a nail in the coffin.

She thought back to Christmas Day when she had realised that she loved her, and through fear, she had thrown that love away. Was it now too late to make amends, to tell her exactly what she felt, what she hoped their future could hold?

Catherine placed her lips softly on Georgina's. "You may not know this but I love you." She said in a voice no more than a whisper. "I realised I loved you months ago but I was frightened of the consequences. It feels as if I have always loved you. Please don't die. Please wake up so I can tell you."

"I'm so sorry I hurt you on Christmas Day. That was the day I fully understood what love was all about. I was too scared to admit it to myself let alone you so I hid behind the mask of that damn contract. Being with you is more important than that piece of paper. I would walk away from it now if it meant you would wake up. I don't care about it as long as I can have you in my life."

Catherine brought Georgina's hand to her lips, kissed it gently, said, "Wake up. Please wake up."

Horrible thoughts started to swirl in her mind. *What if she never wakes up.* She had heard of these cases. A fear coursed through her. "Please let her wake up," she pleaded to whoever or whatever would listen. "I need her. I want her. She is my life."

The steady beep of the machines answered her back.

A while later Catherine stood up and stretched her legs. She wandered to the window and could only see the rooftops of the surrounding buildings. The light was beginning to fade and the orange glow of sunset reflected from a couple of windows, reminding her of the glow of the fire. She shook away the thoughts and turned around.

Catherine ambled to the bed and stood over the sleeping figure. Again her heart felt like it was being pulled out of her body with the love she felt towards the woman lying motionless on the bed.

Catherine bent down placed her face close to the prone woman and whispered, "I love you. Wake up."

She planted another kiss on Georgina's lips and was surprised when the lips opened and tried to kiss her back. Catherine pulled away quickly, not wanting to be caught in a compromising predicament.

Georgina started to moan and move her fingers as though awareness was seeping back into her body and was trying desperately to feel things that will ground her. Her eyes fluttered open and she started to turn her head. She looked around, as though she was seeking to make sense of the environment she found herself in. Confused and unsure she closed them tight again.

Catherine watched her intently and began stroking her hand, and whispered words of encouragement.

Georgina frowned as she tried to piece together any recollections lingering in the back of her mind. She breathed deeply and felt the strange sensation of something in her nostrils. She raised her hand and tried to remove whatever it was that was causing the discomfort. A hand gently stopped her and she heard the same voice. Unable to grasp the words but the reassuring tone halted her from removing the offending article.

Her brain began to ask itself silent questions. *Where I am, and why, who or what I am, how did I get here, and what's going on.* To which, as yet, she had no answers.

Georgina felt some of her senses begin to awaken, as though her eyes had closed for just a second, had nodded and the sudden movement had startled her awake. Feeling that no time had passed, yet knowing that it had.

Georgina coughed and put a hand to her throat. It felt sore. She opened her eyes and realised there was someone nearby but she couldn't focus on the face to register who it was.

In a hoarse voice, she asked, "What time is it ?"

She coughed again.

"About seven o'clock in the evening," came the reply. The voice sounded vaguely familiar but she was too tired to focus her mind.

As she drifted back to sleep, she heard the voice say, "You're in the hospital. Don't move. Let me let the nurse know you have woken up."

Georgina gradually became aware that she was lying in bed, but it didn't feel like her bed. She opened her eyes wide and saw Catherine asleep. Her hand was placed on top of her own. Her head resting on top of her other forearm.

Catherine suddenly sat up as though Georgina's slight movement had jolted her awake. She looked at the woman lying in the bed and smiled the biggest smile she could.

"Thank goodness." Catherine breathed in deeply, closed her eyes and slowly let her breath out. Thanking everyone and everything to whom she had prayed. "You're awake. How are you feeling?"

"Tired," she answered. Her voice sounded throaty and gruff.

Georgina, in a frightened croaky voice, asked, "What happened? Where am I?"

"You're in the hospital."

"Ah yes, the fire." She closed her eyes and took a couple of deep breaths, then the breathing again became a steady rhythm.

A tear trickled down Catherine's face as a wave of love crashed through her, she swiped it away with the back of her hand.

Georgina felt a thumb rubbing her wrist. She fluttered her eyes open and looked to see who was behind the gentle caress. A smile played on her lips when she saw who it was.

"Hi." Catherine squeezed her hand. "How are you feeling. Do you want a drink?"

Georgina coughed and nodded her head. "Mmmm."

Catherine brought the cup to her lips and helped her drink through the straw.

"Thanks." The word came out as a croak.

Georgina coughed as though she was trying to clear her throat. "Sore... dry..." she coughed again.

Catherine again lifted the cup to her lips and placed the straw in her mouth.

"How long..." another cough, "have you..." Georgina rubbed her throat, "been here?"

"Every minute. I came in the ambulance with you."

"What's the time?" Catherine looked at her watch. "Ten past ten at night. Another sip?"

"Please. And a tissue." She took another sip and said, "Thank you."

She dabbed at her eyes with the tissue.

"Your eyes look a bit sore."

"They are a bit irritated. They keep on weeping."

"Try not to rub them."

"It's difficult not to." She then blew her nose."

"Eww. That looks gross." Catherine recoiled, "Imagine what your lungs are like."

"I know." She tried to laugh but ended up in a coughing fit. Her head sunk back into the pillows and again she closed her eyes, taking in deep breaths.

When her breathing had returned to normal, she lay quietly as though she was thinking. A few minutes later, in a voice that didn't quite sound so rough, she said, "I had a dream that someone kissed me."

"Did you?" Catherine said, trying not to sound flummoxed.

"But you say you've been here all the time, so it must have been just a dream."

Catherine blushed profusely. Georgina caught the blush.

"Did you kiss me?" Georgina asked with suspicion.

"I don't know what you mean?" Catherine replied, her blush became deeper.

Georgina smiled at her. "From your reaction, I think you do."

Catherine countered, "And your reaction said you enjoyed

it."

"Did I react?" Georgina sounded suspicious

"You tried to kiss me back." Catherine's lips turned up in a small smile.

"What did you think my reaction would be?"

"I didn't expect any reaction. I only wanted you to know I was here. But your lips moved as though you wanted more. I'm sorry I kissed you, I'm sorry I took advantage of a sleeping woman. I stopped as soon as I realised what I had done. But I wanted to show you how much I cared. And holding and kissing your hand wasn't enough. So I kissed you. And you kissed me back, sort of."

"I remember enjoying those lips touching mine." Georgina face offered a silent acceptance of the apology, then she said, "I was confused. At first, I thought it was someone else. Then I realised the kiss was too gentle and sweet. And I wanted more."

"But I should never have exploited the situation. You were powerless to stop me. I was no more than a predator. And for that, I'm deeply sorry. You looked so peaceful. I was afraid. I thought I was going to lose you. I realised I couldn't lose you. You had become an important part of me. I wanted to kiss you.

Georgina smiled, "I understand. May I kiss you instead? And then I'll forgive you for your indiscretion."

"Of course."

Their lips met chastely. Catherine sat back in the chair as a nurse opened the door. She looked at Catherine and said, "I'm going to ask you to leave as visiting time has been over for two hours."

"I'm not leaving her."

"I'm sorry but you have to allow her to sleep. it will be the best thing for her."

"And I told you, I'm not leaving."

"Okay," the nurse replied. "Why don't you go to the relatives room and we can get you if there is any change."

Georgina squeezed Catherine's hand. "Please." she swallowed. "Do as they ask."

Catherine looked into Georgina's face and she was given a weak smile. "Okay," Catherine replied. "But I don't like it."

Georgina closed her eyes and nodded. "I know."

Catherine stood up and picked up her coat from the arm of the chair. She leant over Georgina again and touched their lips together.

"I'll be back in the morning. Sleep well.

"Thank you." She coughed. "For being with me."

"There's nowhere else I'd rather be."

CHAPTER TWENTY-FIVE

Opening up

Catherine sat in the chair next to her bed. Tiredness was dragging her down as her emotions started to get the better of her. Being grateful that Georgina had emerged from the burning building and survive didn't cut it anymore. Catherine was angry with her for putting herself in that dangerous position.

"Why did you run into a burning building. I don't understand." Catherine asked with a frosty tone.

"Because it was something I had to do." Georgina shrugged her shoulders and replied, as though a tedious question had been asked.

Still not understanding why she did it, a tear rolled down Catherine's cheek as her anger at Georgina began to get the better of her. "I thought I lost you. And yet you are acting as though it was a normal day."

"It was a normal day."

"It wasn't and don't you dare act like it was." Catherine's hackles rose. "You know damn well you acted like a superhero."

"Like a what?" Georgina laughed.

"Like you are doing now. That it is normal for you to run into burning buildings to try to pull a woman out."

"Don't be so melodramatic."

Georgina crossed her arms to guard herself against the tirade she sensed was still to come. She looked Catherine up and down, then met her eyes once more, daring her to speak.

“Melodramatic.” Catherine’s voice grew louder and higher, “Five more minutes and you would have died. You scared me shitless and you’re acting like my feelings don’t matter.”

“Of course they matter. But I did what anyone would do.”

“Don’t be so damn ridiculous. People don’t put themselves in that kind of danger.”

“Some people do?”

“There’s no talking to you when you get like this.”

“Get like what?”

“Stubborn, selfish.”

Georgina felt her hackles rise. “You think I’m stubborn and selfish. Take a look at yourself.”

“I’m angry at you. I could have lost you.” Catherine felt on the verge. Like a barrage of tears had built up and was waiting for the dam to burst. She stood up needing space between them. Another tear escaped and she roughly pushed it aside.

Georgina said softly, “I can see you’re angry and frustrated at me and sometimes anger and fear can make us lash out at people we care about. And I can understand that. As long as it is being said because you care for me, not for some selfish reason.

Catherine’s eyes showed her frustration. “Okay. Let’s go with your argument. You’re saying that my angry and fearful response to you running into a burning building was through my selfishness. So answer these questions for me.”

Georgina gave a slight indifferent shrug.

Catherine wondered why Georgina couldn’t see her point of view so she continued, “Was it selfish of me to be angry when I knew you ran into a burning building? Was it selfish of me to be fearful in case you got hurt? Which by the way you did. Was it selfish of me to be angry and fearful when you were brought out unconscious? I don't call that selfishness. I call that concern for the person you feel deeply about."

Georgina studied the soft curves of her face, her heart softening at the sadness, anger and hurt displayed. "I can understand why you are upset with me. But I could see her. I couldn't hear the sirens. I had to do something. I couldn't leave her in there. I could see she needed help. She wouldn't have been able to crawl that far and she wouldn't have gotten out by herself." She looked down once more, as her face became solemn.

"But you could have died. Five more minutes." Her breath came in ragged sobs. "What would I have done without you."

"Your life would have carried on."

"But without you in it." Catherine sobbed.

"And if I hadn't gone in Jak could have died."

"I know," Catherine said in a plaintive voice.

"As it was, we both got out. We did both get out?" Georgina suddenly asked in fear.

"Yes. You did both get out." Catherine replied and followed up by quietly saying, "Just."

"Is she alright?"

Catherine nodded. "Yes. Thanks to you."

Silence stayed between them as they looked at each other as a range of different emotions played on their faces.

"I'm sorry," Georgina whispered. "I didn't think of the consequences. All I knew was someone needed to act, and act fast. And that someone was me. I was the first person there."

After what seemed like another eternity of silence, Catherine nodded slowly, as though accepting the reason. Then her eyes became slits and a fierceness manifested itself into a steely look.

She raised her voice, as anger overtook any acceptance that

had expressed itself in her thoughts. "No. You didn't think of the consequences."

Catherine turned on her heel and walked towards the door

"Wait... please... don't go." Georgina pleaded.

"You obviously don't want me around. To be a part of your life. Not once did you think about me?"

"I want you more than words can say."

Catherine shook her head. "Actions speak louder than words. And your actions proved that you don't."

Georgina shook her head, "I did think of you," her eyes filled with tears and her face hung in shame. "I made a promise. When the ceiling collapsed and before I passed out, you took over my thoughts. And in those few seconds I prayed that if I came out of there alive, I would make everything right "

Georgina could see Catherine's resolve breaking.

"Please come back here. And I'm truly sorry for the anguish I caused you" She patted the bed next to her. "Please."

Catherine clenched her jaw and anxiously ran her hand through her hair.

"I love you." Georgina pleaded.

The remainder of Catherine's anger melted away under the pleading look Georgina had given her, and the words of love she spoke. All that she was feeling for Georgina rushed to every nerve ending.

Seeing the intensity and devotion in Catherine's expression sent shivers of anticipation flowing through Georgina's veins. At that moment, the look in her eyes changed. The fear and sadness had reformed to hope and anticipation.

Her eyes were so full of tenderness and desire that it was almost tangible. Georgina had looked at Catherine with such love, even though no more words had passed her lips. A love that Catherine desired more than anything. More than the breath in her body. She understood then exactly what had changed between them, and no words were needed.

As Catherine moved back to sit on the bed beside her, Georgina took her in his arms and Catherine melted into her embrace. She put a finger under Catherine's chin and nudged it upwards. "Look at me," she quietly requested, "I want to make sure we are okay."

The corners of Catherine's mouth began to turn up as she faced her, eliciting much the same reaction from Georgina. Both smiles grew contently.

Catherine answered, "I think we're more than okay. But I am more scared of letting you go now. You are an incredible woman who has hidden themself away for too long. You deserve to be happy.

"And you think you can make me happy?"

Hope shone in Georgina's eyes.

Catherine nodded, "I know I can make you happy. Can we at least try? I've realised that I love you. When I saw you being wheeled out on that trolley, your face black and attached to an oxygen mask. My heart felt as though it had been ripped out of me. All the way to the hospital I was praying to anyone, and anything who would listen, that I wouldn't lose you."

"So why did you almost walk away from me again just now?"

"Because the pain of knowing that I could have lost you was too great. And I couldn't get you to understand what the consequences of your reckless actions were. I needed a few moments to pause for breath. I didn't want to argue with you. I wanted to take you in my arms and kiss you. Look after you. Love you." Catherine paused for a moment and said, "I know you have feelings for me. I can see it in your eyes."

"So why have you been so distant from me recently?" Georgina sad eyes showed their pain. "I thought you didn't care.

I thought the only thing that held your attention was that damned contract. That no matter what we felt for each other, that contract would come first."

"It is important to me, and yes, it has been at the forefront of my mind. But so has whatever we have between us."

"Let me get my head around this. You pushed me away and stopped us going out for drinks and meals together because I was at the forefront of your mind. Bullshit."

"I know. It was because I was scared." Catherine tried to express her thoughts, "I didn't understand what was happening to me when I was close to you. You brought out emotions I never thought existed. My emotions were beginning to cloud my judgement. And when my judgement has been clouded in the past, everything has fallen apart. Work, life, love."

She closed her eyes and took a deep breath. When she opened them, she continued, "I couldn't risk it with you, with us. For my own and our preservation, I had to push you away. I thought that if we could get through these last couple of months without the Sword of Damocles hanging over us, then we might have a chance. It seemed as though I was in a precarious position and I had a sense of foreboding that something would trigger a tragedy. And stop me, us, from reaching that goal. And my prize for reaching the goal would be you, would be us."

"But what about safeguarding my feelings." Georgina cut in. "You ran roughshod over them as though that kiss we had at Christmas meant nothing. That we meant nothing. And now you profess you love me. I'm sorry if I'm a bit sceptical."

Catherine nodded, "I see now that I was wrong." She reached out for Georgina's hand. "I should have talked to you about my worries and fears. Please forgive me. I truly didn't want to hurt you. I knew you liked me but until you said it just now, I didn't know you loved me."

Georgina gently pulled her hand away. "At Christmas, you

promised to talk to me. That you wouldn't tell me half-truths. But you didn't keep up your side of the bargain." She shook her head in annoyance. "I had to try to push all romantic thoughts of you from my head. I couldn't understand why you were treating me so. I didn't know what I had done wrong. You started to refuse to go out after work and always made up some lame excuses. That hurt. Even when I asked you what was wrong you ignored me."

"I didn't ignore you."

Georgina started to cough. When she caught her breath she said, "But you didn't speak to me truthfully. Which amounts to the same thing."

"Okay." Catherine acquiesced. "All my thoughts, hopes and fears at Christmas and afterwards, kept arguing with each other. And I couldn't put into words the multitude of emotions that were flowing through me."

"Try now. Let me try to understand what you were thinking."

Catherine did speak for a while. Georgina could see a range of emotions dancing across her face. Some happy, some hopeful, and some full of fear.

"Here goes. These were some of my thoughts." Catherine tried to steady the emotion that was bubbling beneath the surface. "What if a couple of months down the line we found it didn't work for us? If it's a mutual understanding then so be it. But what if it wasn't. What if we had got it together but through circumstances, we lost our friendship, what would have happened then. It would have been easy for you to scupper anything I did to reach that magic number. Then where would I be?" She closed her eyes and rubbed them in her fingers.

"But."

Catherine held up her hand. "No. Don't interrupt." She regained her thoughts. "I knew I wouldn't be exactly homeless. But would I feel comfortable enough to live there? Then what would I do? I couldn't move back to London. I couldn't stay here. Where would I go and what would I do. I didn't want to start over again. I had done that more times than I cared to remember. I would have been the one who would have lost it all. So I thought it would be pointless starting along that path when it could lead to the heartbreak of losing everything. So could I risk everything over what could have been an impossible and pointless dream?"

She looked at Georgina, shook her head and sighed "All those types of thoughts and more kept filling up my mind and I stopped being fully focused on work."

Georgina picked up her hand and squeezed it again, showing understanding and encouragement for her to continue.

Catherine looked deeply into Georgina's eyes. "I always wanted to be honest and truthful with you. I didn't want to tell half-truths and lies. But how could I own up to the emotions I was feeling. Emotions that were alien to me. Emotions that were making me fearful. I knew to be truly happy I would have to try to shake off my fears. And yes, I know everyone is a little nervous when faced with a new circumstance."

She gave a small smile. "You made me want to do my best so the year would pass successfully. From the start, I was soon to realise that not only did I want to work with you and make a go of it. I also wanted your friendship. I valued our time together. You taught me so much about running this place and keeping a tight ship. You taught me more about discipline than I thought I would ever need."

She nodded at Georgina. "I saw that I wasn't doing the best I could. The first meeting after Christmas with the accountant made me realise that I wasn't going to hit the target. And I so needed to reach that target. So something had to give and unfortunately, it was us. I pulled back from our friendship. Not because I wanted to but because I had to."

"And now?" Georgina asked quietly.

"I'm being completely truthful now. I'm scared. Scared of the consequences of being with you. We were edging towards that point of no return where we would end up in one or other of our beds. That we would, as Sue would say, get down and dirty."

Georgina gently asked, "And I will ask again, what about now?"

"Now I'm more scared of losing you than I ever was about losing the business."

A look of understanding passed between them.

"When I was finally allowed in here to see you." She gave a small huff and anger flashed across her face. "I can't believe they were not going to let me because I wasn't family, so I said we were partners."

She shook her head in annoyance and Georgina gave her hand another squeeze.

Gathering her thoughts, she continued, "When I was allowed in to see you, you had all these wires and tubes going everywhere. You looked so pale. You had this bluish tint to your lips. Your face was clean but there was evidence of soot around your nostrils and hairline. And you stank." She smiled.

"Your breathing was ragged and an oxygen mask was still covering your mouth and nose. Nobody would tell me exactly what was going on. All they would tell me was that they were monitoring your progress. You looked so vulnerable. At that moment the only thing that mattered was you."

"I'm not vulnerable now," Georgina replied. "I've woken up with all my faculties intact. I may have a bit of a cough and, apart from this monitor thing on my finger, I'm not attached to any machine. Give me a few days and I'm going to be fine"

"I know." Catherine paused for a moment. "I've thought

long and hard."

Georgina butted in and tried to bring some levity to the situation. "I bet that was difficult."

Georgina started coughing.

"Hah, serves you right," Catherine said dismissively but smiled. "But yeah, sometimes too long and too hard. I have known you now for more than eleven months and gradually, through your personality, your kindness, your humour, the way you spoke, the intensity that you listened, the sparkling passion of your eyes, I knew my heart had been taken. It was as though an invisible cord had blinded us together. And even though I tried to cut the strings, this bond today is stronger than it had ever been. I love you, Gee. I don't ever want to lose you."

"You haven't."

"I almost did." Catherine's voice caught in her throat. "I could have lost everything. You have given me so much and all you tangibly received from me was my signature for a year."

"And that signature has been like me winning the lottery." Georgina looked lovingly into Catherine's eyes.

"My heart is telling me to give us a go. I have fallen in love with you. I know I've never been with a woman before but that does not stop me from loving you. You are all I have ever wanted in a friend, a companion. You took a leap of faith bringing me into your life. Let me take a leap of faith by opening my heart to you"

Georgina nodded, "What this past year has taught me is to grab life by the horns because you don't know when you are going to lose everything." She squeezed Catherine's hand. "So I'm going to ask you. When I get out of here and feel well enough, can I take you out? May I woo you? We'll take it slow and go out on date nights."

"What if I don't want to take it slow. We've been taking it

slow since the first day we met."

"Okay. Let's take each day as it comes and see what happens."

"Okay. But at least let me kiss you again, and not a peck on the cheek."

Catherine leant in and they enjoyed an exquisite kiss.

CHAPTER TWENTY-SIX

Visiting times

The door flung open. "How's the wounded sold..." Georgina and Catherine broke apart from their passionate kiss. Rachel looked embarrassed that she had walked in on their embrace. "Sorry. I didn't mean to interrupt you," she said and then smirked. "I'll come back later."

"No Rachel. Come here. We've got something to tell you." Georgina patted the bed. "Come and perch here."

"We've decided to think about taking our friendship further. Going out on dates. That sort of thing."

"No shit Sherlock." Rachel looked between the two women, grinning like a Cheshire Cat. "About bloody time. I thought you two would never get it together. You've both been trying to hide your attraction for so long. You've both been skirting around each other. Bren and I have been kept amused by it for ages. We thought at the Christmas shindig that you were finally going to get some action. Then a couple of days after, it was as if someone had thrown a bucket of water over the pair of you."

The two women looked at each other shaking their heads. Rachel nodded at them, "Good. I'm pleased for you both."

"So you've been laughing at us." Catherine sat with her mouth open.

"Not laughing. But smiling because it was sweet and endearing."

"We're too old for sweet and endearing." Georgina cut in.

"You're never too old for sweet and endearing. But in your case, Georgie, I can see why you said it." Rachel's infectious laughter caused Catherine to laugh as well.

"Humph." Georgina retorted, as she tried to be hurt, but failed miserably. "We're going to take things slow and see what happens if you must know."

"Good. But if you go any slower, you'd stop."

Rachel started to laugh.

"What now?"

"I've just remembered. Bren now owes me a fiver. Result. Cheers you two."

Both Georgina and Catherine groaned.

Rachel continued, "Now your romantic exploits are out of the way, what has the doctor said?"

"We're waiting for the doctor to come around. I was told he'll be making his rounds soon."

Georgina suddenly turned to look at Rachel, as if the thought had just come to her. "Who's minding the coffeehouse?"

"I left Maddie there." She paused, not wanting to say the next words but knew that she had to. "When we got there this morning, we realised we couldn't open."

"Why?" Catherine demanded.

"There is a little bit of water damage by the toilets."

"I'm sure the punters would have understood." Georgina knowing that they were rarely used during the morning rush.

"I'm sure they would have. But that's not why we couldn't open."

"So what is the problem?"

"It's the other damage."

"What other damage?" both Catherine and Georgina said together, shock registered in both their voices.

"You know we closed to the public as soon as you smelt the smoke and noticed the fire. Then we had the firemen traipsing through to get to the back so they could rescue Georgina, Jak and Faith."

"Yes?"

"So the floor is filthy."

"Okay. That can easily be cleaned. And?"

"Well, one of the window ledges out the back caught alight and caused the glass to break. It's boarded up now and will have to be replaced."

"And?"

"That's how the water damage in the toilets happened."

"For goodness sake. What has stopped us from opening." Georgina growled in annoyance and again started to cough.

Rachel continued, "Some fire investigators were sifting through the debris. I presume to work out the cause of the fire. We asked them some questions, such as how long the smell will linger, was there any structural damage to the party wall and other such things.

"What was their response?" Catherine said dejectedly.

"We invited them in provided them with coffee, but it was from a jar of instant from Jakob's I'm afraid."

"Instant?"

"Yeah. Instant "

"The window was to the stock room and the smoke that billowed in has tainted the stock. Having both front and back door open didn't help either."

Both women gasped.

"All the stock?" Georgina asked in a shocked voice.

Rachel nodded. "Sorry, we had no stock to sell so had to close up. We hadn't restocked the shelves. Remember, Georgina, we were just about to do it when you smelt the smoke."

Catherine said, her mouth agape, sounding shocked, "So all our stock in that room is ruined."

Rachel nodded. "And I couldn't risk anything behind the counter. I did try one of the coffees, but it didn't taste quite right. So yes, all the stock."

Catherine let out an audible sigh. She composed her features then asked with worry, "And my flat?"

"There is smoke damage on the wall in the corridor and part of the shop. I think a deep clean and airing will be needed. The fire was upstairs on the estate agent side so it should be alright. Although the smoke did drift in. I doubt your flat would have suffered much, if at all. Perhaps there will be a smell of smoke. But I doubt it's nothing a few open windows won't solve. But I would check any foodstuff you have lying around. It might be tainted and you don't want an upset stomach. You could also try spreading some of that carpet freshener stuff around if there is."

Catherine and Georgina looked at each other in shock.

"I need to get back and get things sorted." Georgina tried to raise herself from the bed but she was riddled by a coughing fit.

Catherine started to grab her things. "I'll go."

Rachel placed a restraining hand on Catherine's and shook her head.

"I left Maddie at the shop with both front and back doors open, letting in a through draft. The extractor fan is on maximum so hopefully, the whiff of smoke will soon dissipate. We put a table in front of the door with an apology sign. The neighbours and locals have been brilliant. Really supportive. I told her not to start cleaning down the counter et cetera. In my opinion, you will need a deep clean company to come in."

"I have to go and check." Catherine started to get up.

Rachel shook her head, "Plenty of time later today. You are needed here. Let's hear what the doctor has to say first."

Catherine looked at Georgina for an accord. "Sure?"

"Sure. I want you here in case I can come home." Georgina then turned to Rachel and asked, "Have you heard how Jak is? Faith is?"

"Yeah. I bumped into Sal in the corridor. Faith is fine. Her hubby picked her up after she was checked over. Jak is a bit more in the wars but Sal expects to able to take her back to her house soon. She's shaken up. She has a bump on the head, a broken arm, which will stop her cutting hair until it's healed. Her ankle wasn't broken but badly sprained ankle, which stopped her walking and putting any weight through it. She also suffered some smoke inhalation. But without your bravery, stupidity, call it what you want, it could have been much worse."

Georgina scrunched up her face. "Let's not go there again."

Catherine huffed.

Georgina looked at Catherine and said apologetically, "I had to go and help."

"I know you did," Catherine answered softly and patted her arm, showing that she was almost forgiven.

Rachel raised her voice in disbelief, "But it was a burning building."

"With a friend who I could see collapsed on the floor," Georgina replied in her defence.

Rachel continued, showing her discomfort, "I know, but you scared the shit out of me."

"And I scared the shit out of myself." Georgina looked across at Catherine who raised her eyebrows

"Hah. Now she agrees with me." Catherine said as she squeezed Georgina's hand.

Georgina gave a small smile in acceptance of her stupidity, "I'm sorry. But I didn't think. I just reacted."

At that moment a nurse walked in. "Ms Turnball. I see you are feeling better. Ladies will you give us a moment so I can run some tests. Why don't you go to the cafeteria? By the time you come back, the doctor should be ready to do his rounds."

The nurse was still there when the two women came back.

Catherine asked, "Has the doctor been?"

Georgina nodded her head

"Bummer. I wanted to hear what he had to say. She turned to Georgina and asked, "Well?"

"He said he is pleased with me."

"And." Catherine gave Rachel a smirk, "Getting anything out of her is as easy as pulling teeth."

Rachel rolled her eyes and replied, "Don't I know it."

Catherine turned back to Georgina. "Come on Gee. What was said? Did they say why you were unconscious for so long?"

"I have had a slight concussion and mild toxic anoxia.

"What is that when it's at home," Rachel asked as Catherine frowned.

"Mild toxic anoxia happens when you take in toxins or other chemicals. In my case some smoke inhalation. My oxygen dropped below a certain level and my blood wasn't carrying oxygen effectively around my body. For some reason, my oxygen levels took longer to return to normal."

"And that means?"

The nurse replied, "You have to be aware of these symptoms. Lack of attention, concentration, coordination and short-term memory loss. It might also seem as though they have a slight concussion. Dizziness, disorientation or a sore head."

Rachel asked, "Are you sure he didn't say backside. Cos she's a right pain in one."

The nurse tried hard to contain her smile.

"Oi." Georgina tried to swat Rachel arm, who pulled it easily out of the way. "I have to stay in for another day as a precaution. They want to keep a check on the concussion."

"But if there was someone at home?" Catherine asked. "Surely you could go home if there was someone at home to look after you."

"They want me to stay in overnight. The doctor said about monitoring oxygen levels. Tomorrow if the checks they do come back satisfactory, and there is someone at home, then I could leave."

"That fixes it. You are coming to stay with me. I'll keep a check on you. I can do whatever is necessary for the shop and check on you at regular intervals."

"You can't do that."

"I can and no arguing."

"Nurse, is it true that Georgina can come home if she has someone with her."

"As Georgina said. She has to stay until tomorrow. Her oxygen level is still a bit low. And concussion is a funny thing it can suddenly affect you."

"So if she was staying with me, or me staying with her, she could leave tomorrow."

"We'll see what the doctor says on his morning rounds but I don't see why not."

"Problem solved." Catherine nodded. "You want to spend as

little time in hospital and I have a spare bedroom. I can pop up and check on you throughout the day. Or one of the others can. So no more arguments."

"But."

"And no buts." Georgina turned to Rachel and pleaded, "Rachel, help me out here."

"Not after you tried to hit me. And stop being so stubborn."

Catherine interrupted Rachel with a guffaw. "Stubborn. Hah."

Georgina looked at her in irritation. Catherine continued, "Told you."

Rachel looked between the two women, not understanding what had passed between them. So she continued, "Yes. Stop being stubborn and let this woman look after you. I'm sure she can make you comfortable. Then the pair of us can take it in turns checking on you. I'll see if Buwan can get the old buzzer system working."

Catherine grinned "Outnumbered. You have no choice. Tomorrow, if you are allowed out, you will be coming home with me."

The nurse spoke, "Now we got that sorted, out you both go. I need to continue running some more tests,"

The two women started towards the door.

"and check on the burn. Georgina, will you turn over please."

Catherine's hand went to her mouth and moved back towards the bed. "Burn, what burn? I only thought that you were knocked out."

"When the ceiling started to collapse about us some burning wood landed on my shoulder blade. Hence a small burn. I was fine. I lifted it off me and forgot about it When the bigger debris started falling and I pushed Jak away I got the bang on the head. I can remember thinking that Jak was lucky that a fireman was there to catch her, that I wanted you there to catch me." She glanced at Catherine and gave a smile. "After that, I passed out."

The nurse said to Georgina, "You have more than one small burn. It is fairly substantial. You also have quite a few superficial ones on your back. I would have thought you would have felt them."

"I can feel them. I thought it was because that beam trapped me and I was bruised." Georgina admitted as she started to cough.

Catherine looked at her back.

"Stop looking at my bare bum," Georgina exclaimed, her voice sounded hoarse.

"Then stop flashing it at me," countered Catherine.

Feeling a little embarrassed Georgina continued, "I thought you were meant to leave the room."

"And I need to know how to treat them. So stop your wittering." Catherine asked the nurse who was stood the other side of the bed, "So what do I have to do with them."

The nurse replied, "These dressing only needs to be kept clean, dry and changed regularly. Make sure the area around the burn does become infected. If it does go to the treatment room at your local surgery. But there shouldn't be any problems. Now out. You can come back in when I've finished."

Rachel asked Catherine as they were walking to the door. "Do you want me to have a quick check on your flat? I think it will be fine but just in case."

"Do you think you could do that for me? It would be one less worry for me to deal with."

They stepped out into the corridor and the door closed quietly behind them.

Catherine continued, "Do you know where the spare key is?"

"No."

"You know our storeroom at the top of the stairs."

"The one that is full of smoke-damaged stock?"

Catherine gave a sardonic laugh, "The very same. Well if you go in and close the door, you will notice on the door jamb, a key on a hook at about head height."

"Well, I never. I've never noticed it. And how many times have I been in there."

"And how many times have you closed the door behind you? You wouldn't unless you were having a secret rendezvous."

"And I still wouldn't notice it, if you get my drift." Rachel winked.

Shaking her head, Catherine asked, "Is your mind always in the gutter?"

"Yep." Rachel grinned and Catherine shook her head again with a smile. Turning serious Rachel pulled Catherine into a hug and said, "I'll leave now and check on your flat. Hopefully, that will set your mind at rest."

Catherine returned the hug "Thank you. It will."

"I'll look for a deep clean company to freshen up the coffee-house." A sudden thought hit her. "What about the delivery of sandwiches and cakes. Do you want me to get in contact with Di to warn her that we might not be able to take delivery of her cakes and pastries for a day or two? I did see her first thing and said we'd ring her. What about the different coffee and tea suppliers? Do you want me to ring them?"

"I hadn't thought of Di, nor the deep clean. Please let Di know and will you ring around and find a cleaning company for us. Could you also make a list of anything else you think we should do or get in contact with? My brain has turned to mush."

“No problem. Don’t forget the insurance company.”

“As if I could. This is going to put our premiums up. And Rachel,” she smiled at the younger woman. “Thanks. I’ll phone you. And if I don’t see you later, I’ll see you early tomorrow.”

The two women hugged.

“And until she gets the all-clear from a doctor don’t let her try to convince you she is fit enough to come home,” Rachel stated.

“Don’t worry. I won’t.”

Catherine looked at Rachel’s retreating back. At the end of the corridor, Rachel raised a hand and disappeared around the corner. The door to the room opened and the nurse walked out.

“She’s all yours.”

“I hope so,” Catherine answered quietly.

CHAPTER TWENTY-SEVEN

Leaving hospital

The doctor stood at the end of the bed. The clipboard containing Georgina's charts in his hand. He nodded a couple of times and asked a couple of what seemed to her, irrelevant questions.

Georgina answered the questions with her tone taking on a hint of annoyance. Catherine gently squeezed her hand.

"Why all these questions. They don't seem pertinent to my health."

"Oh but they are," he countered. "I'm seeing if you have any confusion. I can see you know where you are. You recognise the people around you. You know what happened, apart from the time you were unconscious. I'm seeing if any more of your memory was affected, and that you could form proper sentences."

Georgina looked at him, not saying anything.

"You say your headache has gone away," he asked.

Georgina nodded. "I felt a bit fuzzy yesterday but I'm good today."

"The hoarseness in your voice is still there, but it sounds much better than yesterday. You're coughing a bit more than I hoped and I can see you are having some trouble breathing deeply." The doctor checked through her symptoms.

"I'm not," she insisted.

Catherine again squeezed her hand.

"Lean forward." He placed his stethoscope against her back. "Breath in. And out."

Georgina immediately started to cough and the doctor looked at her with raised eyebrows.

Georgina said frowning, "So what do I need to do if I want to get out of here today?"

"You need to get plenty of rest. Try to sit in a reclined position. And when you go to sleep, make sure you prop your head and shoulders up with pillows to help you breathe easier. Avoid being around anyone who smokes. I don't want you to breathe in any second-hand smoke. Avoid things that may irritate your lungs, such as extremely cold, hot, humid, or dry air."

Georgina nodded.

"You must also carry out all the bronchial hygiene therapy you were given. And by that, I mean your breathing exercises. Finally, you must have someone with you, checking on you for the next eighteen hours."

Catherine groaned and Georgina looked at her.

"What? She asked. Catherine sighed, "You can still smell the lingering smoke in my flat."

"So we'll go back to mine then." Georgina huffed.

"Can't do that either. I've arranged for a cleaning company to come today, and yes, Rachel is dealing with them. But also the insurance rep is coming to assess the damage caused. I have to be there for that. I will also be getting rid of the damaged stock and double-checking that the order I hastily put in last night is correct. I have got a couple of people measuring up and giving us a quote for a replacement window. If we want to open the day after tomorrow, I need to be at the shop, not your house. Sorry."

Georgina leant back into the pillows and groaned.

"We can put off opening for another day if I stay with you," Catherine suggested.

"We can't do that. We could lose customers. They could get out of their routine and go elsewhere."

"I know. Sorry, but that's the state of play." Catherine said apologetically.

Georgina looked at the doctor almost pleading into his eyes, "So doctor. You won't sign the release papers unless I have someone with me in my house."

"I would advise against it."

"But you couldn't stop me."

"No, I couldn't." The doctor shook his head in agreement. He turned and strode out of the door.

"Don't you dare sign your release papers," Catherine stared angrily at Georgina. "What harm will another night in here do?"

"But I don't want to stay here another night."

"I know you don't. But I'm going to be tied up with the shop. So is Rachel."

Georgina almost pleaded when she asked, "What about Maddie?"

"What about Maddie?"

Georgina continued her train of thought, saying, "She was a carer. Couldn't you ask her to look after me whilst you busy yourself at the shop? And when you've finished there, you can take over."

"That's a really good idea." Catherine nodded in agreement. "But you have forgotten one thing."

"And that is?"

"Maddie and Alison have gone up to the Lake District for a few days."

Georgina closed her eyes and groaned.

Catherine reached down into her bag and brought out her kindle. "Here. Borrow this. And relax whilst you can."

"I need my glasses."

"You can change the font size. Here. Let me show you."

Catherine adjusted the font and gave it back. She stood up and gave Georgina a quick kiss. "I've got to go. People to see. Phone calls to make. Is there anything I can bring you when I come back later?"

"No." Georgina huffed.

"So you don't want your glasses, favourite magazine or a chocolate bar." Catherine raised her eyebrows.

"Please." Georgina grinned

Georgina stood at the doorway of the master bedroom. She felt short of breath and held on to the doorframe for support. The stairs up to Catherine's flat had worn her out. A distant memory invaded her thoughts.

She hesitated for a moment then said, as she turned back into the corridor, "I think I'd rather take the guest room."

"You don't have to."

"I know I don't, but I think I do."

"Why?" Catherine questioned, not understanding.

Georgina took a deep breath and replied, "Because we have both been through a whole gamut of emotions over the last few days. And I am not going to contribute more to those emotions. We said we'd take each day as it comes, so let's do that."

"But I thought..."

"I know what you thought," Georgina sighed, "But I'm tired

and I need to sleep. Climbing the stairs has worn me out."

"So go to sleep in my bed."

"Sorry. I can't." Georgina took a deep breath and held her resolve. "I need my own space."

"It's a king-size bed. You'll have enough space. Don't let me worry needlessly." Catherine's eyes showed pain and sadness.

As no response was forthcoming, she shrugged and said, "Whatever..."

"I'll leave my door open."

"What about tonight? I have to check on your concussion throughout the night. If you are sleeping in my bed, I can open my eyes check on you then fall back to sleep."

Catherine looked at the retreating back and wondered how and why everything changed. She moved over and sat on the edge of the bed and felt a tear escape from the corner of her eye.

"I want to care for you."

"I know you do. And I want us to care for each other. But today I need some space."

"I don't understand."

"I don't expect you do, but let me sleep on it and we'll take it from there."

She continued walking to the guest bedroom.

"Why?"

"I thought I could, but in this moment of I can't."

"Fine," Catherine shouted.

"Fine," came the annoyed reply.

Catherine stomped down the back stairs. Went up to Rachel behind the counter.

"That bloody woman."

Rachel put her hands on Catherine's shoulders and pushed

her down onto the stool.

"Calm down."

"But..."

Rachel pressed a finger to her lips. She turned her back and made a coffee. She handed it to Catherine and said, "She loves you, but whatever has happened you got to remember she needs to have some control over her life. Being here in this shop is her life. We have taken it away from her for a few days. Whatever she has done or not done is because she has lost that control. Let her come around in her own way. Also..."

"Also what?" Catherine demanded.

"Where did you ask her to sleep?"

"My bed of course. Why?"

Rachel raised her eyebrows as if she expected Catherine to understand. When no realisation was imminent, she replied, "I expect she had her reasons. So don't try to force it. Now drink your coffee. Then if you are going to stay down here make yourself useful. Haven't you got some phone calls to make?"

"Don't you start on me as well?"

"You knows I loves ya." Rachel countered back.

"Humph."

A moment later after Catherine had blown on her instant coffee, Rachel asked, "Are you taking your coffee into the office to make those calls, staying out here to help me restock the shelves with the mugs and plates, and put everything else back in its rightful place, or just going to sit there looking gorgeous?"

"Sorry. I was miles away. I'll make those calls as quickly as I can then help with the shelves." Catherine answered and gave Rachel a smile and a nod of understanding.

Rachel smiled back, giving her shoulder a reassuring squeeze.

Catherine looked around the room, and said, "Those cleaners have done a really good job. You wouldn't realise there was any mess. We'll have to give them a good review. And perhaps a few coffee vouchers."

"Nice idea. And yes they have done a good job."

"Right," said Catherine as she stood up. "I'll go and make those calls now. Hopefully, I won't be long."

Half an hour later Catherine came out of the office.

"All sorted?" Rachel asked.

"As best as I could."

"Anything more I can help with?"

"Keep doing what you have been doing. I would like us to reopen tomorrow. Hopefully, the coffee supplies should be coming within the next ten minutes. The teas will be coming soon after. Then we can properly sort everything out." Catherine sighed, "I'm going up to check on Gee. Give us a shout if the coffee order comes."

"Tell Georgina, if she tries to come downstairs, she will have me to answer to."

Catherine laughed, "Okay. As if that would stop her."

Catherine looked at the clock. Two thirteen. She didn't know this time existed. She wondered what had woken her. The streetlight outside her window threw shadows across the room, forming dancing demons.

She heard a noise. A cross between a howl and a whimper. Georgina. The thought flashed through her mind. Catherine suddenly jumped up and, feeling a little dizzy from the sudden movement, held onto the chest of drawers. When the dizziness subsided, she rushed into the spare bedroom. Walking to the side of the bed she looked down on the sleeping woman.

Her face portrayed peacefulness, and then it contorted into

terror. Her mouth opened and words were formed but no sound emerged. Then an ear-splitting scream pierced the air.

Catherine placed a hand on Georgina's shoulder and quietly said, "Shh. It's okay. You're safe here. You can wake up if you want to. I'm here. "

Georgina started to become agitated and her eyelids blinked but didn't open. Georgina could hear a voice coming out of the depths of her consciousness.

"Slowly open your eyes," Catherine murmured. "You are safe here."

Georgina knew she wanted to obey the voice without question, but her eyelids felt heavy. Instead, they continued to flutter.

"Come on babe, open your eyes," Catherine pleaded.

Georgina heard the voice getting closer. She slowly opened her eyes and was briefly blinded by the light from the street. She blinked rapidly and saw the calm face of Catherine smiling back at her. Her emotional state began to overwhelm her, her face contorted and a few tears escaped from her eyes. Catherine scooted onto the bed and wrapped an arm around her in a hug. Her other hand caressed her hand.

"You're safe. I'm here."

The simple gesture of a hug warmed Georgina to her core. She felt like she wasn't alone anymore. That there was someone who cared, and at that moment, she was happy. Georgina smiled weakly. But it was a smile that spoke of possibility and hope and promise. Her fragile emotional state spilt out and tears began cascading down her cheeks.

Leaning down, Catherine placed a sweet, delicate kiss on Georgina's lips.

"I'm here. I'm not going anywhere." Catherine said as she placed other gentle kisses on her cheeks, nose and forehead.

Gradually the tears dried.

"I'm sorry," Georgina spoke.

Catherine laughed, "Not as sorry as me. It's gone two o'clock. And I got to get up early in the morning."

She kissed Georgina sweetly again as Georgina laughed softly and returned the kiss in kind. There was a contented and comfortable pause as the two looked into each other's eyes, both smiling big and warmly. They embraced once more, and they held each other tightly.

"What happened?" Georgina asked.

"You were having a nightmare, but I'm here now." She pulled Georgina back into her embrace.

"I'm sorry." Georgina began to look embarrassed. "I've ruined your beauty sleep."

Catherine smiled. "That's not difficult."

"I'm alright now. Thank you I feel sleepy." Georgina felt her eyes getting heavy.

Catherine nudged Georgina's shoulder. "May I sleep in here with you, otherwise I don't think I'll get off again. I'll be awake worrying about you."

Georgina pulled the covers back and scooted over with a groan.

"Why the groan?" Catherine asked.

"Backs playing up. Come on. Into bed."

Catherine suddenly felt awkward. Apart from Sue and the twins she had never shared a bed with another woman. Especially a woman she had feelings for.

"What's wrong?" Georgina asked.

"Umm." Catherine didn't answer.

Georgina smiled deeply into her eyes.

Catherine looked embarrassed. She said quietly, "I've never slept in the same bed with another woman as a grown-up. Us girls did as kids when we were having sleepovers. I'm embarrassed."

"And you're embarrassed because...?"

"I might cuddle in."

"And that will be a problem because..." Georgina left the sentence hanging.

Catherine "You told me you wanted space and cuddling into you is not giving you space."

"That was earlier when I was having a wobble. The last time I slept in that room was with Laura."

"Oh my goodness Gee. I didn't think. How insensitive is that? Why didn't you say? I'm so sorry. It must have brought back a myriad of emotions for you. No wonder you reacted as you did."

Georgina smiled and patted the bed. "Are you going to get in? I promise nothing more than a cuddle will happen. But even if I wanted to I'm not in the best of health. I feel so tired."

Catherine replied as she lay her head on the pillow. "We have the rest of our lives to see what happens between us." She turned to face Georgina. "We have waited almost a year to be at this stage in our relationship. I'm sure we can wait a while longer."

"Thank you for your understanding. I didn't think I would feel so tired." Georgina smiled weakly, "I'm sorry about earlier. About sleeping in your room. It was just..."

Catherine put a finger to Georgina's lips. "Shh. I understand."

"We just have to work out how our relationship is going to happen. I'm not going to throw away my chance at love because I can't sleep in your bedroom."

Georgina yawned and Catherine smiled as she pulled her into an embrace.

"Who said anything about sleeping." Catherine laughed "Goodnight sleepy head. Sweet dreams." Catherine said softly, as Georgina softly purred, and wrapped herself in Catherine's arms.

CHAPTER TWENTY-EIGHT

Re-opening

Catherine placed a coffee down on the table and said, "No matter how busy we get, you are sitting there. Do you understand?"

Georgina nodded her head and rolled her eyes.

"Promise." Catherine looked into Georgina's eyes, trying to portray that for once she was in total control and would brook no argument.

"I promise. So stop treating me like an invalid."

"So stop being stubborn. And until you are given a clean bill of health, you are one. So sit there. Drink your coffee. Acknowledged our friends and customers, and don't leave your seat. I don't want to have to keep making sure you are being sensible whilst we are busy." Catherine caressed Georgina's cheek with her hand. "Please."

"Okay." Georgina acquiesced.

"You'd better," Rachel's voice broke in. "Or you'll have me to deal with as well."

"Ooh. Scared." Georgina retorted but smiled at both Rachel and Catherine. "I promise."

Catherine walked over the door and said over her shoulder to Rachel, "Ready."

"As we'll ever be," came the usual riposte

Catherine slid the bolts back and propped the door open. She greeted a couple of customers who were waiting for permission to enter. She stepped aside and said, "Please come in."

"Hi, Rich," Rachel spoke to the first customer. "And what can I get you? The usual or are you going to try something different."

"Just the usual, cheers Rach." Richard replied, "So glad you weren't closed for too long. I need my caffeine fix in the morning and the stuff they serve at work is disgusting."

"Well, it's good to be back."

"Hi Mrs T. How are you doing? I heard you helped pull the young lady out. Brave of you."

"Only did what anyone would do," Georgina replied.

"Not everyone would. Anyway. Good to see you up and about with no damage done."

"Thanks, Rich."

The morning rush continued with plenty either acknowledging or making a point of speaking to Georgina. After a while, Georgina stood up and said to Catherine, "I'm going back upstairs if that's okay. I'm feeling a little tired."

"Okay. I'll be up to check on you soon."

"You don't have to."

"I know," Catherine smiled, her eyes were full of concern.

A couple of days later Rachel frowned as she looked at her friend. "Are you okay? You look a bit frazzled."

"I'm fine, honestly." The corners of Catherine's lips turned up into a smile, but it didn't reach her eyes."

"I can sense something is not quite right. Come on spill."

"I'm worried," Catherine said as she lifted the tray out of the dishwasher.

Rachel stopped wiping the table and looked towards Catherine, "Why's that, Cat?"

Sighing Catherine replied, "This fire has changed everything."

"I thought things between you and Georgie were going well."

"They are. Lots of kissing and cuddling."

"So what's the problem?" Rachel asked. "Worried about the next step."

"No. Nothing like that."

Rachel raised her eyebrows.

"Well, maybe a little." Catherine declared, with a shy smile.

"So go with the flow. Don't force it." Rachel replied, "She loves you."

"And I love her," Catherine admitted. "This is huge for me."

"When the time is right. It will just happen. Don't overthink it." Rachel paused for a moment. "Answer me this. Have you ever thought so hard about going to bed with a bloke?"

"Honestly?"

"Yeah."

"No."

Rachel probed Catherine's memory, "Not even the first time."

"Oh, then I did." A blush crept over her cheeks.

"And why was that?"

"Because I wanted it to be perfect."

"And was it."

Catherine burst out laughing, "Good grief, no. I had no idea what I was doing."

"But did you enjoy it?

"It was alright I suppose. Not quite the toe curl I was told to expect, but yeah it was okay." Catherine nodded engrossed in her memory.

"So making love for the first time doesn't have to be perfect. It rarely is. You don't have to know exactly what you're doing, just that you are giving and receiving pleasure."

Catherine's cheeks blushed red again.

"Over time you will find out what works for the pair of you."

"Thank you," Catherine said. "I think I need to set aside some time for sex counselling every now and then. Even talk to you or Sue. Perhaps then I'll be better at it."

"Maybe you haven't been with the person meant for you. Stop overthinking it. When the time is right it will happen."

The two women turned back to work. Rachel noticed that a frown was still etched on Catherine's brow.

"Are you going to tell me what else is troubling you?"

Catherine took a deep breath. "It's this place. Being closed for those few days without any sales has put a stop on our profits. Then having to restock virtually everything, having to pay for the deep cleaning and completely a new window out the back. It's just too much."

Rachel continued tidying the tables, "That, surely, will come from your insurance claim."

"It will." Catherine paused as she tried to hold her emotions in. "But we're paying for all that now and it will take more than a couple of weeks to be reimbursed. You know how these companies work. Quick to take your money but take forever to pay it out. And I haven't that time."

Rachel walked towards the counter. "Why? Surely the business's finances can stand the wait. Or should I be worried as well?"

"You haven't anything to worry about." Catherine shook her head. "The business can easily stand the wait. But I won't be able to."

Rachel frowned not understanding. Then gradually realisation dawned.

"This will stop you from reaching the magic number, won't it?"

Catherine nodded.

"And to think, when I last met with the accountant, I was so happy. Then I made that stupid comment about a catastrophe. Well the thirty or however many minutes it was when next door was on fire, became that catastrophe. It has truly scuppered my plans for the future."

"Oh, Catherine. I don't know what to say." Rachel's hand flew up to her face as though she was trying to hide from the words Catherine had spoken.

"Neither do I."

Rachel touched her hand on Catherine's arm and asked, "Does Georgina realise this? Does she understand the implications?"

Catherine shook her head, "I don't think so. Remember she hasn't been here in the shop since the fire. She knows about all our outlays. She knows that the insurance company have said the claim is valid. But I doubt she has thought of the implications for this month. She hasn't the investment to worry about as I do. I can see all my hard work for the year pouring down the drain, following the water needed to put out the fire."

"That's not right. You have or would have reached the target easily."

"The contract says at the end of twelve months, not the end of thirteen months when the claim comes through."

"So what are you going to do?"

"I don't know." She shook her head and gave a wry smile. "Ask Gee for a job. But at least I'm not being thrown out of my home."

"Oh Cat. I didn't realise."

Catherine shrugged her shoulders and sighed. She tried to lighten the mood, "Lucky you." She nudged Rachel's shoulder. "You only have to put up with me being your boss for another couple of weeks."

"It's so unfair. Let me hug you."

Catherine melted into Rachel's arms. She took a couple of deep breaths and puffed out her cheeks. "However, aside from my business woes, I have been more troubled by Georgina's health."

"In what way?" Rachel moved to arm's length and frowned. "I thought she was recovering well."

"To a certain extent, she is."

Rachel replied, "By the way that was a good shout making her take a few days off. So why are you worried?"

"I didn't make her. We all did that by coming in and covering her shifts. But I did change the rota so she has the next three days off and has been banished from the coffeehouse."

"I bet she didn't like that." Rachel gave a small laugh.

Joining in with a smile, Catherine replied, "She didn't have a choice. Fait accompli and all that."

"Sneaky. So why are you worried about her health?"

"Her cough is persisting."

"Is she doing her breathing exercises?"

"As far as I'm aware. She should be doing them in the morning and evening. But since the stubborn, independent woman moved back home yesterday, I can't keep a check on her."

"You'll have to ask her and make sure she does them. Tell her you are scared about her health."

"I will. But you know her. She will fob it off as nothing."

"Make her realise she has to think of others not just herself. What did the physiotherapist say?"

"She has to go see them tomorrow."

Rachel looked into Catherine's eyes and noticed they were beginning to fill, so she pulled her back into a hug.

"Can you cope for a few minutes? I need to take a walk and clear my head. And perhaps check on Georgina."

"Of course." Rachel nodded. "Take as much time as you need."

"Why didn't she stay a couple of days more? I wouldn't have to worry about her through the daytime as well as everything else." Catherine let out a huge sigh.

Rachel shook her head. "You should tell her that we might not reach the target."

"It's not her problem."

"It is and it's ours."

"No it's not," Catherine said as she walked out the door

"It affects her. It affects all of us."

"No. It affects me."

"So you are going to keep her in the dark again and not talk to her."

"For the moment," she replied and walked outside, where even the sunshine couldn't lift her mood.

To herself, Rachel said, "Not on my watch you're not. There was too much of that after Christmas."

That evening Catherine walked around to Georgina's house again and pressed on the doorbell. Georgina opened the door and said, "I wasn't expecting you. Not after seeing you earlier."

"Sorry. If you have other plans I'll go."

Georgina reached out an arm to stop her from walking away.

"No. Nothing like that. I wasn't expecting anyone. This is a pleasant surprise. Now is better than tomorrow. Will I still be seeing you tomorrow?"

"Of course. Try keeping me away."

Georgina stepped aside. "Please come in," she said. "I was only chilling out and reading but if you want to watch a film, we could do that."

They kissed as they passed each other.

"As long as it's not The Sound of Music." Catherine laughed.

Georgina rolled her eyes. "Your choice. I'll watch anything except horror."

"And there was me thinking of something retro. Perhaps along the lines of The Texas Chain Saw Massacre. Yeah, that would be a nice cosy film to snuggle up to."

Georgina swatted her arm. "Even the title makes me squirm. I was thinking of a rom-com. Something we can smile at."

"An oldie or a recent one?"

"An oldie, but not too old, like me." Georgina laughed which turned into a cough.

"Have you done your bronchial hygiene therapy for tonight?"

"I was about to start them when you rang the bell." Catherine shook her head and studied her.

"I was," Georgina said trying to convince Catherine.

"You've got to push yourself, Gee. I don't want to worry about you every single minute."

"You haven't got to worry about me."

"I do and I will, until I know you have fully recovered,"

Catherine replied. “So for me, if not yourself, please do your exercises regularly.”

“Okay. Help me with them now. Then we’ll see a film.”

Catherine nodded, “What about Love Actually?”

“Good choice. Go and put the kettle on, fill up the bowl, and make me a cup of green tea.”

“Yes milady. Anything else milady.” Catherine asked as she walked to the kitchen.

“Bring me in a towel as well as the bowl, please Cat,” Georgina shouted to her back.

Catherine waved her hand in acknowledgement.

Fifteen minutes later Catherine said, “You can take your head from under the towel and drink your tea before it gets too cold.”

Georgina emerged from under the towel, face flushed with the steam. She wiped the sweat that had trickled down her temples in the towel. She picked up the mug and drank it down in one gulp.

“How was that?” Catherine asked.

“Hot,” Georgina laughed, then coughed.

“So what’s next?”

“The deep breathing ones.”

“Do you need any help?”

“Not until the end,” Georgina laughed.

Catherine looked at her curiously.

“You’ll see.”

Georgina sat back in her chair, placed her hands on her stomach and did a set of repetitive deep breathing. The next set saw her huffing out her breath, ending with a cough. The third set saw her breathing deep, holding and a slow release.

She then sat down on the floor with a groan, knees creaking.

"Chuck me a couple of cushions, love."

After she dodged the cushions that had been aimed at her head, she collected them and put them under her hips. She did her sets on her back, sides, then stomach. Groaning each time she turned over.

Catherine started to giggle.

"What are you giggling about?" Georgina asked.

"You sounded like Meg Ryan in When Harry met Sally, with all that groaning and moaning."

Georgina picked up one of the cushions and threw it towards Catherine but it landed harmlessly at her feet.

"And that is why I need you," Georgina admitted.

"What?" Catherine continued smiling, "So you can learn how to throw a cushion at me."

"Funny." Georgina pulled a face. "Help get me off the floor."

"How do you normally get up."

Georgina grimaced again.

"Gee? Is this why you haven't been doing all of them?" Catherine asked.

Georgina put her head in her hands and showed her embarrassment by saying, "Yes. Because at the moment I feel too weak to get up off the floor by myself. There that's why. Satisfied now."

"Oh, Gee. Why didn't you say, I would have helped?"

"I didn't want you to think I was getting older. That I couldn't do things like I used to. Why would you want to team up with someone who would struggle to get up off the floor?"

"Come on. Give me your hands." Catherine placed her feet in front of Georgina's, grabbed her hands, pulled her to her feet and into a tight embrace and said, "We are all getting older. We will have to adapt, that's all."

"But..."

"No buts. We will face everything together."

A wave of guilt washed over Catherine as she told her they would face things together and she was hiding something so huge. *Next week. I'll tell her next week when she's feeling better. Yep. That's what I'll do. I'll tell her next week.*

"Are you ready to watch the film and kiss and snuggle?" Catherine asked as she walked Georgina over to the settee.

Georgina looked into Catherine's eyes and said, "If I was feeling well enough, I would be wanting to make love to you, with you, right here, right now."

"You... you know I've n...never with a woman." Catherine finally got out, and yet her heart gave a flip at the thought.

"I know. You've told me often enough."

"That doesn't worry you?"

"Why should it? Nobody has until they do for the first time." Georgina took both Catherine's hands in hers. "You cannot control who you fall in love with. And I do love you. We started as friends, and now we are on the way to being lovers. We've gotten to know each other pretty well thus far." Georgina smiled, "And sweet and passionate kisses will have to suffice until I feel better. Until I can show you how much I love you."

Georgina planted a tender kiss on Catherine's lips. The kiss became more passionate. Georgina drew away, breathless, and said, "Goodness woman. Have you any idea what you do to me."

"No. But soon I'd like to find out." Catherine's stomach promptly rumbled.

Georgina chuckled. "Haven't you eaten?"

"Hold that thought." Catherine got up and walked to the door. She reached into the bag she had dumped there and said, "I've brought pizza and wine. Let me put it in the oven and we can eat it while watching the film."

CHAPTER TWENTY-NINE

Almost there

"I'm fine," Georgina replied. "I can do my fair share. I don't need to be mollycoddled anymore."

"Humour me. Please." Catherine pleaded

"The doctor has given me a clean bill of health. I've been working the easy shifts for a week now and it's two weeks since I was released from the hospital. I can run up the stairs. Well, I can run up as well as I could beforehand." She laughed. "I only have to do deep breathing if, and when, I think I need to. So I insist on working the busy shift. Don't treat me as though I'm fragile. I'm fine."

Catherine looked at Rachel for back up.

But Rachel said, "Sorry Cat. I'm with Georgie on this one. I know you care about her but you can't wrap her up in cotton-wool for any longer."

"Rachel, can you hold the fort for a while. I need to speak to Cat. Give us a shout if it gets busy."

Rachel nodded

"Cat, will you come into the office for a moment."

Catherine turned to Rachel and said, "This seems ominous."

Rachel shrugged her shoulders as if to say, 'don't ask me.'

Georgina and Catherine walked into the office and sat in their respective chairs.

"What's on your mind. I'm sorry if you think I'm mollycoddling you, but the thought of losing you is still tearing me up. When Maddie called and said there was a fire next door and you had disappeared. It frightened me to death. I got here as quick as I could. I even had words with the driver of the bus I was on and ran the fastest and farthest I've done for years. As I get there you are being loaded into the ambulance. At that moment I thought I lost you."

"You've told me this before. I'm fine now. You heard the doctor. No lasting damage. Will you please stop hovering around me, like a mother hen? I know you are worried about me. But I'm good. I might be older than you and reaching the twilight years of my working life. But I'm not decrepit."

"Okay. I'll change the rota for next week when I work on it later." Catherine capitulated.

Georgina sighed and gave Catherine a big smile. "Did you know this time last year I was thinking of going part-time? Now, look at me. Asking for the harder shifts. Who'd have thought."

"You were thinking of going part-time. I never knew that."

Nodding, Georgina replied, "I wasn't enjoying going into work each day. I felt sad and lonely. It wasn't fun anymore. It had become a drudge. At that time I was feeling my age. I was feeling older than my age. I was going home alone, getting up, coming here, going home. Every day, no different from the previous. I thought about giving it all up but as I had ten more years before I could collect my pension. I couldn't jack it in."

"You were thinking of selling?" Incredulity inflected Catherine's voice.

"Yes. But then you came along." Georgina beamed. "We are almost at the year mark and I have no worries about you reaching the target. I'm looking forward to next year and the following years. I feel invigorated."

Catherine grimaced as she still hadn't told Georgina that the insurance company were dragging their feet. She had to tell her now.

Georgina continued, completely unaware of the turmoil that was going on in Catherine's head. "You have been the kick up the backside I needed. When Laura died, I feared that I would lose everything we had built up. There was no way I would have coped looking after this place by myself. And yet I hated the idea that Laura had foisted some stranger on me. But you were impressive almost from day one. You took to this business like a duck to water. You were the type of person this place needed. If I haven't told you before I want to tell you now. Thank you for giving us a go."

"I've loved virtually every moment." Catherine smiled at her. "And I found someone to love." *And I'm hiding a secret that will put it all in jeopardy.*

"I had lost the love of my life and I had this fear that I would never again find love. I feared that I had become so set in my ways, so unlovable. That I was too old to start again. And yet as I look into your eyes, I know that isn't true. I am ready to take our relationship to the next phase and I hope you are too."

A smile grew on Catherine's face, and her fears began to disappear. "I am. I'm scared though." *Tell her. Tell her what you are truly scared of.*

"Me too." Georgina answered, "I might not be your first love, and you might not have been mine, but I would like to be your last partner, last lover. Both in business and pleasure. My first kiss and my first love have long since been forgotten but that first kiss with you is lodged in my memory in the never to be forgotten section."

A far-away look came into her eyes as she smiled at the recollection.

Catherine smiled, "I remember the first time I looked at your face. You were gawping at me. I didn't quite know what to think. Then you smiled. And in that second, the pull towards you was real."

"I know. Rachel told me I was gawping." Georgina walked around and stood behind Catherine. She placed her hands on her shoulders and said, "During the next few months I ignored the pull, thinking it's a ridiculous notion, an impossible dream. We allowed our friendship to grow. And I felt myself being drawn even closer to you. Even though I knew the risks."

"What risks," Catherine asked.

"That my friendship, and love, wouldn't be reciprocated. That I would be in the same situation as I was with Laura."

"From what I've heard I'm nothing like Laura." *Oh yes, I am.*

"You're not. You are kind, funny, considerate and I will always show my appreciation and love for you. I promise I will give you my full attention even when my mind is trying to take me elsewhere. I promise to start showing you my affection in all the little things I can do for you. I promise I will never hide anything from you."

Catherine swallowed hard and felt a blush forming on her cheeks. She had to tell Georgina they wouldn't make the magic percentage. *Tell her now.*

"Gee," Catherine took hold of both her hands. "I have something to tell you?"

"You can tell me you love me any day. I will never shy away from hearing those words."

She looked into the gorgeous eyes filled with love and couldn't spoil the moment. "Gee, I love you."

"I love you too."

Tomorrow. I'll tell her tomorrow.

Georgina continued "I love you and I want to say and hear

those three words every day for the rest of our lives. That's the commitment I give to you. I have only one regret and that is I didn't meet you sooner so I'd be able to love you for longer. You make me complete. Please can I stay the night?"

Georgina took Catherine's smiling face in her hands and kissed her tenderly on the lips. The understanding flowed between them. "And you still look at me the same way you did that first day. The day I started to live again"

"How did Georgie take it?" Rachel asked Catherine as the rush died down.

"I didn't tell her. The time wasn't right."

"I don't believe you." Rachel almost shouted out loud. "You still haven't told her. I didn't take you as a coward."

"I couldn't." Catherine ran her hands through her hair.

"What stopped you?" Rachel asked shaking her head. "This excuse had better be good."

Catherine smiled as she remembered. "She professed her undying love for me."

"Did she?"

"And she asked if she could stay over tonight." Catherine grinned in anticipation. "How could I tell her after that?"

"She wants to stay over?" Rachel asked in amazement.

"Yes, and I want tonight to be special. To be memorable. I don't want to spoil what I hope will be the start of a wonderful relationship. I'll tell her tomorrow or the next time I see her. But I don't want to tell her at work it has to be when we are by ourselves."

"You'd better."

They didn't speak for a little while.

Catherine spoke again, "I'm still hoping the insurance money will come through."

“Is it likely to?”

“No,” Catherine admitted with a sigh.

“So tell her. Or I will.” Rachel said, with a steely going in her eye.

“Give me a break.”

You’ve had enough breaks already. Tell her. It’s not fair on her. She’s expecting you to be her business partner.”

“I know.”

CHAPTER THIRTY

Being true

Catherine's doorbell sounded and she rushed down the stairs, one at a time, as fast as she could.

"Coming," she shouted, ten steps from the bottom.

She reached the door, took a deep breath, and tried to control her nerves.

"Hi," she said shyly as she opened the door. She stepped aside and said, "Go on up."

As they entered the living room Georgina gently pushed Catherine against the closed door. She asked, "May I kiss you properly now?"

"Mmm-hmm."

Their kiss became more passionate and their hands began to roam.

They broke the kiss and Georgina professed, "I've waited far too long to do this."

Catherine nodded her head, her heart pounding against her ribs. "I'm frightened," Catherine admitted. Her voice coming out little more than a whisper "What if I can't satisfy you."

"But what if you can?" Georgina looked at Catherine, with eyes full of love. "I'm scared as well, you know," she said softly. "I've only ever been with five different women. And since Laura, it's the first time for me too."

"Is it?" Catherine sounded dubious.

"I might be a lesbian but we aren't all nymphomaniacs."

"I'm not suggesting you are. I thought you would have been with more women. I just surprised."

Georgina groaned and said, "For goodness sake woman. Will you be quiet and let me kiss you?"

Georgina's lips rested on Catherine's who slowly opened her mouth, and allowed Georgina to gently explore with her tongue. As though she was searching for a release to her pent up need. A need she felt spreading throughout her body.

Catherine moaned in her mouth.

Georgina revelled in her taste, the softness of her lips, the way their tongues fought each other. All Catherine could feel was the acute awakening of her body, the roiling in her stomach and the amazing sensation between her legs as she felt her juices begin to flow. Something she hadn't felt in a long time. Her moan became deeper, longer. Tickling the lips of the woman who was extracting these sensations from her.

They broke away and Catherine murmured, "Oh God. I think I've died and gone to heaven. What have you done to me? Nobody has made me feel like this by kissing me."

"You wait to see what else I can do with my tongue," teased Georgina.

Catherine almost fainted on the spot with the desire that pulsed through her body. She shivered as warm, gentle hands pushed under her shirt, and up her ribs. Her hands began to explore the body in front of her with tender caresses. Georgina stopped her hands roving as they reached Catherine's boobs. She stared into Catherine's eyes and asked a silent question. Catherine nodded and let a smile ingratiate her features as she closed her eyes.

Georgina displayed a sly grin, running her finger down Catherine's chest, lingering on each hardening nipple underneath the confines of the bra. She teased the surrounding skin, then squeezed them gently, causing Catherine to bite her lip, as her cheeks began to flush.

Georgina expertly undid the buttons on Catherine's shirt and pushed it off her shoulders. Catherine quickly pulled her arms from the sleeves and let the shirt dangle from the back of her trousers.

Georgina's hungry eyes devoured the sight in front of her. She moved the flimsy material aside that was encasing the objects of her desire. She lowered her head and her mouth covered one breast. She began to slowly lick and tease her nipple, sucking until it hardened under her insistent attention. Her fingers rolled, pinched and circled the other one as Catherine wriggled with desire, until it too, was swollen and hard under the touch.

Georgina moved her mouth to her other breast as she allowed her hands to rove lower, caressing her sides. Catherine squirmed as her hands touched her ticklish spots. Georgina inched around the inside of her waistband and fumbled slightly as she released the button on Catherine's trousers. The zipper soon followed, and her rounded belly escaped from its imprisonment.

Her eyes locked on Catherine as she again silently asked for permission. Knees cracked as Georgina knelt in front of Catherine. She pulled the tight-fitting unwilling cotton fabric over Catherine's hips. She pushed the trousers down to her ankles and Catherine impatiently kicked them off. Smiling Georgina found her mouth inches from Catherine's core.

Every muscle in Catherine's body tensed with excitement as she felt Georgina's breath through the flimsy material surrounding her modesty. Georgina kissed through the material and she smelt the aroma of Catherine's arousal.

Georgina's hands reached up and cupped Catherine's breasts, squeezing her nipples gently. She kissed along the bikini line as her hands took special care sliding across all her dips and curves, exploring every inch as she mapped out her intentions. She teased and tormented Catherine with her touch. Whimpering, Catherine parted her thighs, as her body quivered with a desire that she never knew she was capable of.

Georgina moved the fabric of her knickers to the side and gently stroked her fingers in Catherine's folds. Catherine bit her lip as she felt Georgina gently push a finger inside her wetness. Catherine moaned softly, and spread her legs wider. Desire took over. Wanting and needing more she thrust her hips forward, trying to capture the instrument of her pleasurable torture.

"I think you are overdressed." Georgina laughed as she halted her ministrations and removed the offending material. Catherine discarded the bra that had been pushing up her exposed breasts.

Georgina placed her hands on Catherine's hips as she admired her flushed naked body in front of her. "You're beautiful."

Georgina planted kisses on the top of Catherine's thighs, and said, "You smell exquisite. I want to taste you."

Rooted to the spot, the door and Georgina's hands on her hips kept Catherine standing. Georgina dipped her tongue around the swollen, crimson folds, savouring the tang of arousal.

"Bloody hell," Catherine muttered, whilst Georgina's tongue continued to lick and lap up the juices.

Georgina looked up into her eyes. "Are you okay?" she asked, her voice husky with desire.

"Mmhm." Catherine moaned in delight

"You smell and taste so delicious," she said between licks.

"Don't stop. Please don't stop." Her hands wrapped in Georgina's hair and held her tight.

"Never." She murmured as she sucked and quickened the

thrust of her tongue. She pulled on her hard, swollen, clit as she took it into her mouth.

“Mmhm.” Catherine moaned as she writhed in contentment.

She slipped in one then two fingers and found her rhythm, stroking and plunging.

Whether it was because it had been the first time anyone had done anything like this, or if it was because of the woman kneeling in front of her, she didn’t know. Nor did she care. She was dripping and had no worries about being dry, about being hurt. Georgina's fingers were slipping into her with ease.

“Oh…” Catherine ground down on Georgina’s hand, as her inner muscles started to grip Georgina’s fingers like a vice.

“Ah…” She moaned, her lips parted as flung her head back in ecstasy. “I’m… fuck…” she screamed.

Her chest started heaving, as her muscles contracted. Unable to control the wave of divine pleasure which had assaulted her senses. Each intense pulse of release lifted her to heights of sexual bliss she had never experienced before. She came, came and came again, and as each orgasm overwhelmed her, swamping her senses.

“Oh fuck…” Catherine placed her hands on Georgina’s shoulders and pushed her away for fear she might lose total control of her legs and pass out with happiness.

Georgina stilled her fingers and tongue, looked at the woman in front of her, radiant in the afterglow of fulfilment.

“What have you done to me?” Catherine whispered, not trusting her voice. She slid down the door and pulled Georgina into a tight embrace. “I never believed I could feel this good. I’ve never come like that before, in fact, that’s only the first, second and third orgasm I’ve ever had.”

“Ever?”

Catherine nodded.

"I'm so sorry. I would have at least let you lie down and be comfortable." Georgina gave a shy smile as she kissed the top of Catherine's head. "But I couldn't stop myself. Your kisses, your passion, flicked a switch in me. I couldn't wait I had to show you how much I love you."

"I know."

"You okay?" Georgina asked.

"Mmhm." Catherine buried her head in Georgina's shoulder and burst into tears.

"Oh Cat babe. Don't cry."

"These are happy tears," Catherine admitted through her sobs. "That was wonderful. I can still feel you inside me. My clit is still throbbing and my legs have turned to mush."

Georgina grinned.

Catherine grinned back. "And my nipples are still hard enough to poke out someone's eye."

Georgina gazed lovingly at Catherine's boobs. She put a finger under Catherine's chin and kissed the mouth of the woman she desired.

Catherine could taste herself on Georgina's tongue and lips. "So that's what I taste like."

"Mmm-hmm. And I'd like to taste your juices again if you'll let me."

Catherine could feel a blush take over the whole of her body as a flush of desire swept through her. She hid in Georgina's shoulder.

She suddenly pulled away and said, "There's something wrong here. I'm totally naked and you still are wearing all your clothes."

"Whose fault is that? I was too busy undressing you, touching you, savouring you and loving you to think about undressing me.

"I think we should remove everything of yours and take this somewhere more comfortable, don't you?"

"What a good idea. But you're going to have to help get me off the floor cos I think my knees and back have locked."

Catherine helped Georgina up and gently led her towards the bedroom?

"Mine or the guest one," Catherine asked, remembering Georgina's reaction when she stayed here last.

Georgina stopped and claimed Catherine's mouth. Pulling apart she said, "Yours. I want to exorcise all my ghosts and demons and can think of no better way than making love to you again, wrapping my body around you and waking up in your arms."

Georgina guided Catherine into the master bedroom. She tenderly pushed Catherine onto her back, she moved to straddle her hips.

"Not so quick, lady," Catherine ordered. "Trousers off before anything else."

Georgina shimmed out of her jeans, kicked off her shoes and flung her socks away. She climbed back onto the bed and this time straddled Catherine's hips with no more complaints.

Catherine reached up and pulled Georgina's shirt over her head. She stretched around to unclasp her bra and was greeted by darkened areola, contrasting the lily-white skin. She gasped, "Wow." and closed her mouth around the dark pink nipple. Georgina thrust forward and pressed into Catherine's mouth. Gasping as a scorching tongue flicked over it repeatedly.

"And you've never touched a woman before?" gasped Georgina.

Catherine peered at Georgina from under her eyelashes, with a slight shake. She grazed her teeth over the nipple, causing Georgina to groan out loud. Catherine leant across and licked, kissed and nibbled at her other breast.

Catherine leant further and, wrapping her arms around Georgina, making her roll over on her side. She pushed further and rolled Georgina on her back. Catherine began a slow exploration of Georgina's body with lips, tongue and teeth.

Kissing her way downwards she removed the last piece of offending clothing. She kissed her way back up Georgina's body and each moan that was generated by Georgina was reciprocated by one of her own. Georgina writhed beneath her, as Catherine sent a scorching fire coursing through her veins. Catherine used her mouth and fingers, and tried to memorise Georgina's body by touch, stopping at different points to leave a heated kiss or a gentle nip. Their bodies moved together as if each motion, each touch, had been practised for years.

Georgina closed her eyes in ecstasy, savouring the added sense of being unsure where the next touch would come from. Her stomach flipped at the sudden feel of hot breath against her ear. Teeth tugged at her earlobe and Catherine's tongue tasted the sensitive area of her neck. She was utterly ruined when Catherine husked into her ear, "You're beautiful."

"Oh my goodness," Georgina let out a gasp. "Please Cat."

Georgina took hold of Catherine's hand and push it downwards.

"I need you to touch me. Please."

Catherine wasn't sure how to proceed or what was expected. The experience was out of the ordinary for her, and it made her feel a little bit lost. "What do you want me to do? Help me."

"Inside. Go inside." Georgina pleaded as she pressed Catherine's hand down between her legs.

Georgina knew she was already wet and it would take much to send her over the edge.

"You want me inside you?"

"Yes," Georgina breathed. "Please, Cat... I want you... I need you..."

Catherine's fingers entered Georgina's warm, wet spot for the first time. She started with one, two and then worked up to three, her fingers diving deep inside her.

Georgina cried out in delight, as she bucked hard against Catherine's hand. Her thumb found Georgina's clitoris, and as soon as her thumb touched against it, a shuddering, strangled cry came out of Georgina's mouth. Her thighs clamped together, trapping Catherine's fingers deep inside. Her back arched, as she could feel her body readying for the release. The orgasm took hold as all of her strong muscles clamped then released in a steady pulse around Catherine's fingers.

She whimpered as she bit down on Catherine's shoulder as the orgasm wracked through her body. Georgina's moan slowly gave way to heavy breathing as she fought to draw enough oxygen into her body.

"Shit," Georgina exclaimed. "That was amazing."

"I was going to say the same thing." Catherine smiled, feeling pleased with herself.

Georgina sighed blissfully as she played with Catherine's hair. She was finally feeling at peace. And making love to Catherine was everything she'd hoped it would be.

Catherine nuzzled her nose against Georgina's cheek as they recovered from their lovemaking. Catherine turned to Georgina and said, "You've brought so much love into my life in such a short time." She paused for a moment and added, "I never thought I would find love like this."

Georgina smiled, "Exactly how I feel. You took the words right out of my mouth.

"Let me have your mouth again so I can see what else you can do."

"I think my tongue could show you quite a few more

things."

"Oh, can it?" Catherine raised her eyebrows.

"And to show you how grateful I am for all the love you have given me. I'd like to roam my lips and tongue all over your body again."

Soon each woman were again giving themselves completely to the other. Georgina revelled in the freedom to show Catherine what had been missing.

Later that night the two of them were wrapped happily together, their arms and legs intertwined. Their gentle snores were the only sound to break the silence.

CHAPTER THIRTY-ONE

Day of reckoning

Catherine had been lying awake for what seemed like hours. She watched the sleeping figure of Georgina as she gently puffed out rhythmic breaths. She looked so serene and peaceful, as though she had no care in the world.

Catherine on the other hand had been dreading today. Her face was neither serene nor peaceful.

She looked over at the clock. Ten minutes before the usual rude awakening. She gently and quietly removed herself from Georgina's intertwined limbs. She leant over to the clock and turned off the alarm.

She padded over to the bathroom and, as she reached the door, looked back at the sleeping figure.

"I'm sorry," she said in a whisper. "I should have told you weeks ago. Rachel's correct I am a coward."

Georgina stirred and, as though, her subconscious realised the person she was snuggling had gone, turned onto her back. Her quiet puffing of breath turned into a gentle snore.

Catherine's fingers went to her mouth and she could still smell and taste the lingering delights from the previous night. Catherine smiled at the gorgeous woman who had again received and given so much pleasure.

The doubts began to creep into her consciousness. Had she been correct in hiding the true consequence of the fire next door? Over the past couple of weeks, she had resigned herself to losing her share of the business. She knew that solid foundations were now in place. She hoped that Georgina would still want to work with her. So what if she didn't have a vested interest, she could still play her part as an employee.

She knew the jeopardies involved when she signed that contract a year ago and she had been willing to take the risk. All her hopes had been resting on the insurance company coming through. And when the post arrived yesterday her prospects had been dashed.

Had she hidden her disappointment well enough? Rachel had picked up her mood and had kept touching her arm and giving her hugs. Georgina seemed oblivious.

She glanced again at the clock. Four hours until meeting the accountant. Six hours before Georgina and herself met the solicitor. She hoped she wouldn't embarrass herself by breaking down in tears. They were already gathering in the corner of her eyes.

So what if she lost the coffeehouse. She would still have this flat, and hopefully Georgina.

She turned and entered the bathroom. She turned on the taps, and when the water reached the correct temperature, she stepped under the spray and got ready to start the first day of her new life. Tears sprung from her eyes and her body was racked with silent sobs. She let the water wash away the offending tears.

As the water continued to pummel onto her shoulders, a steely resolve entered her body. She turned off the taps and stepped from the shower. She dried herself off, straightened her back, and walked back into the bedroom. She glanced at the sleeping woman who was unaware of the turmoil that played around in Catherine's mind.

She quickly dressed and ate a piece of toast and drank some coffee. Walking back into the bedroom she leant over and kissed the sleeping figure.

"Good morning sleepy head. Don't forget we've got to leave here at eleven-thirty."

"What time is it?" Georgina groaned as she hid her head under the pillow.

"Ten minutes until opening time. There's a coffee on the bedside cabinet. Don't let it get cold."

She lifted a corner of the pillow and gave Georgina a kiss.

"Eleven thirty." Catherine reminded her.

"As if I could forget," came the mumbled reply.

Georgina lifted the pillow off herself and sat up. Catherine's eyes roamed over the body of her lover and smiled, realising the person she loved was in her bed. And everything between them felt right, felt natural. But would it survive today? She sighed.

Georgina, in a voice that sounded more awake, said, "I've got to go home first though, I'll be parked up around the corner. Love you. See you later."

"Love you too." Catherine gave her another kiss and wandered down the stairs to start the next chapter of her life.

Catherine walked around the corner and saw Georgina leaning against the bonnet of her car. Eyes closed soaking up the weak rays of the sun. Catherine wandered over to her and Georgina opened her eyes as if aware of her approach.

She smiled and Catherine smiled back as she kissed her cheek.

"Ready?" Georgina asked.

"As ready as I'll ever be," came the reply.

Georgina clicked the doors open and both women climbed

inside.

"How did the meeting with the accountant go?" Georgina asked.

"Exactly as I expected it to," Catherine replied, as she tried to smile warmly at her lover. But the smile felt false because it was. It didn't reach her eyes.

Georgina looked across and patted Catherine's knee, and said, "I'm almost as nervous about this meeting as I was a year ago."

"You and me both," Catherine responded with a sigh. She felt her resolve slipping.

"I don't know why I'm nervous. All we got to do is sign a couple of papers."

"About that."

Georgina pulled out onto the main road, "You know my rules, when I'm driving on the main roads conversation stops. I need to concentrate."

Catherine sat silently beside her, with her arms folded across her chest.

They pulled into a parking space right in front of the solicitors' office. Before Catherine had the chance to say anything, Georgina was out of the car. As soon as she shut the door, she heard the locks click into place.

"Hey, wait for me," she shouted to Georgina.

She rushed to join her as she heard the receptionist say, "Ms Munden, Ms Turnball. Mr James is waiting for you. Would you like to follow me?"

Catherine touched Georgina's arm as they were following the receptionist, and said, "I've got something to tell you."

"Let's get these papers signed first. We will have plenty of time to talk afterwards."

The receptionist knocked and opened the door, and said to

the man behind the desk, “Mr James. Ms Munden and Ms Turnball are here.”

Rupert James stood up and extended his hand. “Ladies,” he said. “Please take a seat. My, this year has passed quickly.”

The two women sat down.

“You don’t want me to witter on. You’re here to sign the papers.”

He shuffled a few papers on his desk and said, “I received the email from your accountant earlier. And as you know the five per cent profit margin was not achieved.”

Georgina gasped. In a state of shock, she asked, “How close did we get?”

“Four point Nine three,” the solicitor stated bluntly

Georgina sighed and squeezed Catherine’s knee. “I’m so sorry, Catherine. We got so close.”

“Not as sorry as me,” Catherine sighed. “I’ve known since the fire that we wouldn’t make it. Not unless some miracle occurred. Shit happens.”

“So why didn’t you tell me.”

“I tried nearly every day. But I didn’t want to see the look in your eyes that I’m seeing now. I didn’t want to disappoint you.”

“You have never disappointed me.”

Rupert cleared his throat, turned to Catherine and said, “Within the terms of the agreement, the half share that was left to you by your aunt will, by default, revert to Ms Turnball. I need you, Ms Munden, to sign here,” he pointed and he put a cross. He lifted the top sheet and pointed and again put a cross. “And here.”

Without looking at the documents, Catherine signed where she had been asked.

“Ms Turnball, I will ask you to countersign, here and here.”

Georgina signed in the respective places.

Rupert James picked up the papers and said, “My work here is done. Thank you for doing business with me. If you need our services again, please do not hesitate to get in touch.”

He stood up and shook hands with both women.

Georgina parked in virtually the same place as she had earlier. Neither woman had spoken but Georgina had squeezed Catherine’s knee. They got out of the car and walked side by side towards the coffeehouse. As Catherine neared her front door she turned to Georgina and said, “I think I need some time by myself.”

“Nonsense,” Georgina responded. “What you need is your friends around you.”

She pulled Catherine into the coffeehouse.

The place was full of people and she was greeted by all her friends, who either sat on the chairs or stood around the room. Georgina nodded to Rachel and the background music was turned off. Puzzlement was shown in Catherine’s frown.

"What's going on?" Catherine asked.

Georgina smiled and as she knelt on one knee in front of Catherine, a small groan escaped her lips.

She took hold of Catherine’s hands and said, “Today, you not only signed a paper that acknowledged the year agreement had reverted to its default setting, but you also signed another one where you agreed to become joint owner of this place.” She waved her hands around the room.

She took a deep breath, “And now in front of all our friends I want to ask you one last favour.”

She paused to look deeply into Catherine’s eyes. She held a small box which she opened and presented to Catherine and said, “I want to spend the rest of my life with you. Partners in business and in pleasure. I’m not asking you to marry me to-morrow but one day in the future will you also do me the honour of becoming my wife. I love you, Cat."

Catherine pulled Georgina up into her embrace and shouted, "Yes. Yes. Yes. And I love you too." Tears sprung from the corners of her eyes. She knuckled them away, as she kissed Georgina deeply.

Catherine and Georgina were immediately surrounded by their friends. Sounds of bottles being popped could be heard and a glass of champagne was placed into each of their hands. The bell above the door could be heard above the hubbub and a voice rang out.

"On behalf of all your friends gathered here today we would like to say congratulations."

Catherine looked towards the voice and screamed, "Sue... When did you get here? How did you know?"

With a grin that split her face, she said, "I stayed at Georgie's last night."

"Last night?"

Georgina looked at her and said, "You're not the only one who can keep secrets. We planned all this last week when a little bird told me what was happening. But that conversation is for another time." She raised her glass and said, "To my business partner and future wife. I love you."

"And I love you too," Catherine replied as she burst into tears.

Today was the start of their new journey, partners in both love and business. Both excited yet unsure where their journey was going to take them. They had been drawn together by chance, by the action of two very different women many years ago. But it wasn't an accident that they were together now. The bond between them started to grow from the first second they met. It was the precise thing they each needed and deserved.

Georgina loved Catherine and Catherine loved Georgina.

And nothing was going to come between them again. No contract, no fear of the unknown, no past relationships. All they needed was each other. Their partnership was not in the fine print but was in the actions of the heart. They needed nothing more to bind them together than the love that passed between them. A love that needed no words.

THANK YOU

Thank you for reading this novel and I hope you enjoyed it. If you did then please help other people find it and to enjoy it as well.

Recommend it: I would appreciate it if you would recommend this book to friends and reader's groups.

Review it: Please review this book by telling people why you liked it. Reviews and recommendations are the lifeblood of any Indie writer.

Every time you leave a positive review for an author you become the little voice that whispers "You're doing a good job. Don't you quit."

I love hearing from my readers. You can contact me on my Facebook page at
https://www.facebook.com/tapurkis.author/

Visit
https://teresapurkis.weebly.com/

Or
https://www.amazon.com/author/teresapurkis

BOOKS BY THE AUTHOR

Fiction
Coming Home Series

Coming Home
Back For Good
Where She Belongs

Christmas In The Canaries

Deliverance

Non-Fiction
My Bristol: The History and The Culture

ABOUT THE AUTHOR

Teresa Purkis

Teresa spent her working career as a Teacher of Mathematics and Physical Education.

She was born in Bristol, England and has lived with her Civil Partner for over thirty years.

Teresa is thoroughly enjoying her retirement as it gives her time to gain different experiences and learn new skills and crafts.

She enjoys discovering exciting places to visit, mainly through cruising holidays. As well as writing, Teresa likes playing lawn bowls and darts, in addition to watching her local football team Bristol Rovers.

Teresa has an interest in photography and has spent many an hour taking in the sights and sounds of the City she loves.

Printed in Great Britain
by Amazon

69784332R00193